PROTECTING MAGGIE

SEAL OF PROTECTION: ALLIANCE
BOOK 4

SUSAN STOKER

Edited by Kelli Collins

Cover Design by AURA Design Group

Manufactured in the United States

CHAPTER ONE

Maggie Lionetti stood in front of the empty cabinet for several moments. All that was in there was a can of beans and some flour and sugar. And Maggie hated beans. They belonged to her roommate, Adina, who'd been gone on deployment for the last three months.

Sighing, she closed the cabinet and grabbed a glass instead. She filled it with water and went to sit on the couch. She was very grateful to her friend for letting her stay in her apartment while she was gone, but she hadn't realized how tough life would *really* be as a convicted felon.

Convicted felon.

The words rang in Maggie's head, making her shudder. Never in a million years would she have thought this was where she'd be. In her "before life," which was how she thought about it now, she'd been a pharmacist. She'd worked her butt off to get her degree and become one of the best pharmacists in the area. She had loyal customers who wouldn't go anywhere else to get their prescriptions filled. She'd had money in the bank, a nice condo, and lots of friends. At least, she'd *thought* she had lots of friends.

Turns out they'd all disappeared once she'd been arrested. Maggie knew she couldn't really blame them.

She still remembered the feeling of the handcuffs around her wrists and how she felt when she'd been put in the back of that police car. Humiliated, confused, terrified.

Those feelings had only magnified when she was booked into the local lockup after being fingerprinted and getting her mug shot taken. After being released on bail, she was fired from her job, and without any money coming in but still plenty of bills to pay—while also trying to find a lawyer who would take her case—she found herself completely broke and desperate in a matter of months.

In the end, without any support from friends and no family to lean on, she'd had to settle for a public defender. She didn't really hold the lawyer responsible for her three-year sentence. He'd done what he could. The evidence was stacked against her from the start.

And when her ex-boyfriend had taken the stand for the prosecution, her fate was sealed.

She'd gotten out early, on account of overcrowding and good behavior, but she wasn't allowed to leave California until her probation was over. She had to meet with her probation officer regularly and stay out of trouble. Now Maggie was trying to rebuild her life, and she was extremely grateful to Adina for giving her a place to stay, but she was finding it impossible to make ends meet.

She couldn't get her old job back—no one would hire a pharmacist who'd been convicted of drug smuggling—and finding *any* kind of job that paid a decent living wage was next to impossible for a felon.

So Maggie had resorted to doing what her probation officer and likely anyone who hadn't been in her situation before—hungry, desperate, depressed—would frown upon.

She was impersonating Adina. Using her Uber credentials to make enough money to get by. Barely.

She didn't like doing it, lying to the people who hired her, pretending to be her roommate, but Uber wasn't going to let *her* open an account. Not with the felony thing on her record. So she had to lie. It was either that or starve.

Feeling her stomach rumble with hunger, Maggie gulped the water down, hoping it would fill her belly at least a little, tricking it into thinking it had gotten something of substance, then stood. She put the glass in the sink and headed for the door, grabbing the car keys along the way.

She'd managed to make enough yesterday to fill Adina's old Honda Accord with gas, and she hoped today's tips would be more generous so she could go to the grocery store and get more than ramen. The thought of a huge salad made Maggie's mouth water, but fresh vegetables were expensive. She'd have to do really well today to splurge on something like that.

Sighing, Maggie made sure the apartment door was

locked behind her—the last thing she wanted was someone breaking into Adina's place while she was gone—and headed toward the stairs. Today would be another long day behind the wheel, but what other choice did she have?

* * *

Maggie was tired. The day had been shit. Almost everyone she'd picked up had been stingy with their tips. And they'd been assholes to boot. Driving people around seemed like it would be a cushy job, but she had to put up with rudeness, people telling her how to drive, telling her she was going the wrong way, or being irritated with her because there was traffic...as if she could do anything about that.

She was at the end of her rope and decided that she'd pick up one more fare, then go home to the empty apartment, maybe try to choke down the beans that she hated. They were protein, right? Good for her.

Pulling up the info on her last pickup of the day, she saw it was at a grocery store she'd passed earlier. The one she'd planned to go to after work if tips had been good, to buy dinner. It felt as if karma was laughing at her.

The name of her fare was Remi Stephenson, and she was relieved that her pickup was a woman. That didn't mean she wouldn't be treated like shit—women could be just as awful as men—but at least the odds of her being accosted or sexually harassed were less.

Maggie pulled into the parking lot and saw a woman standing not too far from the entrance of the store looking down at her phone. She had several bags at her feet, the reusable kind. It was a dead giveaway that she was probably her fare. She pulled up next to her and rolled down the window. "Remi?" she called out, wanting to make sure she was really the person who'd ordered the Uber before unlocking the doors.

"That's me. Adina?" the woman asked.

Hearing her roommate's name was always a little jarring. She merely smiled and clicked the automatic locks. Remi picked up her bags, opened the back door, and got in. Then she took a quick picture of the identification card on the back of the passenger headrest.

"My boyfriend hates when I take an Uber, but I don't like to bother him or his friends," Remi said with a small apologetic smile.

Maggie didn't like when people took pictures of the ID card. Thankfully, it didn't have Adina's picture on it, but it had her information—name, Uber license number, things like that. Things that could get Maggie in big trouble if it ever came out that she was impersonating her friend. But at the same time, she approved when women like Remi took steps to protect themselves. No one could be too careful these days. It made her laugh a little that, in the past, people were warned never to accept rides from strangers, and today they *paid* strangers to drive them around. It was ironic.

"It's okay. I'd do the same if I was in your shoes," Maggie said as cheerfully as she could. She recited the address that had been put into the app to verify that's where Remi wanted to be dropped off.

"That's me," Remi said with a smile as she turned around to grab the seat belt. Thankfully the address wasn't too far away.

Maggie did her best to make small talk. Sometimes the people she picked up wanted to chat, and other times they simply stared out the window and ignored her. But Remi seemed friendly enough.

"Are you having a good day?" Maggie asked as she pulled out of the parking lot.

"I am. I spent the morning with one of my good friends and got a lot of work done. She brought me home, but then I started thinking about how I wanted to surprise my boyfriend with a chocolate cake."

"Oh, that's nice," Maggie said. And it was. She'd never had anyone surprise her with anything before. Well...not a *nice* surprise. She refused to think about *that* day, about what a surprise it was when the cops who'd pulled her over on the interstate had pulled that bag out from under her passenger seat.

"I'm not much of a cook, *or* a baker, but my boyfriend works really hard. He and all his friends do. He's a SEAL. And yes, I'm allowed to tell you that." Remi giggled.

Maggie found herself smiling. It was hard not to around someone like the woman currently in her backseat. She exuded friendliness and happiness. It was a nice change from what she usually dealt with.

"Anyway, he's been working really hard lately, and I wanted to do something nice for him. And if I called any of his friends to give me a ride to the store, they'd probably text him and let him know, then the surprise would be ruined."

Maggie wrinkled her nose a little at that. It seemed a little...stalkerish...for a friend to immediately go and tell the boyfriend what his girlfriend was doing and where she was going. She must not have hidden her reaction very well, because Remi chuckled.

"I know, that seems weird. But trust me, with the things my friends and I have been through, not to mention the stuff my boyfriend sees in his line of work, it's perfectly normal. He's protective."

"Must be nice," Maggie blurted, then immediately regretted it. Her voice sounded a little too...wistful for her peace of mind. She didn't regret not having a man in her life. She'd had enough of guys. She was perfectly capable of taking care of herself, thank you very much.

Her stomach chose that moment to growl, as if publicly calling her out on that particular lie. It wasn't as if she was doing a very good job of taking care of herself at the moment. But she'd manage. As soon as she was allowed, she was getting out of this state, moving somewhere that had a lower cost of living, and she'd figure out how to get back on her feet.

"It is," Remi said nonchalantly, politely ignoring the way Maggie's stomach had rumbled so loudly. "Anyway, he'll bluster and ask what the hell I was thinking, taking an Uber to and from the store, but then I'll present him with the cake I made and all will be well."

Maggie grinned. "That'll actually work?" she asked.

Remi giggled. "Okay, probably not. But when all I'm wearing is one of his button-down shirts—and nothing else —I'll definitely be forgiven."

Maggie couldn't hold back the burst of laughter at that.

"But seriously," Remi said, still sounding chipper and happy. "I declined two rides before yours because they were from men. I know that sounds sexist, but I prefer women drivers. I know that women can be just as horrible as men, but I do what I can to stay safe by taking pictures of the licenses and using the new safety features in the ride-share app."

"Smart," Maggie said, meaning it.

"One of my friends was kidnapped by two women she knew, and they tried to sell her into sexual slavery. So I *know* women can be horrible. But I still feel safer in a car with someone of my own gender."

Maggie gasped. Remi had dropped that bomb so nonchalantly. "Is she okay? Your friend?" she couldn't help but ask.

"Oh, yeah. Josie's great. She's amazing. A four-foot-nine dynamo. She's adorable and you can't help but want to stick her in your pocket and take her home, but she's tough as nails. I love her so much. She's who I was visiting this morning. She can type like the wind too. I mean, seriously, I've never seen anyone type as fast as she can. She's made a career out of it. I love going over to her place and sitting at her table to draw while she types. I don't know, somehow the vibe she sends out makes me feel more creative."

The woman switched topics faster than Maggie could keep up. "You draw?" she asked.

"Yeah. I have a cartoon. It does pretty well. It's dorky as hell, but people seem to like it."

"Cartoon?"

"Uh-huh. Pecky the Traveling Taco."

Maggie's mouth dropped open. "Oh my God, seriously? You draw that? I love Pecky!" Looking in the rearview mirror, Maggie saw Remi blush. It was unexpected. This woman was extremely talented. And she was in *her* car! It felt surreal.

"Thanks."

"Wow. I've never driven a famous person around before," Maggie said, only slightly teasing.

"Oh please," Remi told her. "I'm not famous."

Maggie begged to differ. She wanted to tell her that all the women she'd been incarcerated with loved her cartoon strip. Practically the only time everyone got along was when they were laughing about Pecky's latest shenanigans. That taco had been a bright spot in what had been an otherwise pretty miserable two years.

"You make a difference," she said in a serious tone. "I mean it. You might think what you do is just a hobby or for fun. But it means something to a lot of people."

Remi didn't blow off her words. Instead, she leaned forward in her seat and said, "Thank you. That means the world to me."

Maggie pulled up to a small house. It was adorable and looked nothing like what she imagined the creator of

Pecky the Traveling Taco would live in. She turned to Remi. "Good luck with the cake. I hope your boyfriend isn't too upset with you for taking an Uber."

"Oh, I'm sure Vincent will forgive me. As I said, he just worries. Honestly, it feels nice. Even though I can take care of myself, and *did* for quite a while, it's nice to know someone has my back now." She gathered her bags and opened the back door. "Thanks for the ride and letting me ramble on."

"You're welcome."

"I hope you're going to get a break to get something to eat. Don't be embarrassed, but I heard your stomach growl."

Maggie couldn't stop the mortified blush from heating her cheeks. "I'm headed home now. You were my last ride of the day."

"Good."

"Um...Remi?" Maggie blurted before she could shut the car door.

"Yeah?"

"Anytime you need a ride...I'm happy to help out. My number is on the license you took a picture of. You know, if it would make you and your boyfriend feel safer."

"Oh, that's so nice! Thank you. I don't use Ubers much, but if I do need a ride in the future, I'll definitely call."

Maggie nodded. She was feeling a little sad that this would probably be the one and only time she saw Remi. She didn't really expect her to call for a ride in the future, but it had been a long time since she'd felt any kind of connection with another person. Remi was down-to-earth, funny, and open. Even being around her for the short time it took to drive her home made Maggie feel more like her old self. Less hard, less cynical.

Then Remi held out a folded bill. "Tip," she said with a smile. "I like to give cash because I don't know if Uber takes a cut of it if I do it on the app."

"Thanks. Have a good evening," she told her with a smile.

Remi nodded and said, "You too. Bye!" She got out of the car and headed up the walkway to the door of her house.

Maggie closed out the trip on the ride-share app, then pulled away from the house. At the stop sign down the street, she unfolded the bill Remi had given her.

She blinked. Sure she was hallucinating.

Nope. It wasn't just a one-dollar bill or a five.

Remi had given her a hundred and fifty-dollar tip. On a ten-dollar fare.

Tears swam in Maggie's eyes. That was more money than she usually made in three days of driving people around. It meant she could go to the store and get more than just ramen. She could get that salad she'd been craving.

Remi had no reason to give her so much money. She probably felt sorry for her, but Maggie couldn't even be embarrassed about that. She needed that money more than Remi could possibly know. But then again, maybe she *did* know.

Turning left toward the grocery store instead of right, toward her apartment, Maggie let the tears she'd been holding back fall down her cheeks. Because of the generosity and kindness of a stranger, she would get to eat tonight. A real meal. And some of the hopelessness and depression lifted from her shoulders. Suddenly, the world didn't feel as if it was against her anymore. Maybe this was a sign that things were turning around.

Maggie wanted to believe that, but life had a way of lifting her up, then slamming her back down when she least expected it. A hundred and fifty bucks wouldn't last long, but for tonight, at least, she was going to put her worries aside.

CHAPTER TWO

"I have a situation."

Shawn "Preacher" Franklin sat up straighter, snapping out of his funk. He'd collapsed onto his sofa after arriving home from the naval base earlier, too on edge to make something for dinner, and he'd been there ever since. He loved being a SEAL. Loved his country. Loved his teammates. But lately, he'd been feeling...unsettled.

Seeing Kevlar, Safe, and Blink with their girlfriends, women who softened their prickly edges, had him wanting what *they* had. Not their specific women, of course, but someone he could share his thoughts and feelings with at the end of each day. But the thing was, when it came to relationships, Preacher was unlike most SEALs.

He believed in soul mates.

He'd been raised to believe there was one person out there just for him, that he'd know her when he saw her...

and that being with anyone sexually before he'd met his soul mate was disrespectful.

Being a virgin at thirty-something was practically unheard of. *Especially* for a Navy SEAL.

He'd been given the nickname Preacher by some guys in boot camp. When they'd heard that he was waiting for his soul mate, that he wasn't interested in picking up some random frog hog at the local bar during his time off, they'd laughed and given him the moniker.

It wasn't as if he'd never been tempted. But every time he decided that his old-fashioned values were ridiculous, and he should just get it over with and fuck someone already...

He couldn't do it.

He wasn't ashamed of his beliefs either. But he *was* becoming discouraged by them. He was afraid he'd already missed her. That maybe he hadn't recognized his soul mate when he'd met her in the past.

Or worse—that he'd never find her at all.

That was the dreaded thought going through his head when Kevlar called. But hearing the serious tone of his team leader on the phone had all thoughts of loneliness flying from his brain.

"What's wrong?" he barked.

"Sorry, I didn't mean to sound so dramatic," Kevlar answered in a sheepish tone. "But I learned something disturbing tonight and wanted to run it by someone."

"I'm listening," Preacher said, feeling his heart rate slowly decrease. There had been enough "situations" lately with Wren, Josie, and Remi that he couldn't help his immediate battle-mode response.

"Remi went to and from the store today via one of those ride-share apps and—"

"Wait, why didn't she call someone? Is she okay? Did something happen?" Preacher asked, interrupting his friend.

Kevlar chuckled. "All questions I asked *her*. She's fine. Nothing happened. And she said she didn't want to bother anyone. That she wanted to surprise me with a chocolate cake. Believe me, I made sure she understood that it wasn't a bother to call one of our friends to help her out. Anyone would've been happy to give her a ride somewhere."

Preacher frowned. "Right, so...if nothing happened, what's the situation?"

"Remi got along great with the driver—of course she did...she's Remi. But she did what I've taught her to do, taking a picture of the driver's info, just in case. The driver also encouraged Remi to call her if she needed a ride in the future. Here's the thing," Kevlar said, getting to the point. "The driver's name was Adina Cornett. And that's the info that was on the placard Remi took a picture of."

"Isn't Adina the woman who works in supply?"

"Yes—and she's deployed, which is why we haven't seen her around."

"Shit," Preacher said.

"Exactly. There's someone driving around in what I'm guessing is Adina's car, using *her* name, and probably robbing her blind while she's deployed."

"So what are we going to do about it?" Preacher asked. "Are we calling NCIS?"

"I thought we'd see what we could find out on our own first," Kevlar said.

Preacher smiled, feeling a surge of excitement flow through his veins.

"The fake Adina told Remi to call her anytime she needed a ride. I'm thinking we might need a ride home from work tomorrow."

"Will Remi go along with this?" Preacher asked, sounding skeptical.

"She's not happy with the deception. Told me that the fake Adina was really nice. That she liked her a lot. Warned me to go easy. Said she probably has a perfectly good reason to be using Adina's name and car."

Preacher snorted.

"That was my response," Kevlar agreed. "She also gave this woman a hundred and fifty-dollar tip."

"Seriously?" Preacher asked.

"Yes. She reassured me that she wasn't pressured to do so. Just that she felt a connection to the woman and she seemed down. Oh, and the icing on the cake? Her stomach was growling almost continuously."

Preacher wanted to roll his eyes, but it wasn't as if someone could fake something like that. Yes, perhaps she'd held off eating in the hopes that her body would make its needs known audibly. But that wasn't likely. And Remi wasn't the kind of woman to be taken advantage of. She was one of the sweetest women Preacher knew, but she'd grown up with money and was pretty good about recognizing someone who was only being nice to try to get some cash out of her.

"I'm in," he told his friend.

"I'll see if Smiley wants to come with us too," Kevlar said.

Preacher winced. Smiley was a little rough around the edges, he'd probably scare the crap out of Fake Adina... which was probably Kevlar's intention. By the time the ride was over tomorrow, the woman would definitely think twice about whatever illegal scheme she was perpetrating. "Maybe Safe or MacGyver would be better?"

"No. I want this woman intimidated. I want her to regret what she's done. She can't go around using someone else's name and car to steal. And who knows how deep this goes."

"Should we try to get a hold of Adina?" Preacher asked.

"I will. After tomorrow," Kevlar said.

"All right. I'll see you in the morning."

"Thanks for listening and not telling me I'm crazy or too overprotective of Remi," Kevlar said.

"You are both of those things," Preacher said with a laugh. "But if Remi doesn't mind, why should I?"

Kevlar chuckled. "True. Later."

Preacher clicked off his phone and pressed his lips together. His mind was whirling with the info Kevlar had just shared. None of them really knew Adina, they just worked with her in a professional capacity. But knowing she was deployed and someone was taking advantage of her didn't sit well with him, just as it hadn't with Kevlar. Tomorrow, they'd figure out what the hell was going on and take whatever steps were necessary to stop the fraud.

* * *

Maggie had been surprised to hear from Remi so soon, especially after she'd admitted that she didn't use ride shares all that often. But she was happy to get the return business. Today had been slow, and everyone she'd given a ride to had been a stingy tipper. It was depressing to only get a dollar tip on a fifteen-dollar ride, but it wasn't as if she could do anything about it.

She'd already spent most of the tip money Remi had gifted her yesterday, but she'd managed to get quite a few groceries. Tuna, generic cereal, some bread that was on sale, some dented cans of vegetables, and she'd splurged on some hamburger and made a huge cheesy casserole the night before, along with one of the best salads she'd had in ages, which should last her for several meals.

Adina's car desperately needed a tune-up, and that was next up on Maggie's list of things to do. Without the car, she'd be dead in the water, literally. It was the only thing keeping her from starving.

Remi had asked to be picked up near the gates of the huge naval base, and when Maggie pulled up to the curb outside the pawn shop where Remi had said she'd be waiting out front, she didn't immediately see her.

Instead, as soon as she stopped, Maggie saw three men

walking down the sidewalk with purpose in their steps. All three were wearing the blue camouflage uniforms the Navy issued their personnel.

It wasn't until it was too late to take the car out of gear and step on the gas that she realized they were coming toward *her*.

One of the men got into the front seat, and the other two got into the back. Maggie's heart was pounding so hard it almost hurt. She'd been in some close calls over the last three months, but she'd never felt as threatened as she did right this minute. These men could easily overpower her. If they wanted to hurt her, there wouldn't be anything she could do about it.

"I don't have any cash on me," she said quickly, "but you can have the car."

"We aren't going to hurt you or rob you. We just want to talk," said the man who was sitting next to her in the passenger seat. He had green eyes, wavy dark hair, and a closely trimmed beard and mustache. The men in the back had frowns on their faces and were staring at her with looks so intense and scary, it was all Maggie could do to keep breathing.

Her hand was on the door handle, and she was two seconds away from bailing and running as fast as she could. But leaving Adina's car would be a disaster...so she hesitated.

"Talk?" Maggie managed to squeak out.

"Yeah. What's your name?" the man sitting directly behind her asked.

Looking in the rearview mirror, Maggie saw him staring at her. He was leaning forward as he spoke, while the other man in the backseat was taking a picture of the Uber license affixed to the headrest. It had Adina's information on it, except for the phone number, which Maggie had taped over with her own. She didn't like the way he was scrutinizing the license—and suddenly she had a feeling these men had figured out she wasn't who she said she was.

"Adina," she stammered out. "Adina Cornett."

"Bullshit," the man behind her barked. "We know Adina. We work with her on the base. She's almost ten years younger than you, blonde, has blue eyes, and is several inches taller than you, as well. And she just happens to be floating around the Middle East on a ship right about now. So you need to start talking—fast. Why are you pretending to be her, driving her car, and doing who knows what the hell else with *her* name?"

Maggie swallowed hard. She knew this day would come. Riverton was a fairly large city, but it wasn't LA. She was bound to come across someone who knew Adina at some point. Her friend had a fairly unique name, and the man was right, Maggie looked nothing like her.

She tried to come up with a rebuttal. To figure out what she could say that would get these men out of her car and to leave her alone, but nothing plausible came to mind.

"Well?" the other, kind of mean-looking guy in the backseat, asked. He'd taken his attention from Adina's license and was now staring at her as well.

Maggie opened her mouth to say something, she had

no idea what, but the normally reliable Accord took that moment to sputter and die. The engine cut off—and the silence that filled the car was almost oppressive.

It was the last straw. Maggie had no idea what was wrong with the car, just that without it, she was totally screwed.

She gripped the steering wheel and stared straight ahead, trying really hard not to burst into tears. She didn't figure it would help her cause with these men. "Maggie. My name is Maggie Lionetti."

"I'm Preacher. Kevlar and Smiley are in the back," the man next to her said in what almost sounded like a gentle tone. But Maggie wasn't fooled. He was probably trying to get her to let down her guard before he called the cops. If he did that, she was going back to prison. She'd been told time and time again by her probation officer what would happen if she screwed up.

"How did you get the keys to Adina's car?" Kevlar asked.

Maggie felt cold. Some of the horrible things she'd gone through behind bars flashed through her brain. The near assaults, the fights, the verbal abuse. She couldn't go back. She *couldn't*.

"Maggie?" Preacher asked.

They weren't going to give up. Weren't going to simply get out of her car and leave her alone. Overwhelmed with grief, the pressures of the last three months pressing in on her, Maggie broke.

"Adina's my friend. She's my *only* friend. I met her...

recently. I needed a place to go a few months ago, and she offered to let me stay with her. I took her up on it. When she was deployed, she said I could use her car, and she knows I'm using her Uber account. We talked about it. She agreed." Her words were fast and succinct, and Maggie refused to look at any of the men in the small vehicle as she talked. She heard the rustle of their clothes as they shifted in their seats but didn't take her gaze off the street in front of her.

"Why'd you need a place to stay? Do you not have another job?" Smiley asked.

Maggie had never heard a name so incongruent to a person's countenance. The man hadn't smiled once. He looked downright frightening.

And it *definitely* seemed like they weren't going to leave her alone until she told them everything.

Fine. They wanted to know? She didn't have anything to hide. Not really.

She huffed out a long breath and turned her head to look at the man next to her. Preacher. He looked nothing like a man of the cloth. Not that she really knew what they were supposed to look like. But out of the three men in the car at the moment, he seemed the least...hostile.

"I was in jail. I served nearly two of my three years. Got out for good behavior and because there weren't any more beds available for the more violent offenders. I met Adina before I went in. She wrote me every single week. Picked me up when I was released.

"I couldn't get my old job back when I got out, and I

had no money, no place to stay. It's almost cruel how the system works...yes, you're released, but the odds of going right back behind bars is huge because of how impossible it is to rebuild an honest life back in the real world. Lucky for me, I had Adina. The deployment was a surprise, but she generously said I could stay at her apartment while she was gone. Drive her car. And it was actually *her* idea for me to take over her Uber account. It's given me a way to make a few bucks. To eat.

"I'm not stealing from Adina, I swear. Yes, I'm using her ride-share account, but I can't get my own because of the felony on my record. Do you know how hard it is to find a decent job when you've been convicted of a crime?" She barked a harsh laugh. "No. Of course you don't. Well, I can tell you, it's nearly impossible. And for the record, I'm innocent. You won't believe me, no one does, but it's still true."

She was practically panting by the time she ran out of words. She desperately wanted these men to believe her, but the odds of that were extremely low.

"You know we can get in touch with Adina and verify your story, right?" Kevlar asked.

Turning, Maggie looked at him. "Do it. Ask her. She'll verify everything I just told you."

"What'd you get put behind bars for?"

"Smiley," Preacher said in a warning tone.

Maggie wasn't surprised. It wasn't as if Smiley hadn't asked what all three men were thinking.

"I'm no threat to society," she said tiredly. "I know you

won't believe this either, but I was set up. I needed to go up to the LA area for my job, and my boyfriend asked if I would bring something to a friend for him. I had no problem with that, and the friend was going to meet me at the pharmacy where I was going to be for work. I got pulled over on the way up there, and for some reason the cop decided to search my car. The bag my boyfriend gave me had drugs in it. A *lot* of drugs. I got three years for transporting with the intent to sell. No one would believe that it wasn't my bag, and that I wasn't bringing drugs to LA to sell them."

You could hear a pin drop in the car, it was that silent.

"Assuming the boyfriend is now your *ex*-boyfriend," Kevlar said dryly.

Maggie couldn't help it. She snorted. Loudly. "Obviously. Look, I don't like using Adina's credentials, but I have no other way of making money to feed myself. And I don't have to pay rent, but I'm still trying to pay my share anyway. I would get out of Riverton altogether if I could, but I'm not allowed to leave the state until my probation is over. I'm literally stuck here. I'm trying to do my best but it's just not enough. It's never enough." The last three words were whispered.

Maggie wanted to ask if they were going to turn her in. To Uber. To the cops. To her probation officer. But the words were stuck in her throat. Not for the first time, she wished she had never met her ex. But she had. She'd been swayed by his larger-than-life personality and impressed by the fact that he was a high-ranking naval officer. She'd learned the hard way that not all military members were upstanding citizens.

She could only pray the ones sitting in her car at the moment were more compassionate than her snake of an ex.

"What's wrong with the car?" Preacher asked.

She glanced at him, then shrugged. "I don't know," she admitted softly. "I've been saving up to take it to the shop. It's been acting weird. Sputtering and turning off by itself when I stop."

Preacher shared a look with the men in the backseat before he turned back to her. "Give me the keys."

Maggie blinked. "No."

"I'm not going to steal this piece of shit," Preacher told her. "I want to talk to my friends, and I have to make sure you won't take off when we get out...if this thing even starts again."

She wanted to continue to protest. To beg them all to just leave her alone. To tell them that she'd stop driving for the ride-share app. But she couldn't. Unless she wanted to work for a strip club, which she definitely did *not*, she needed to keep taxiing people around.

"Give him the keys, Maggie," Kevlar ordered.

To her surprise, she found herself doing just that. What did it matter? These men literally held her life in their hands. If they turned her in, she was going right back behind bars. The last thing she wanted to do was piss them off any more than she already had.

Her fingertips brushed against Preacher's palm when

she dropped the keys in his hand—and to her shock, she felt a tingle shoot up her arm.

She snatched her hand back as if she'd been burned. She wanted to cradle her hand against her chest but refrained, barely. She'd learned through her time behind bars that to let anyone know what you were thinking or feeling was dangerous.

She did her best to wipe all emotion from her face...but she had a feeling she'd failed miserably when Preacher spoke.

"Breathe, Maggie. We just need to talk for a moment."

Breathe. Right. As if.

She sat frozen as the three men got out and slammed the doors behind them.

Despair hit Maggie all over again. They weren't going to believe her. No one did. They probably thought she was a master drug dealer or something. That she was using the Uber job as a cover for delivering drugs to people all across the city. She was screwed. She might as well prepare herself to put on the horrible jailhouse pants and shirt she'd been forced to wear for the last two years.

The tears she'd managed to hold back finally sprang to her eyes and fell down her cheeks.

CHAPTER THREE

Preacher stepped away from the vehicle and waited for Kevlar and Smiley. They huddled against the brick wall of the building near where Maggie had parked.

"I believe her," Kevlar said without preamble.

"Me too," Preacher agreed.

The two men looked at Smiley. He was the skeptic of the team. The guy who always came up with the worst-case scenarios.

To Preacher's surprise, he nodded and said, "She's not lying."

"So what do we do?" he asked.

"I'm going to send a message to Adina's commander, just to verify her story, but in the meantime, I'm thinking she's not going to get far with that piece-of-shit vehicle," Kevlar said.

Preacher looked over at the car in question and

frowned when he saw Maggie slumped over the wheel. He felt a pang of guilt for the way they had tricked her. Despite how bad it looked, she didn't seem to have nefarious intentions in using Adina's name and Uber license.

There was also something about the woman that made him want to hug her close and reassure her that everything would be all right.

Which was crazy. But that didn't change how he felt.

"I'll follow her home to make sure she gets there okay," he blurted.

Both Kevlar and Smiley studied him intensely.

Finally, Kevlar said, "It might not be smart to get involved with a felon."

Irritation swam through Preacher's veins. "I didn't say I was getting involved with her. And I'm just making sure she gets home all right, not planning on parading her through the naval base, shouting her criminal history to everyone I pass," he said tightly.

To his surprise, Smiley chuckled. "I'd pay to see that," he said under his breath.

"Right, sorry," Kevlar said without hesitation.

"Besides...can you really see that woman as a drug dealer? We pressed her just a little and she caved. If she's dealing drugs, I'm secretly a math genius who's on the verge of solving the world's most difficult equation," Preacher said sarcastically.

"Is there such a thing?" Smiley asked.

"No clue. Probably."

"Can we stick to the topic at hand?" Kevlar asked.

"We are," Smiley told him without missing a beat. "Math. Preacher brought it up."

He shared an amused grin with his teammate. "Beyond my math ability, or lack thereof...are we gonna do something about her situation?"

Kevlar took a moment to think about his answer before sighing. "Remi really liked her. I'm not sure it's in her best interest to keep doing what she's doing though. If her probation officer gets wind that she's impersonating Adina and using her license to work, that could be bad for her."

Preacher nodded. "We know a lot of people. I'm guessing we can get her some help. Maybe find her a job."

"You think she'll accept our help?" Smiley asked.

Preacher turned to look back at Maggie. She looked so dejected. As if she was just waiting for something bad to happen. He met his teammate's gaze. "Yeah, I think she will. She's pretty much at rock bottom. She needs proof that not everyone is out to get her."

"After I verify with Adina that she's allowing Maggie to live in her apartment, I'll give Wolf a call."

"I'll do it," Preacher told his friend.

"All right. You want to see if the car'll start? If it does, just go with her, in case anything else happens to the vehicle on her way home. We'll head back to the base, and I'll bring your vehicle to you. Just text me the address of the apartment complex where she's staying," Kevlar told him.

"Thanks. I appreciate it." What he *really* appreciated was his friends not telling him that he was stupid for

SUSAN STOKER

involving himself in Maggie's life. Yes, Kevlar warned him that it might not be a good idea, but he would've blatantly told him he was being a bonehead if he *really* thought Preacher was making a mistake.

But Preacher had a gut feeling that she needed someone in her corner. The story of her arrest for drug smuggling sounded almost too over the top to be true, but he wasn't an idiot; he was well aware that plenty of people were put in prison for things they didn't do or on trumped-up charges.

Smiley clapped him on the shoulder and Kevlar gave him a chin lift, then they turned without another word and headed back toward the base and their vehicles. Preacher headed to the Accord and got in. He held out the keys. "Let's see if she'll start, shall we?"

Maggie sniffed and didn't hide the fact that she'd been crying. Preacher's heart lurched in his chest. He hated that she'd been crying but didn't comment on it.

She wiped her cheeks with her shoulders and reached for the keyring. She stuck the key in the ignition and for a second, he didn't think the engine was going to turn over, but it finally did...with what he imagined was a long groan from the overworked car.

"So?" Maggie asked, turning to look at him. "What now? Are you going to turn me in?"

"No."

She looked surprised. "No?"

"Nope," Preacher confirmed. "Right now, I'm going to

30

escort you home. My friends will bring my car to your place."

Maggie stiffened and she sat up straighter. "If you think you can fuck my life up even more than it is already because I'm at a disadvantage here, you're wrong. I can and *will* defend myself, and I might go back to prison for assault but I'm not going to let you touch me."

Preacher was genuinely horrified that she thought he might blackmail her or otherwise hurt her. He leaned back against the door, away from her, and shook his head. "I just want to make sure you get home all right. That's all. I swear."

Neither said anything for a tense moment. Then Maggie asked, "Why?"

"Why what?"

"Why do you care? I'm nobody to you. A felon. A convicted drug dealer. Why in the world would you do anything to help me?"

"Because Remi likes you," Preacher said simply.

Maggie frowned.

He tried to explain. "Remi is...she's like a sister to me. She and Kevlar went through some shit, and she came out the other side the same sunny, happy person she was before. And believe me, that's a freaking miracle. We'd all do anything to make sure she stays that way. And given how she talked about you to Kevlar, it was clear that you made an impression on her."

When he paused, Maggie said, "I liked her too. She was...nice. I haven't experienced much of that lately."

"I'm sure. Which is why I want to help you. Besides, my mama would frown at me in disappointment—and trust me, that's the worst feeling ever, to disappoint your mom—if I didn't step in and do what I can to help you out."

"I wouldn't know. I was adopted when I was an infant. And let's just say things between me and my adoptive parents didn't work out. I left home at eighteen and haven't looked back."

"I'm sorry."

"Don't be. I'm fine," Maggie said.

"Right. So...would you be opposed if I called a couple of friends and inquired about finding you a job?"

Maggie stared at Preacher with big brown eyes. Her black hair was pulled back in a ponytail, and her face seemed a little pale to him. It was the disbelief that someone would be willing to help her that ate at him though. No one should be this surprised at the basic decency they were being shown by another human being.

"As long as it's legal, no. And I'll have to tell my probation officer, so it can't be under the table," she eventually said.

"Of course not," Preacher said calmly. "You hungry? I'm starving. We had a long day of boring meetings, and I'd kill for Del Taco. If you swing by one on your way home, it'll be my treat."

"I'm not sleeping with you," Maggie said stiffly. "And if you're setting me up, if you're some kind of serial killer, I won't go down without a fight. I'll get your DNA under my fingernails, scream my head off, and be the last person you ever murder."

"I'm not a serial killer. Can't deny that I've killed before, but they all deserved it," Preacher said bluntly.

To his surprise, Maggie simply tilted her head and stared at him. He wished he knew what she was thinking.

"For the Navy," she said after a beat. It wasn't a question.

"For the Navy," Preacher confirmed. "I'm a Navy SEAL."

That got a reaction out of her. "You are?"

He couldn't help but chuckle at her response. "It's that surprising?"

"Well, yeah. You don't look how I imagined a SEAL looking. You're..." Her voice trailed off.

"I'm what?" Preacher asked, genuinely interested in hearing what she thought.

"You don't seem to have the edge I guess I thought someone who does what you do would have."

Preacher shrugged. "Honestly, it's a weird job. We spend a lot of time researching and in meetings and briefings. If I had a dollar for every mile I've spent in the air flying to this or that country, I'd be a millionaire. Sometimes we jump out of perfectly good airplanes, hike for miles and miles, only to expend one bullet, then hike miles and miles back to our extrication point. I've seen some awful things, done things I'm not proud of, but done more things I'm *extremely* proud of.

"I don't like the bureaucracy, but love the men on my

team as if they're my brothers, and I love serving my country. I dislike bullies, and I find the way the poor and women and children are treated around the world absolutely abhorrent. I support the rights of people to practice any kind of religion they want, but not oppression in the name of any religion. I love animals, kids, and my family. And I know that last part's kind of a tangent, but I'm trying to reassure you that I'm not going to hurt you, Maggie. I just want to help."

"Can I take a picture of your ID?" she asked after a brief moment.

In response, Preacher reached for his wallet. He pulled out his Navy ID card and held it out to her.

"Shawn Franklin," she said with a small smile, right before she clicked a picture of the ID. She handed the ID back to him and said, "It's such a...normal name."

Preacher chuckled.

"Are you really a preacher?" she asked.

"No. Not even close," he told her.

"So it's the opposite? You have that nickname because you're a manwhore or something?"

"No. Not even close," he repeated.

Maggie frowned. "Then why?"

"Maybe someday I'll tell you. I'm hungry. Can we please get going so I don't waste into nothing here in your front seat?" This wasn't the time or place to get into the reason behind his nickname. He could always tell her what he fell back on when others wanted to know how he got it...that he was the moral compass of his team. For some reason, he didn't want to lie to this woman. But he didn't want to tell her that he was a freaking virgin either. So yeah, that was a conversation for another time and place, if it happened at all.

"Okay. Shawn? Can I call you that?"

The hair on the back of his neck stood up. Preacher was well aware that Remi, Wren, and Josie all called their men by their real names instead of their nicknames. He hadn't thought much about it...but now, hearing his given name on Maggie's lips made him yearn anew for what his teammates had with their women. "Yeah. You can call me Shawn."

"I really will fight you with everything I have if you try anything."

Preacher nodded seriously. "Noted."

She looked around and, seeing the coast was clear, pulled away from the curb. "There's a Del Taco not too far from my apartment."

"Sounds good. I'll text Kevlar and let him know we're stopping to grab dinner before heading to your place. Can I have your address, so he knows where to pick me up?"

Maggie nodded and gave him the info he needed to pass on to Kevlar.

The trip to Del Taco was uneventful, except for when he doubled what Maggie ordered so she'd have enough for leftovers. Hamburgers and fries weren't the best heated up the next day, but he didn't think she'd care. She tried to protest but he ignored her, enjoying how she didn't hesitate to dig into the bag once they'd left the restaurant.

She pulled into the parking lot of the apartment complex where she was staying and turned off the engine before looking at him. "I...are you really not going to turn me in? To Uber or my probation officer?"

"I'm not going to turn you in," Preacher told her.

"I need this job. It's the only way I've found to make any kind of money that isn't working in fast food or something dangerous, like stripping or working at one of the all-night convenience stores. Not that a fast-food job isn't good enough, it's just..."

"I understand. I'm going to call some people tonight. If you'll trust me, just a little, and not do any ride-share jobs tonight or tomorrow, I'll get back to you and let you know what I've found. Can you do that?"

Maggie nodded. "Thank you. And for the record, if it doesn't work out, I'm still appreciative that you tried."

"Why wouldn't it work out?" Preacher asked.

She shrugged. "When people find out that I'm a convicted drug dealer, any interest they had in hiring me seems to dry up."

"That won't be the case here," he reassured her.

Maggie simply shrugged. "Even still, I appreciate the effort."

Preacher was frustrated that she clearly didn't believe him. But he supposed he couldn't blame her. Not after what she'd been through. "I'm going to give you my number. If you need anything, and I mean anything, you call me. I'll do what I can to help."

She looked confused—which irritated Preacher all over

again. Hadn't *anyone* offered to help her in the recent past? Other than Adina? He supposed not, based on her reaction.

They exchanged numbers, and just seeing her name in his contacts made Preacher feel...he wasn't sure *what* he felt. Content? Excited?

"Thanks again for dinner. Are you going to be okay waiting out here until your friend comes?" she asked.

Preacher couldn't help it. He asked, "Seriously? The Navy sends me across some of the most dangerous borders in the world, and you want to know if I'll be okay waiting in a well-lit parking lot for the ten minutes it'll take my buddy to get here with my car?"

Maggie blushed, but she lifted her chin and said, "Yeah."

He chuckled. "Then, yes, I'll be fine."

They both got out of the Accord, and Maggie clutched the bag of food in front of her almost defensively. "Well, thanks again. For everything. Dinner, not calling the cops. You know...not being a serial killer."

This woman had made him smile more than he could remember doing in a long time. "You're welcome. I'll be in touch, Maggie. And for the record, not everyone is an asshole like your ex."

"Thank goodness," she said with a small snort. Then she gave him an awkward wave and headed for the door to the building. It wasn't until she was safely inside the apartment complex that Preacher relaxed a fraction. He looked around. The area of town was fairly safe and the parking lot had a lot of lights. Both of which made him feel better.

Why he should care so much about a woman he'd just met, he wasn't sure. But he couldn't deny the feeling. His mind spun with ideas for who he would call to try to help Maggie get a job.

He was still thinking about his options when Kevlar pulled up. He got out and let Preacher get behind the wheel.

"All good?" he asked.

"All good," Preacher confirmed.

"Still feel the same? That she didn't do what she was accused of?"

"Even more so," he admitted. He simply couldn't see Maggie transporting drugs to sell. Maybe he was being naïve, but he didn't think so.

"Right. So...are we taking the car in to be looked at?"

Preacher smiled. That was one of the many reasons he respected his team leader. "Yup."

Kevlar sighed. "You know after they hear Maggie's story, Remi and the others are probably going to want to befriend her. Not sure I'm comfortable with that," he said.

"Of course they are. Remi's a good judge of character."

"I know, but I'm still worried."

"Good luck telling her you don't want her contacting Maggie," Preacher said with a small grin.

"Shit," Kevlar said, blowing out a breath and running a hand through his hair. "You honestly don't think she's a danger?" he asked his teammate.

"No."

"I'll see if I can convince Remi to take things slow. Maybe start out by getting to know her by text or something. Give us a chance to check the situation out."

Preacher grinned wider. He had a feeling Remi wasn't going to want to "take things slow."

It felt right to bring Maggie into their fold. If anyone needed a friend, it was that woman. She was prickly and untrusting, but he couldn't blame her. He couldn't imagine what two years behind bars had been like. But today, she'd crossed paths with the right people. He and his friends would make sure she'd be okay.

CHAPTER FOUR

Maggie lay on Adina's couch and stared up at the ceiling. Her belly was full, she'd actually had a good night's sleep, and it felt great to take a day off from stressing about finding a job, getting enough money to eat, and wondering if Adina's car was going to finally break down for good.

Speaking of the car...she'd gotten a text from Shawn a short while ago, asking if she would allow him to take the car to a trustworthy mechanic he knew. She hadn't responded yet, because she wasn't sure she wanted to get any more involved with Shawn or his friends than she was already. Trusting someone, especially a man, wasn't something she was comfortable with. Roman Robertson hadn't even blinked when he'd set her up. The four months they'd been dating had apparently meant nothing to him. She was just a means to an end. And it stung. A lot.

So Maggie couldn't help but wonder why Shawn was so

keen on helping her. She was relieved he and his friends hadn't gone to the police about her using Adina's ride-share profile, but at any time, they still could.

The smart thing would be to block Shawn's number and pretend she'd never met him. *Especially* because he was in the Navy. But the man knew where she lived. He could easily call her probation officer and rat her out. At this point, the best thing would be to let him do his act of charity and slowly ease her way out of his life. She shouldn't have let him accompany her home last night, but she'd been weak. Had been relieved the three men hadn't seemed to want to get her in trouble. But now she was regretting all her decisions.

Then again, if he was being honest, and he really could find her a job, she couldn't afford to block him.

Hating that she'd be beholden to anyone, she sighed. Then she sat up and reached for her phone. She needed to reply to Shawn's text.

Maggie: Okay.

Deciding it would be best to keep things short and to the point, she was satisfied with her response.

Shawn: That hurt, didn't it?

. . .

Maggie couldn't help but smile at that.

Maggie: A little. *grin*

Shawn: Look, I get it. You don't know me. But I swear I'm on your side.

The jury was still out on that, but Maggie was determined to keep things between her and Shawn professional. If he wanted to be a do-gooder, she'd let him help her. It wouldn't matter in the end. The second she was able to get out of this state, she was gone.

Maggie: All right.

She was purposely being stand-offish in the hopes he'd get the message. That she didn't want anything from him... other than any connections he wanted to use to get her a job.

Shawn: Right. I've arranged for a tow truck to pick up the Accord later this morning. The guy I know who works there will take a look and let you know what he finds.

Hopefully it won't be anything major. Kevlar spoke with Adina's commander, and she verified everything you told us. I wasn't worried, but I thought it might make you feel better to know that. I also talked to a friend of mine, and if you're interested, you have an interview this afternoon. I can pick you up and bring you there, then take you home after. Let me know.

The message was long...and Maggie got the impression that she'd somehow hurt his feelings. Why she cared was a mystery, but she did.

Maggie: This is hard for me. After what happened, it's almost impossible to trust anyone. And yes, I'm very interested in the job.

Shawn: Don't you want to know what it is?

Maggie: It doesn't matter. At this point I'll do just about anything other than taking my clothes off for men to ogle my body...not that I look down on women who do that, it's just not for me.

Shawn: It involves clothes, but not taking them off. Is three o'clock okay for me to pick you up?

Maggie couldn't help but be intrigued.

• • •

Maggie: It's not as if I have a full calendar. LOL. Three is fine.

Shawn: See you then. Oh…and I hope you don't mind, but I gave your number to a couple other friends of mine. Women. They're the girlfriends of some of my teammates. I told them not to go overboard, but I'm guessing they will anyway. I'd apologize, but they're good people. See you later.

Maggie stared at the words on her phone screen. He'd given her number to other people? She should be pissed about that, but she didn't have time to think much about it —because just then, her phone vibrated in her hand, scaring the crap out of her.

It was a group text. Apparently, these women weren't the kind to procrastinate.

Unknown, Unknown, + 1 more: Hi! It's Remi! We met the other day when you picked me up at the store!

Unknown, Unknown + 1 more: And I'm Josie.

Unknown, Unknown + 1 more: And I'm Wren. We just wanted to write and say hi!

Unknown, Unknown + 1 more: Yeah, hi!

Unknown, Unknown + 1 more: I want to apologize for my role in yesterday. My man and his friends ambushing you. He was worried that you were a con man. Or woman. I told him he was wrong, that you were sweet as could be. The only reason I agreed to arrange that pickup was because I was sure that you'd win over Vincent and the others. And I was right. :)

Unknown, Unknown + 1 more: Remi, how come you always get to meet the cool people first?

Unknown, Unknown + 1 more: Maybe because I get out of my house more than you do, Wren.

Unknown, Unknown + 1 more: Good point.

Unknown, Unknown + 1 more: Do you forgive me, Maggie?

Maggie's fingers were moving before she thought about it.

Maggie: Of course.

Unknown, Unknown + 1 more: Good. Because I would've felt awful if you were traumatized or something.

Maggie: I'm not traumatized.

Unknown, Unknown + 1 more: Thank goodness. Wanna go to lunch with us?

Maggie stared down at the phone. Were these women for real? In her experience, people weren't this friendly. Especially with someone they didn't know.

Something occurred to her then.

. . .

Maggie: Did your boyfriend tell you about me? That I'm a felon? That I just got out of jail a few months ago? That I was in for two years for a drug conviction?

Unknown, Unknown + 1 more: Yeah. But Vincent also told me that you said you didn't do it.

Unknown, Unknown + 1 more: For the record, girl, that sucks.

Unknown, Unknown + 1 more: I wonder if there's someone we can get a hold of to see about clearing you. Because the whole thing sounds like BS to me.

Maggie's eyes instantly filled with tears. She literally didn't know these women, had only met Remi once, and they'd already shown more faith in her than people she'd known for years. When she'd been arrested, all of her so-called *friends* had disappeared into thin air. Everyone except for Adina.

She quickly added the numbers of the women into her contact list.

Wren, Remi + 1 more: So...lunch?

Maggie: I'd like that, but I don't have a car at the moment. Ironic, huh?

Wren, Remi + 1 more: No problem! We can pick you up. Bo got a ride to work with Flash today, so I can use his Wrangler.

Maggie: Okay.

Wren, Remi + 1 more: Send me your address later. We'll be there around noon. Will that work?

Maggie: Yeah. Without a car, I'm not working anyway.

Wren, Remi + 1 more: Okay. See you at noon then!

Wren, Remi + 1 more: This'll be fun!

Wren, Remi + 1 more: I have one more cartoon to sketch out then I'm done for the day. Can't wait to see you again, Maggie!

Maggie felt as if she were in an alternate dimension. She couldn't really afford to go to lunch. Having people interested in being her friend didn't make her money woes disappear. She had a little bit of the money left that Remi had tipped her, but fixing Adina's car wouldn't be cheap. The three women were so welcoming and nice though, it was impossible to say no.

She missed having friends. People to hang out with. To laugh with. To just coexist with. Maggie had no problem being alone, she liked it actually, but she'd spent the last two years while incarcerated locked in her own head. It would be nice to hang out with someone other than herself for the first time in a long while.

Inevitably, her thoughts went back to Shawn. He'd been the one to give the other women her number. What was his angle? He'd said he wasn't looking for sex, but *all* men wanted that...didn't they?

Deciding to turn him down flat if he offered to pay to fix whatever was wrong with Adina's car made Maggie feel better. She didn't need a guy to "save" her from her life. A man had put her in the predicament she was in now, and she'd be damned if she repeated her past mistakes.

She'd figure out a way to pay for the car herself. Somehow.

* * *

Right at noon, through the window of her apartment, Maggie saw a black Jeep Wrangler pull into the parking lot. She could see three women in the vehicle, so she quickly sent a text to the group, letting them know she was on her way down. She grabbed her purse and locked the door behind her before heading down the stairs.

She'd second-guessed this decision a dozen times since she'd agreed to go to lunch, but she couldn't back out now. She exited the building and saw Remi standing by the Jeep.

"Hi!" she said happily as Maggie approached.

"Hi," Maggie returned. Then, to her surprise, Remi stepped forward and hugged her. Unexpected tears sprang to her eyes. How long had it been since she'd been touched with kindness? Since she'd gotten a hug? Years.

"We thought Hob Nob Hill sounded perfect for today. I hope that's okay?" Remi said when she'd pulled back.

Maggie shrugged. "I don't eat out a lot. I'm sure it's fine."

"It's more than fine!" the woman behind the wheel of the Jeep said. "I'm Wren, by the way. And it's amazing. Laid-back comfort food and not a pretentious atmosphere.

My favorite is the Iowa Porker. It's a huge, deep-fried pork tenderloin sandwich. I can never eat it all, but Bo doesn't mind because he gets the leftovers."

Maggie couldn't help but smile at that. She climbed into the backseat next to Remi.

"I'm Josie. It's nice to meet you."

"Same," Maggie said.

The talk on the way to the restaurant was casual, and Maggie was relieved that she didn't need to participate much in the conversation. The three women seemed to genuinely like each other, and she got the impression that it had been a while since they'd gotten together. She said as much and was surprised when Remi laughed.

"I saw Wren two days ago, when we worked together in the morning, and Josie came over last night and we watched a movie."

"Oh," Maggie said. "I just thought...it seemed as if you guys hadn't talked in a while."

"This is just how we are around each other," Josie said with a smile. "On our own, we're each kind of shy, believe it or not. But when we get together it's as if we're different people. Outgoing and talkative."

Everyone chuckled, and Maggie even joined in. She could understand that. Once upon a time, she was the same way. Reticent around strangers, but she came out of her shell when she was around people she knew and liked. But life had changed her. Now she felt as if she were on the outside looking in. Knowing in her bones that if people knew who she was, what she'd been accused of, where she'd spent the last two years of her life, they'd turn their backs on her. She felt tainted. Even though she hadn't done what she'd been accused of, the feeling was still there.

Wren pulled up outside the small restaurant in downtown Riverton and said she'd be right in after she parked. They went inside and were immediately seated at a booth. The interior of the restaurant was quirky and casual, which was a relief for Maggie, since she was wearing jeans and a T-shirt.

Wren joined them and, after a small discussion about the choices on the menu, they put in their orders with the waitress. Maggie was a little worried about the prices, as they weren't exactly cheap, but she decided to hell with it. She deserved this little moment of happiness. She'd worry about where her next meal was coming from later.

"So," Josie said after the waitress had brought them drinks. "On a scale of one to ten, how overbearing were the guys yesterday?"

Maggie grinned. "They weren't bad."

All three of the other women rolled their eyes.

"Right. They can be intimidating when they want to be. I think it's in their SEAL genes or something."

"I really am sorry for being a part of their ambush," Remi said. "I knew Vincent was concerned about the Navy woman he knows, but I didn't realize he was going to bring Preacher and Smiley with him to confront you about it."

"It's okay," Maggie said.

"It's not. But I'm relieved that things seemed to work out. How do you know Adina?"

The conversation flowed easily. Maggie relaxed as the topic of her incarceration didn't come up. She could pretend that she was a normal woman out for lunch with her girlfriends.

Their lunches were brought out, and Maggie's eyes widened at the size of the portions.

"It's no wonder Americans are so overweight, huh?" Wren said with a chuckle.

Maggie had gotten a Reuben sandwich and the fries were literally overflowing off her plate. The Iowa Porker sandwich Remi ordered was the same, except it was the breaded and deep-fried pork tenderloin that was hanging over the bun *and* plate. The BLT Wren got was so thick, there was no way she was going to be able to get her mouth around it. And Josie's cobb salad was as big as her head.

At least the problem of what she was going to eat for dinner or lunch tomorrow was solved. She'd have enough leftovers for at least one more meal. Maybe two. And the food was delicious. Probably because all she'd been eating for weeks was ramen and hotdogs, but still.

Between bites, Wren said, "I hear you'll be back in this area later this afternoon to talk to Julie."

Maggie looked at her blankly.

"You didn't know Preacher was bringing you for an interview with her later?" Remi asked.

"I mean, I knew he had talked to someone for me about a job, but I don't know the details," Maggie admitted, feeling kind of stupid for not asking more questions.

"Julie is awesome. She's married to a former SEAL

commander. She has this amazing secondhand shop here in downtown Riverton. She helps high schoolers get formal clothes at cost or for free for their dances and stuff, as well as more casual clothes for those who need it. She really helped me when I first arrived in town," Wren said.

"Me too," Josie agreed.

Shawn's comments about clothes made a lot more sense now. But learning who her interview was with and for what kind of job didn't make Maggie relax. "I don't know anything about fashion," she admitted quietly.

But none of the women looked concerned. "Oh, it doesn't matter," Remi said with a casual wave of her hand.

"It doesn't," Wren insisted, when she saw the skeptical expression on Maggie's face. "Julie hasn't always had an easy time of it. She's the daughter of a former senator and was raised with a silver spoon in her mouth. It wasn't until she was kidnapped and taken south of the border to be a sex slave that she realized there was more to life than tea parties and crumpets."

"Crumpets?" Josie asked with a small laugh. "What the hell are those?"

"I have no idea," Wren admitted.

"I don't know either, but now I have a great idea for a Pecky cartoon. He makes friends with a crumpet and has no idea what he is," Remi said.

Everyone laughed, but Maggie was still worried about the interview she had with this Julie person later.

Remi leaned in and put a hand on Maggie's arm. Again,

it felt strange to be touched in a friendly manner, and not grabbed by a guard or a fellow prisoner.

"Julie's great. And so are all her friends, who I'm sure you'll meet sooner or later. Caroline and all the others are wives of former SEALs. We've all learned so much from them. And knowing they've made it, have successful relationships and families with men who did the same thing that our boyfriends do? It's reassuring."

"So...Preacher, huh?" Wren asked.

Maggie frowned at the other woman.

"You and Preacher?" she clarified.

She quickly shook her head. "Oh, no. I've only met him once."

"And yet, he arranged to get your car fixed, gave us your number, and he suggested the job with Julie..." Wren said, her voice trailing off suggestively.

But Maggie shook her head again, speaking more firmly this time. "No. It's not like that. I just met the man yesterday. I don't know anything about him. That's not what this is. *At all*. I'm not looking for a boyfriend. Not that he's even interested in me that way." It felt as if she was protesting too much, but the last thing she wanted was these women thinking there could be anything between her and their friend.

Maybe that's why they'd invited her out today. Because they assumed she and Shawn had something going on?

Disappointment hit her hard. Of *course* there was a catch to the invitation to lunch.

"Preacher's different," Remi mused. "He's still badass,

like all the guys on the team. But he's...reserved. He doesn't flirt. Doesn't go to the bars to pick up women. From what Vincent has told me, he's never even known him to have a girlfriend. So for him to have taken the lead in helping you out...it means something."

Maggie wasn't interested in hearing about Shawn's love life—or lack thereof. "You don't understand. As soon as I can, I'm leaving California. I'm not looking for any kind of relationship."

Wren and Josie both sat back in the booth, looks of surprise and...disappointment...on their faces.

Shit. Maggie hadn't meant to infer that she didn't want their friendship, but it appeared that was exactly what she'd done.

"Oh, we get it," Remi said, gesturing to the other two women. "None of us were interested in a relationship when we met our guys either. I met Vincent when we were stranded miles off the shore of Hawaii. We were left to die in the ocean. The *last* thing I was thinking about was any kind of relationship with the guy who was stranded with me. And Wren was drugged while on a date, and Safe happened to be there to help her. And Josie..." She paused and reached out to squeeze the other woman's hand. "She was left to rot in an Iranian prison, where Blink was dragged into the cell next to hers as a POW.

"Trust me, none of us expected, or were looking for, any kind of relationship either. We were all simply trying to survive. But here's the thing—sometimes the exact thing you need shows up when you least expect it. You might not have known you needed someone at your side, but suddenly he's there, and suddenly you can't imagine living one more day without him."

Maggie swallowed hard. She felt horrible for these women. She'd been feeling so sorry for herself for being in jail, but what Wren, Josie, and Remi had been through sounded like it was so much worse. "I'm sorry," she whispered.

"No, don't be sorry," Wren told her. "You and Preacher might not turn out to be anything other than friends. But who doesn't need more friends?"

She was right. Maggie had been so worried about keeping Shawn at arm's length, she hadn't considered he could be another potential friend. Look at her right now. She was having lunch with some women she'd never met, yet already genuinely liked. Who was to say she wouldn't end up feeling the same way about Shawn? She could certainly use some more people on her side.

The fact that he was in the Navy was hard to overlook, but the odds of Shawn and Roman knowing each other were slim...she hoped.

"You're right," she said, doing her best to smile reassuringly at the others.

"Of course we are," Remi said with a grin.

Maggie's phone vibrated in her purse at her hip, and thinking it might be Shawn—it was unlikely it would be anyone else, since the only other people who had her number besides Adina and her probation officer were sitting at the table around her—she reached into her purse to see who was calling.

It was from an unknown number.

"Do you guys mind if I get this?" Maggie asked. If it was her probation officer, she couldn't afford to blow off the call. And if it was someone calling for a ride, she'd need to tell them she wasn't working at the moment.

"Of course not."

"Go for it."

"No."

Clicking on the green button, Maggie brought the phone up to her ear. "Hello?"

"Heard you got out. Congrats. If you say anything about me to anyone, you'll regret it. If you try to pin what happened on me again, you'll find out just how much of a peon you are. Keep your mouth shut, bitch."

Then the line went dead.

Maggie felt sick.

"Are you all right? You're white as a sheet," Remi said in concern.

How had Roman gotten her new number? She'd blocked his cell number just in case, the one she'd had from before...and now it was obvious that he'd been keeping tabs on her. Probably waiting for the day she got out just so he could threaten her. How in the world she'd ever thought she loved the guy was a complete mystery. He was nothing but a bully. An asshole with power.

"I'm okay," Maggie whispered, feeling anything but.

"No, you aren't," Remi said, as Josie waved over their waitress.

"I'll go get the car," Wren said.

"No, I'm fine," she insisted. But the three women ignored her fake protests.

And the truth was, she was *anything* but fine.

With a single phone call, Roman had made it clear she'd never be free of him. At any time, he could do something that would get her thrown right back behind bars. He could plant drugs in her car, her apartment, then call her probation officer. She wouldn't be safe until she left this state, and him, far behind her.

And maybe not even then.

Before she knew it, Remi had paid for their lunches— ignoring Maggie's protests that she could pay for her own sandwich—Josie had gotten the waitress to package up their leftovers, and Wren was waiting at the curb when they exited the restaurant.

They were halfway back to her apartment when Maggie's phone rang again. Dread rose within her, but she pulled it out and looked at the screen.

She blinked when she saw who was calling.

Shawn.

The relief she felt was immense and immediate. "Hello?"

"Are you all right? Remi texted me and said you got a phone call that freaked you out."

Maggie's gaze flew to Remi. She looked a little sheepish and shrugged in apology.

"Maggie?" Shawn's impatient voice sounded in her ear.

"I'm good."

"You sure? You want to postpone the interview today?"

"About that. I'm not sure I know enough to work in a clothes store. I'm more of a science kind of person."

"I talked to several of my friends. Caroline's a chemist, and she was willing to see if she could help you get hired on with her company, but after talking to her, we both thought the best fit would be with Julie. If you really don't want to consider it, I'll figure something else out."

Now Maggie felt bad. "No, that's okay. I'll at least talk to her."

"Good. Now, do you need to postpone it?"

He was being really...nice. "No. It's fine."

"Fine. Right. I've been told that when a woman says something's fine, it's really not."

To her surprise, Maggie found herself giggling. "That's probably true, but in this case, I mean it."

"Okay. I'm going to say this, and it'll probably sound like bullshit or a line, but I'm being earnest. You can talk to me, Maggie. I know we just met, but if I can do anything to help, you just need to say something. And if you aren't comfortable talking to me, there are three women in that car with you who have been to hell and back and would understand *anything* you might be going through."

Maggie wasn't sure about that. They had supportive boyfriends who she had a feeling would protect them with everything they had. Look how Remi's boyfriend had acted when he'd found out Maggie was using Adina's name and ride-share account. He wasn't even dating Adina, and he'd done what he could to make sure Maggie wasn't stealing the other woman blind.

Her situation wasn't anything like what these women had apparently been through. They didn't have someone out to get them, and who wouldn't blink at putting an innocent person behind bars to protect themselves.

"Okay," she said belatedly.

She heard Shawn sigh, and she felt bad yet again. "I'll be there around three. Hopefully I'll have heard about your car by then too. Text if you change your mind about the interview."

"I will. Shawn?"

"Yeah?"

"Thanks."

She wasn't sure what she was thanking him for, but she wasn't surprised when he simply said, "You're welcome. See you later."

"Are you mad?" Remi asked as soon as Maggie had hung up. "About me telling him about the call?"

Was she? Surprisingly, Maggie found that she wasn't. "No."

"Good. You want to talk about it?"

"Not really."

"All right. But we're here if you do. We might be flighty and kind of weird, but we're good listeners. And we have some badass boyfriends we can sic on someone if you need it."

Maggie couldn't help but laugh at that. Roman

Robertson was no laughing matter, and yet here she was, doing it all the same. The last thing she'd ever do was put any of the SEALs close to these women in Roman's crosshairs. She didn't exactly know what his job was in the Navy, but he'd told Maggie his title when they'd first met, which had meant nothing to her. She'd had to google naval ranks to see where he was in the pecking order. She no longer remembered his title, but she recalled that he was pretty high up there.

"Thanks," she told Remi.

The rest of the ride home was a little less tense, and Maggie was genuinely sad to say goodbye to the trio. They vowed to keep in touch, and invites for future lunches and movie nights were promised.

When Maggie unlocked her apartment door a couple of minutes after waving the women off, she felt much lighter than she had after Roman's call. More human. Less like a monster who'd been locked behind bars for so long. She felt as if she was a seed bursting through the soil in the spring after a long hibernation for the winter. That was cheesy as hell, but appropriate.

Her life was complicated. With her lack of funds, the car being in the shop, Roman's reappearance in her life and his threats, the budding friendship with Remi, Wren, and Josie...and Shawn.

She still wasn't sure what to think about him. She didn't know the man, not at all, and yet she'd still allowed him to arrange to have Adina's car picked up, find her a job, and he'd gone out of his way to give her number to women who he was positive would take her under their wings. It was strange how little concern she had at the moment, considering the amount of control she'd given to a relative stranger.

Maggie supposed she'd have time later today to find out more about him.

It hit her then that she'd be alone in his car with him. He could literally do anything, drive her anywhere. But then again, she'd been alone with him last night too, and every day she accepted a customer on the ride-share program, she was risking her safety.

If it came down to trusting Shawn or a stranger, she had to admit...she'd pick Shawn every time.

It was that thought that truly surprised Maggie. What was it about him that made her want to instinctively throw out her convictions about never trusting another man?

She had no idea. But the idea was frightening.

Sighing, Maggie put her leftovers in the fridge and pulled out the cash from her wallet, counting it, trying to mentally make a list of what she needed to stay afloat for the rest of the month. She was making it...barely. Back in her before life, she'd had a healthy balance in her bank account, was a respected pharmacist, and had very few worries at all.

It was crazy how life could change on a dime. Time would tell if opening herself up to Shawn and the women would come back to bite her. But for the first time in ages...she felt a smidgen of hope.

CHAPTER FIVE

Preacher wasn't sure this was a good idea. Helping Maggie get a job? Yes. Getting involved in her life? No.

But he couldn't stop himself. There was just something about her that made him reluctant to stay away. Flash had offered to take her to My Sister's Closet for her interview with Julie, but it had only taken Preacher one-point-two seconds to decline.

He wanted to spend time with Maggie. Get to know her better. She'd gotten under his skin in less than twenty-four hours, and even though he knew he was setting himself up for heartbreak, Preacher was going out of his way to see her again anyway.

The woman had said herself that she was getting out of California as soon as she could. She'd been burned by a man—not just burned, incinerated. But the fact that Remi had texted him during lunch because she was concerned about Maggie told Preacher that she was special. Remi had a tender heart, so if *she* didn't like Maggie, there was no way she'd get him involved.

There was also a lot about the situation with Maggie's ex that concerned him. The most important was not knowing his name. He could always contact Tex and see what the computer genius could dig up about the man. If he was willing to throw his girlfriend under the bus and have her convicted for transporting drugs, there was no telling what else the man had done...or might still do.

But first things first. Maggie needed a job and Julie was eager to meet her. Both donations and customers had picked up for her secondhand clothing boutique, and she said she'd welcome an extra set of hands to help out.

After pulling into the parking lot of Maggie's apartment, he sent her a text letting her know he was there. Preacher would've preferred to go to her door and walk her down, but her trust issues prevented her from giving him the apartment number. Which was smart.

Compromising, he stood at the passenger door, waiting for Maggie to arrive. It didn't take long.

The day before, he'd been too concerned about finding out who she was and why she was using Adina's car and information to give people rides to take in much else. Today, his gaze traveled over Maggie from head to toe, studying her carefully. She was quite a bit shorter than his six foot three, maybe around five-five or five-six. Was probably in her mid-thirties, like him. She had shiny black hair that, like yesterday, was pulled into a long ponytail at the back of her head. It swung back and forth as she walked toward him.

She wore a pair of jeans that hugged her shapely legs... and as much as he hated himself for noticing, her tits were more than a handful. The T-shirt she had on accentuated her shape even as it fully covered her. Others might describe her as having an average figure, but in Preacher's eyes, there was nothing *average* about her. She looked healthy.

And at present, she seemed as if she didn't have a care in the world. Which made the old saying about how you couldn't tell what someone was going through by their outward appearance all the more true.

"Hey," Preacher said as she approached. He struggled to push away his thoughts about her figure...and how badly he suddenly wanted to see what was under all her clothes.

"Hi," Maggie returned. She stopped a good six feet away and simply stared at him.

"What?" he asked, confused at the way she was looking at him.

"Nothing. You just...you look different without your uniform on."

Preacher relaxed and chuckled. "I don't mind the camo, but since I wear it twenty-four-seven when we're on a mission, I try to wear civilian clothes when I can. You ready?"

She nodded, but said, "No."

Preacher had reached for the door handle of his car but

hesitated at her response. "You change your mind?" he asked.

"No. Yes. I don't know."

He couldn't help but chuckle a little. "That was as clear as mud."

She gave him a sheepish look. "It's just...I need a job. I don't like using Adina's account for Uber because it could send me straight back to jail, but all of this seems...I don't know...too good to be true?"

Preacher did his best to look relaxed. The thought of this woman being locked up again felt *wrong*. "This isn't a pity job," he told her. "You'll earn the money you make. Julie is an angel, but she works extremely hard and expects anyone who works for her to do the same. From what I understand, it's extremely rewarding to see women and girls find the perfect dress or outfit for whatever function they're going to, or to provide a family that's lost everything in a fire what they need clothes-wise in the short term, or to attend fundraising events and come away with buttloads of cash...but it's hard work. If you accept this job, you won't be sitting on your ass every day. You'll be sorting through donated clothes, going to high schools to give presentations, and dealing with the random customers who come into the shop."

"Wow, way to make the job sound appealing," Maggie said with a laugh.

But Preacher didn't even crack a smile. "I'm sure some days it's a shitshow. But it's the days when you see a girl who's never been able to afford something as simple as new clothes feel pretty, when she tries on a designer dress for the first time, that are the real reward."

Maggie tilted her head as she met his gaze. "Is that how you feel? With your job? I mean, I know it's not designer dresses, but I'm sure some days are horrible, yet the satisfaction you must feel when you rescue innocent people or take out a horrible terrorist who wants to kill as many people as he can has to be overwhelming."

Preacher blinked in surprise. She wasn't wrong. Not at all. "Yeah," he said with a small nod.

"Okay. Let's do this. I still don't know how good I'll be at this clothes thing. I have no fashion sense at all, couldn't tell a Walmart dress from a Louis Vuitton, but I'm not afraid of hard work."

Preacher was proud of this woman. She didn't seem the hysterical type or prone to drama. She did what needed to be done and didn't expect a pat on the head for it. He opened the door to the car and gestured to the seat. "Your chariot, my lady."

She chuckled and stepped forward.

Something clicked within Preacher right then. A yearning to do the same thing for this woman years from now. Holding open her door right before they set out for one adventure or another.

It was improbable as hell, but suddenly he knew—Maggie was the woman he'd been looking for his entire life.

Just as suddenly, he also knew that convincing her to

give him a chance would be the most difficult thing he'd ever done. But she'd be worth the effort.

He wasn't an idiot. He knew without a doubt that the chances she'd lower her guards enough to let him in were extremely slim. And why would she choose *him* when there were so many other men out there who were more experienced, had safer jobs, and were better-looking?

Even though there was a very small percent of a chance that she'd even consider going out with him—forget about deciding to spend the rest of her life with him—Preacher would do whatever he could to make her see that he was one of the good guys. He wasn't like her coward of an ex. He'd never let her take the blame for something he did. She needed someone to stand up for her, and next to her, and even in front of her sometimes.

And he wanted to be that man.

Instinctively, Preacher knew he was meant to be hers.

Shutting the door, he closed his eyes for a moment. The overwhelming thought of the journey he had ahead of him almost made him change his mind. But he'd never backed down from a challenge. From something that scared him. And Maggie Lionetti terrified the crap out of him. She might just be everything he'd ever wanted, and one wrong move could result in him losing her before he even had her.

Opening his eyes, he strode around his dark blue, sensible Chevy Malibu and hoped like hell everything with Julie would go all right today. Helping Maggie become more self-sufficient, shore up her self-esteem, was the first step in helping her get back on her feet. He could wait to court her until she felt stronger on her own. Maybe.

* * *

Maggie shook Julie's hand and returned her wide smile. This was happening. She'd been skeptical about the job... until she talked with the owner of the adorable boutique. From the front, the store looked high-end, fancy, like nowhere Maggie would ever want to work. But beggars couldn't be choosers, and she'd pretty much already decided she had no other choice but to take the job.

Then Julie had taken her into the back of the store, and Maggie had gotten a look at the chaos back there...and she'd understood a little more about why Julie needed help. There were bags of clothes *everywhere*. And still more were hung up on racks in every nook and cranny of the space. Even as Julie explained how things worked—incoming donations, requests for clothes from the Red Cross and other organizations, weekly donations to homeless shelters, and the visits to high schools with dresses for the girls to choose from—the bell over the front door tinkled regularly, and she had to go greet whoever had come in looking to browse or shop.

The woman *definitely* needed help.

But the thing that impressed Maggie the most was how unruffled Julie seemed. She needed and wanted the help, but she also made it clear that working here wouldn't be an all-consuming thing. She herself went home at five o'clock every day. Spending time with her husband was more important than anything else. And from the little Maggie knew about the woman's story, she wasn't surprised. Like Remi, Wren, and Josie, Julie had been through her own trauma and had found out the hard way what was important in life. Friends and family. Not working a hundred hours a week.

By the time they were done talking, an hour and a half had gone by. It felt more like she'd just spent time with a good friend rather than being in an interview. Maggie found herself eager to start. The pay was quite a bit lower than what she'd been making before she'd been arrested, but definitely more than she'd been earning driving people around. And the good thing was, it was one hundred percent legal, which was a relief.

When Maggie had brought up the fact that she was a convicted felon, Julie hadn't seemed concerned. She'd simply asked, "Are you going to steal from me?"

Maggie had answered with a firm no, and that was that.

It seemed too good to be true, but she tried to push that negative thought to the back of her mind.

"You want to text Preacher and tell him we're done?" Julie asked when they walked back into the main part of the store after shaking hands and agreeing that Maggie would start work in a few days, when she'd gotten her car back and had reliable transportation.

"Oh, I don't want to bother him at home. I can get an Uber."

"He's not at home," Julie said, looking confused. "I'm pretty sure he's down the street in the small bookstore."

"I told him that he could leave though," Maggie said.

Julie chuckled. "One thing you'll learn about a Navy SEAL...they pretty much never do what you think they should. They'll do what they think is right. Every time."

Maggie couldn't wrap her mind around that. Obviously she'd been around the wrong kind of people for way too long. She took her phone out of her purse and sent Shawn a text.

She and Julie made small talk and the next thing Maggie knew, Shawn was walking through the door, the tiny bell tinkling as he entered.

"So?" he asked, looking anxious.

"Preacher, meet the newest employee of My Sister's Closet," Julie said with a huge smile.

"Awesome!" he said, and Maggie could see his shoulders visibly relax.

Had he really been that worried? And was his concern that Julie wouldn't want to hire her, or because of something else?

She didn't have to wonder about that for long, because Julie said, "Jeez, do you look so relieved because I hired her or because she accepted?"

Shawn shrugged. "I had no doubt that Maggie would be an awesome interview or that you'd be happy for the help. But sometimes people don't click."

"We clicked," Julie reassured him. "Right, Maggie?"

"Right," she said. And she was surprised to find that

she wasn't lying. She liked Julie. She was no-nonsense, and what she was doing with her store to help others was inspiring.

"It's late. You're going to take her to get something to eat, right?" Julie asked.

She opened her mouth to protest, but Shawn beat her to it. "Of course." Then he walked over and bent down to kiss the other woman on the cheek. "Thanks, Julie. You're the best."

She rolled her eyes. "I'm the one who should be thanking *you* for bringing Maggie in."

"And I think I'm the one who should be thanking both of *you*," Maggie countered.

"We'll see if you're still feeling that way after your first shift," Julie said with a smile. "Now get. I'll see you later. Text me if anything changes and you need to start later than we decided. Regardless of how things look around here, I'm really flexible. If you need to change your hours or anything, we can work it out."

Things really *did* seem too good to be true. "I appreciate it."

"And I appreciate your willingness to work hard. We'll talk later."

Maggie waved at Julie as Shawn put his fingertips on the small of her back and they headed for the door.

If anyone else had dared touch her after only meeting the day before, Maggie would've told them to keep their damn hands to themselves. But for some reason, Shawn's touch didn't make her cringe. Even the memory of how the guards at the prison would grab her arm and sometimes shove her from behind when she walked didn't make her change her mind about Shawn being at her back.

When they were on the sidewalk, he moved so he was on the side closest to the street as they headed toward the lot, where he'd parked earlier.

"Were you really at the bookstore that whole time?" Maggie asked.

Shawn shrugged. "Pretty much. I did stop into a few other stores to browse before going to the bookstore."

"Did you get anything?"

To her surprise, Maggie could've sworn she saw a blush make its way up the back of his neck into his cheeks.

"It's a bookstore. Of course I did. You can't go in one and not end up buying at least a book or two."

"It's been a long time since I've splurged on something like that, but I used to go to the library all the time. I need to go back. I miss reading." It wasn't something Maggie would've admitted to many people. But again, Shawn made her feel comfortable sharing things she normally wouldn't. It was disconcerting but also felt...good.

"You want to go after we eat? I think there's a branch not too far from your apartment."

Maggie stopped in her tracks and stared up at the man next to her. Coming from any other guy, she would've thought the offer was a precursor to something else. But she was pretty sure Shawn was being genuine.

"What? What's wrong?" he asked, looking around as if

searching for some kind of danger that had her stopping on the sidewalk so abruptly.

"I'm not sleeping with you," Maggie blurted. She'd already told him that, but she felt the need to repeat it... just in case she was wrong about his intentions.

Shawn's worried look morphed into something else. Irritation. Disappointment.

It was the latter that made Maggie feel ashamed of her outburst.

"I know. We've already been over this, but okay. I'll go there again. The thought didn't even cross my mind. I offered to take you to the library because I thought you might enjoy doing something you hadn't done in a while—get a new book. I would've brought you to the bookstore and *bought* you something, but I figured that might offend you. Believe it or not, I've been where you are, Maggie. Not exactly, of course, but broke enough that all I could afford was noodles and, if I was lucky, gas in my car. The last thing I'd do right now is try to seduce you. And honestly, I wouldn't have the foggiest idea of how to go about it anyway."

"Right," Maggie said sarcastically. She was trying hard not to feel horrible for how she was treating this man. He'd been nothing but amazing to her, and she was being a bitch. But she couldn't seem to stop herself. Her shields had been crumbling, and she desperately needed to shore them back up to prevent herself from getting hurt once more. "You're a Navy SEAL. I'm sure women throw themselves at you all the time. But if that's what you think you're going to get out of helping me, you need to think again. I'm not going to be one more notch on your bedpost."

"There *are* no notches," Shawn said.

Maggie stared at him, unsure what he meant. "Uh-huh. Whatever."

"You want to know why I'm called Preacher?" he said.

It was weird that they were standing in the middle of a sidewalk having this conversation, but now that she'd started it, Maggie didn't know how to stop.

He didn't give her a chance to respond. "In boot camp, when we had breaks, all the guys would go to the bars to pick up women. I never went. Not even once. That's not my thing. They started calling me Preacher to make fun of me. But I didn't care. Not then, and even less now. When I sleep with a woman, it'll be because she's the one I want to spend the rest of my life with. Not because she's drunk and wants to brag about sleeping with a SEAL. Call me old fashioned, it doesn't bother me. I know what I want—and that's to wait until I find the right woman."

Maggie gaped at Shawn. Was he saying what she *thought* he was saying? "How old are you?"

He smiled. "Thirty-three."

"And you..." Her voice trailed off.

She wasn't going to ask. Nope, it wasn't her place and it was rude.

But he answered the question she was too chicken to ask anyway. "I told you, I'm waiting. So you have nothing to fear from me in regard to forcing you or pressuring you for sex."

This man was a *virgin*? It was unbelievable. He was...*gorgeous*. Stacked. Handsome. Beautiful, in fact. But more importantly, he was kind. Generous. Nice. A great friend. Loyal. *All the adjectives*.

How in the world could he be a virgin?

Shawn sighed. "Your reaction is exactly why I don't share that with many people. I just don't see the appeal in having sex simply for the *sake* of having sex. I've got some toys, so I'm not ignorant about how it all works. And I have a healthy sex drive. I just usually take care of it myself. I don't rely on women to satisfy my needs. I want a connection with someone before we share something as intimate as sex."

The more he spoke, the more flabbergasted Maggie became. And the more interested. It was somewhat ironic that him admitting he was a virgin made her *more* attracted to him, not less.

"So...you want to go to the library or not?"

He sounded so calm. Not at all worried that he'd told her something extremely personal and private about himself. Yes, he was trying to reassure her that he wasn't out to get into her pants, but still. "Yes," she found herself saying.

"Great. How's Italian sound for dinner? There's an awesome little mom-and-pop place not too far from here. I know the owners. They're amazing. And I guarantee you won't leave hungry."

"Is it possible to leave an Italian restaurant hungry?" she asked.

Shawn smirked. "You'd be surprised."

They started walking again, and as they did, her hand accidentally brushed against his.

"Sorry," he said with a small shrug as he looked down at her.

In that moment, Maggie realized she was seeing Shawn in a brand-new light.

She'd painted him with the same brush as her ex. They were both in the Navy, were very alpha, were comfortable in their skin. But Shawn and Roman were so different, it wasn't even funny. Yes, if they were lined up side by side, they'd seem very similar. But now that she was getting to know Shawn, she could see that they were like night and day.

Roman was the dark night and Shawn was the light of day. And she actually enjoyed being around Shawn. Wanted to get to know him better.

"What do you like to read?" she asked as they walked.

The smile he gifted her with made tingles shoot up the back of her neck. She liked when he looked at her like that. Liked it a lot.

* * *

Preacher's heart felt as if it was beating out of his chest. He couldn't believe he'd admitted that he'd never been with a woman to Maggie. She had to be thinking he was the most pathetic man she'd ever met. Who was a virgin at thirty-three? But he'd needed to do *something* to reassure her that he wasn't being nice simply to get her into bed.

Thankfully, his admission did seem to make her relax, which was his goal. But he was still second-guessing himself. His offer to take her to dinner and to the library truly came with no strings. He simply wanted to prolong their time together.

And it seemed as if she wanted that too. Their conversation flowed and they hadn't had one moment of awkwardness where they didn't know what to say to each other. He'd told her about his family in Maine, how he became interested in the SEALs, and even about some of his less top-secret missions.

In return, he'd heard about her adoption as an infant, and how she'd later found her birth mother, who'd died about a decade ago, before Maggie actually had a chance to get to know her. She had no siblings, adopted or biological. She told him stories about some of the things she'd done in college, and he couldn't remember laughing so much.

After eating too much, and rolling out of the restaurant, they spent over an hour at the library. He could've spent at least another hour but Maggie was looking tired, and she didn't protest when he asked if she was ready to go. She had a stack of books in her arms when they left, which for some reason made Preacher feel proud.

The only dark moment to their evening was when her phone rang. She'd answered it, and then, without saying a word, ended the connection with whoever was on the other end. She refused to tell him who it was, but it was obvious to Preacher that she was rattled by the call. He hated that she didn't trust him enough to talk to him, but it had only been a day since they'd met, even though it seemed way longer than that.

"I'm sorry I don't know anything about your car yet," he told her when he'd pulled into her parking lot.

"It's okay. I'll call tomorrow."

He made a mental note to make sure to get a hold of the mechanic first thing in the morning. He had no idea what was wrong with the car, but he wanted to make sure Maggie could afford whatever it was. He'd already worked out a deal with the guy that he'd charge half of whatever the cost was to Preacher, but he also wanted to make sure the fifty percent that was left was something Maggie could swing.

He hadn't lied when he'd told her earlier that he knew what it was like to have money issues. He was in a good place now, but he wanted to pay forward the favors he'd gotten back then to Maggie.

"I had a good time today," Preacher said...and immediately felt stupid. This hadn't been a date. Not even close. And yet it was still the best time he'd had with a woman in years.

"Me too," Maggie told him.

He wanted to prolong the moment, see if she wanted to do something with him again. But he wasn't sure how to bring it up. He just wasn't very good at this kind of thing. Dating.

"Thanks for introducing me to Julie. And for giving the others my number. Since I've been out, I hadn't realized how isolated I've become."

Her words made Preacher feel good. "You're welcome."

"So..." she said, drawing the word out.

"Right. I need to get going. Got PT in the morning," Preacher said, feeling as awkward as a teenager. "Do you want to go to dinner again with me sometime?" he blurted.

To his relief, Maggie nodded. "Yeah. I think I would."

"Great! I'll call you."

"Okay."

"Okay." Preacher knew he was smiling like a fool, but he couldn't stop. He stepped toward her impulsively and leaned down to kiss her on the cheek. She stiffened but didn't back away from him. "Sleep well."

"I will. You too."

"Call if you need anything."

She scrunched her nose at that. "I'm not going to need anything."

She was probably right, but Preacher couldn't help saying, "You never know. Talk to you later, Maggie."

"Bye, Shawn."

Preacher smiled all the way home.

CHAPTER SIX

"You've been awfully smiley the last few days," MacGyver said. "What's up with that?"

Preacher looked over at his teammate. They were currently doing sit-ups in the sand, and in a moment they'd be up and running down the beach again. It was early, the sun had just peeked over the horizon, and Kevlar was working them hard this morning. And yet, Preacher felt as if he was a new man. The last week and a half had been...awesome.

He'd talked with Maggie on the phone every night, even the ones he'd seen her after they'd both gotten off work. Her job at My Sister's Closet was going great. She said it was hectic, but she enjoyed it more than she thought she would. They'd gotten together three times since he'd taken her for the interview with Julie, and last night, she'd finally let him walk her up to her apartment door.

Things were progressing. Slowly, but any progress at all was a step in the right direction as far as Preacher was concerned.

"I assume things are going well with the chick who was impersonating Adina," Flash said.

"Her name is Maggie. And she was only using her Uber credentials because she couldn't find another job," Preacher said a little testily.

"Are we believing that she was innocent?" Safe asked.

Preacher did his best not to jump down his friend's throat. He didn't sound skeptical, was simply asking a question. But it still rankled. To his surprise, it was Smiley who answered.

"She's innocent," he said firmly.

"How do you know?" Safe pushed.

"When you meet her, you'll know," Smiley said without hesitation. "There's just something about her that screams innocent."

"So...is there anything that can be done?" Flash asked.

"About what?" Kevlar questioned.

"About her doing two years behind bars for something she didn't do," Flash clarified. "Is there anyone we can call to investigate and get her conviction overturned? Wait— does she know who set her up? What's up with *that* person?"

"Yeah, who's the asshole who set her up?" Blink asked, sounding angry on her behalf.

This was why he loved working with these men. They were always ready to throw down for the innocent.

"Preacher? What do you know about the guy? It was an ex, right?" Kevlar asked.

Preacher stood, along with the rest of his team, and headed down the beach at a fast jog. He might complain about these early-morning workouts, but he secretly loved them. They got his heart pumping and his blood flowing. Helped him think more clearly.

"Yeah, it was an ex," he confirmed. "But Maggie and I haven't really talked about it. She's extremely sensitive about everything that happened, and I can't blame her. She lives her life in fear of doing even the smallest thing wrong and ending up back behind bars. It sucks."

"I can imagine," MacGyver said. "Is her ex still around? Like, could he do something that would put her back in jail? Like make a false report to her probation officer?"

Preacher stopped in his tracks. The rest of his team kept running for a moment, before stopping and turning around to stare at him.

"Preacher?" Kevlar called out in concern.

He felt like an idiot. He hadn't even *thought* of that. Preacher was aware that Maggie wanted to get out of California, but he hadn't pushed her for details. He simply figured it was the bad memories and the high cost of living here that made her desperate to leave. But now that MacGyver had brought it up, she had to be terrified that her ex would do something to send her back to prison.

Especially if he'd been the one to put her there in the first place.

And she had hinted during one of their conversations that he was someone pretty high up in the Navy.

His teammates came back to where he was standing.

"What's wrong?" Smiley asked, his brow furrowed.

"He could absolutely do something that would put her back behind bars," Preacher said, answering MacGyver's question. "I think she's terrified of that exact thing happening."

"So what do we do?" Safe asked. "To help prevent that?"

Preacher swallowed hard. "I don't know. Without knowing who this guy is, we're kind of flying blind. She *did* tell me that he's in the Navy."

"What?"

"He is?"

"Shit. That complicates things."

Preacher had thought all the same things his teammates were expressing when Maggie had first admitted her ex was a naval officer.

"You need to find out who he is. Get her to tell you his name," Flash said.

"I don't think it's that easy."

"It should be. Is she protecting him for some reason? Does she still love him?" Safe asked.

"*No*," Preacher practically growled. He knew that without a doubt.

"I don't know. Sometimes it's hard for abused women to

leave their abusers. They think they love him, or her, and want to change them," Kevlar said.

"That's not Maggie's issue," Preacher said firmly. "She's afraid of him. And she's been getting phone calls. She doesn't tell me who they're from, and she hangs up almost immediately, but I can see they're affecting her. Scaring her. Now...I think they're from the ex."

Kevlar frowned. "That's not good."

"No, it's not," Preacher agreed.

"If this guy *is* in the Navy, we'll need proof of anything before we can go to NCIS," Flash said.

"Can't we just bring our concerns to them and have them investigate?" MacGyver asked. "And you don't even have to ask Maggie for a name. If he testified against her, his name should be in the court documents, right?"

"Yes. But I don't want to go behind her back. Not when we've just started seeing each other. It would feel like a huge betrayal of trust. She was *very* reluctant to even tell me that he was in the Navy. If I start investigating her case and find out who this asshole is without her knowledge, I have no doubt it'll kill whatever it is we've started together. I want her to trust me enough to tell me who he is freely," Preacher told his friends.

"I can understand that," Kevlar said. "But if he's threatening her..." His words trailed off.

"Fuck," Blink said under his breath. "It's a no-win situation."

Preacher agreed one hundred percent. He'd been an idiot. Blindly courting Maggie as if she was in a normal situation. But now that he'd stopped to think about it, her situation was anything *but* normal.

"Are you sure you want to get involved with this woman?" Flash asked. "And I'm not asking to be a dick here. She's a convicted felon, there will be a lot of things that will be more difficult or impossible for her, or both of you, if you get together."

Preacher did his best not to lash out at his friend. He was well aware of the consequences Maggie faced in the future because of what happened. She couldn't vote while she was on probation, it would be more difficult to get loans for everything from cars to homes, and she already knew about the difficulty in finding a job.

But the thought of not seeing her again made his skin crawl.

The thing was, Preacher *liked* Maggie. She was funny, kind, and considerate. And she was smart as hell. The more he was around her, the more he *wanted* to be around her. He'd never met another woman who made him feel that way.

"I'm sure," he told Flash belatedly.

"Okay, then we need to figure this out," Kevlar said firmly. "You need to work on getting the name of her ex so we know who we're dealing with."

Everyone else nodded in agreement.

That. It was reason number one hundred and sixty-seven why Preacher would give his life for these men if it came down to it. They were loyal to a fault and had no problem throwing down for someone they cared about.

"I'll see what I can do," Preacher said, already dreading the conversation he knew he needed to have with Maggie. She wasn't going to want to talk about her ex. Not only because talking about him would bring up bad memories, but because he honestly believed she was terrified of the man.

"Right. With that settled, everyone get your asses moving. We have four more miles to run before we can turn around and head back to base."

Everyone groaned but did as they were ordered.

Throughout the rest of the morning, Preacher tried to figure out how he was going to bring up the topic of Maggie's ex the next time they talked, and by the time they arrived back where they'd parked their vehicles, he was no closer to a viable plan.

But his friends were right. Maggie needed help. And she might not have realized what she was getting into when she'd picked up Remi the other week, but she was about to find out that Preacher and his friends weren't just pretty faces. They had some amazing connections and wouldn't hesitate to use them to help someone in need. And Maggie definitely needed someone on her side.

* * *

It was weird how much Maggie was looking forward to seeing Shawn tonight. The three times they'd met up in the last week and a half had been really nice. She'd never felt so...excited to be with someone before. Which, ironically, also made her want to be more cautious.

The memory of what Roman had done was fresh in her mind. How could it not be? Sometimes at night, when she was alone, she could still smell the jail cell where she'd spent two long years. The funk that came with so many people living in a small space felt as if it had seeped into her pores.

The thought of making one wrong decision and being sent back there was enough to make her want to hide under her covers and never come out again.

But when she was with Shawn, she wasn't trying to figure out how and when he was going to screw her over. She could let down her guard and just...be herself. Which was weird in itself, because she was still trying to figure out who the new Maggie Lionetti was. Prison had changed her, as it would anyone. But she didn't know if it had made her stronger or simply more cynical.

Tonight, Shawn was picking her up and they were going to dinner at a place called Aces Bar and Grill. He'd reassured her that it was laid-back and not a typical pub. Adina had mentioned it as well before she'd been deployed. Bars weren't Maggie's thing, but she'd been willing to give it a try.

Now though, she was having second thoughts. When Shawn called earlier, he'd sounded...off. He'd asked if he could come up to her place to talk a little before they'd left for dinner. So of course, she was nervous about what he wanted to talk about. She didn't think he was going to say he'd changed his mind about wanting to hang out with her, because he'd confirmed their plans to go to dinner afterward. But she couldn't think of anything else he'd want to discuss with her that would make him sound so serious.

And yet...she could. The big elephant in the room.

Maggie knew more than anyone that being with her wasn't exactly easy. Her past colored everything she did these days. She never drove over the speed limit, never brought attention to herself when out in public, kept to herself more often than not.

And maybe all of that was too much for Shawn. Maybe he was going to try to let her down easy in regard to them being friends, and was still planning on taking her to dinner as a consolation prize. One last meal together before ditching her.

Maggie's imagination was spinning out of control, and she was on the verge of calling Shawn and telling him she didn't want to see or talk to him anymore—out of self-preservation, not because it was what she truly wanted—when her phone rang.

It scared the crap out of her. She forgot she'd turned up the ringer today, so she could hear it while she was working—thankfully, at her new job, she could take calls and answer texts as long as there weren't any customers in the store. She'd missed a few of Shawn's messages in the last week, and the feeling of disappointment had hit her surprisingly hard, so she'd done what she could to mitigate missing him again.

Looking down, her stomach rolled when she saw

"unknown" on the screen. She wished not for the first time that she could ignore it. That she could send the call to voicemail. But she wanted to be available at all times to her probation officer. The woman wouldn't report her just for letting a call go to voicemail, but Maggie was desperate to do everything in her power to follow the rules that had been laid out for her when she'd been released from prison. Of course, she had her PO's office number saved into her cell, but it was always possible she was calling from a different phone.

She couldn't ignore the call, no matter how much she wanted to or how badly seeing that "unknown" on her screen made her stomach cramp.

Bracing for the worst, Maggie said, "Hello?"

"You're dating a SEAL?" the man on the other end of the line asked, venom oozing from every word. "Are you fucking kidding me?"

"Leave me alone, Roman," Maggie said, getting mad for the first time. It felt good. Usually she simply hung up on him and blocked whatever number he was calling from, but tonight she was done. D. O. N. E. *Done.* "I think you've messed with my life enough. I've kept my mouth shut and will continue to do so. But you need to stop calling me."

"Listen, bitch, you don't tell me what to do. I'm the one holding all the cards. And damn straight you'll keep your mouth shut. I can get you put right back behind bars with one phone call."

Maggie's knees went weak, and she crumpled to the floor right where she was standing. "Why?" she whispered.

"Why are you doing this? You screwed my entire life, Roman! Why are you still messing with me?"

"Because it's fun," was his response.

And the laugh that followed his blunt statement made Maggie realize he wasn't kidding. He really thought this was *fun*. Ruining her life was entertainment for him.

In a flash, she realized how badly she'd messed up. She should've been recording all her incoming calls. To have proof that Roman was harassing her. That he was the one who'd set her up two years ago.

As soon as she hung up, she'd rectify that, find one of those recording apps. She didn't know how they worked, but she'd figure it out. Maybe Shawn would help.

The thought of the man who would be at her apartment at any moment made her stiffen once more. And as if her thoughts of him had transferred somehow to Roman, he spoke again.

"I'm warning you now, if you say anything to that Frogman or his friends, you'll regret it. I'll find out who he is sooner or later and I'll make him regret ever meeting you. I told you that I'm a big deal on this base, and I wasn't lying. I can make sure his team rots in some jungle, or their blood boils in a fucking desert on the other side of the world. Once I know who he is, if I hear even one peep that they're asking about me, it'll be a done deal. I *own* you, Maggie. Don't you fucking forget that."

How could she? He wouldn't let her.

Maggie opened her mouth to once again plead with her ex to leave her alone, but it was too late. The line was dead.

Robotically, she clicked on the number he'd called from and blocked it, despite knowing it would do no good. Roman apparently had an endless supply of burner phones to call her from. She could get another phone number, but he'd found *this* one—a new number she'd gotten after her release—easily enough. She had no reason to doubt he'd find another number just as easily.

She sat on the tile floor staring into space, racking her brain trying to figure out what to do. She could run, leave the state, hide out, but that would only get her in worse trouble. She had no idea how to disappear or get a new identity. Besides, despite what her record said, she wasn't a criminal. Didn't like being in trouble. She was a rule follower, and just the thought of living the rest of her life hiding from the authorities gave her hives.

But Roman's threat against Shawn and his friends rang true. She didn't doubt for a second he could totally screw with their team, and she knew he wouldn't hesitate to do so. The last thing she wanted was for someone else to get hurt or in trouble because of her bad decisions. And dating Roman Robertson was one of the worst decisions she'd ever made. It had literally ruined her life.

She'd be damned if it would ruin Shawn's as well.

Knowing what she had to do made Maggie feel even more helpless and scared.

When a knock sounded on her door, she jerked in surprise. Slowly, she stood, her feet tingling from sitting on them for so long. Woodenly, she walked to the door and looked through the peephole. It was Shawn, as she expected.

Opening the door, she swallowed hard. He looked good. Really good. He wore a white and blue checkered flannel shirt, which should have seemed a little silly in southern California, but it only made him look even more handsome than usual. It also seemed as if he'd tried to actually style his hair, rather than simply running a hand through it, as he usually did. His beard was neatly trimmed, and the smile on his face when he saw her should've made Maggie's toes curl. Instead, it made her feel nauseous, considering what she was about to do.

The smile on his face slowly faded and he asked, "What's wrong?"

Taking a deep breath, Maggie stepped back. "Nothing. Come on in."

Inviting him in was a big step for her. It showed a level of trust that she'd thought had been pulverized because of all she'd been through. But this man had somehow managed to break through her shields and gotten her to trust him in record time. Too bad she was about to ruin that with what she was going to tell him.

They walked into her apartment and, feeling awkward, Maggie turned to Shawn. "Do you want something to drink?"

"No. I want you to tell me what has you so freaked out. Do you not want me here? I can go. Or have you changed your mind about Aces? We can go somewhere else."

That was one of the things she liked most about this

man. He did whatever he could to always make sure she felt comfortable. And he wasn't afraid to come right out and ask her what she was thinking and feeling. In her experience, men didn't do that. They pretended everything was all right, even when it clearly wasn't.

She needed to get this done. Rip it off like a Band-Aid. "This isn't working for me, Shawn. I don't think we should see each other or talk anymore."

To her consternation, Shawn didn't have any kind of outward response to her words. He simply stared at her.

To cover the awkward moment, and her unease, Maggie kept talking. "It's not that I don't like you. I do. It's just... I've got a lot on my plate. You know, with the job you helped me get, and making sure I don't do anything that could violate my probation. Adina will be coming home in a few months, and I need to focus on finding a new place to live."

"I see," he said when she was finished.

But he didn't turn around and leave. Didn't do anything other than stand there and continue to stare at her with those deep green eyes of his.

"Shawn?" she asked, feeling nervous now.

To her surprise, he reached out and took the cellphone she was still gripping like it was a lifeline. She let go and watched as he unlocked it and began scrolling on the screen.

"How did you know my phone's passcode?" she blurted.

"I've been around you enough to see you unlock it a few times."

Well, crap. Of course he had. He was a Navy SEAL. Observant. And she needed to be better at protecting herself. Especially with her ex apparently out to get her.

"He called again," Shawn said. It wasn't a question.

Maggie held her breath as she stared at him. She wasn't sure if she wanted him to figure out all her secrets and convince her to let him stay, or just turn around and leave.

God, who was she kidding—she didn't want him to leave. Not at all. He made her feel safe, which was a hell of a thing after not feeling safe for even one minute of the day for the last two years. Even when she was sleeping, Maggie had been on edge. She and her cellmate had gotten along, but all it would've taken was one argument and she could have found a homemade shank in her chest.

"I can help you," Shawn said softly and evenly. "My friends and I have connections. This is what I wanted to talk to you about. All I need is a name and we can do the rest. You don't have to say anything else, just tell me who your ex is and I'll make sure he doesn't do anything that would get you in trouble again."

Maggie wanted to sink into his arms and tell him all her secrets. But she locked her knees. Roman's call was still way too fresh in her mind. He'd do exactly what he threatened. He'd somehow get Shawn and his SEAL team sent to the far reaches of the world if they started looking into him. They'd be in danger. Hell, if Roman had his way, he'd probably try to get them killed in the line of duty, just so she'd truly not have anyone on her side.

"I can't." She'd meant to stick to her guns and tell him

that her decision wasn't about her ex, but instead, those two little words popped out.

"He threatened you," Shawn said.

And for the first time, Maggie heard emotion in his tone. He was pissed. Not at her, but on her behalf.

She broke. When was the last time someone had been offended and pissed off because of something being done to her? Years.

Tears filled her eyes, even as she shook her head.

"It's okay. You can tell me," Shawn cajoled.

But she couldn't. She'd protect this man from her ex if it was the last thing she did. Maybe it was stupid, it probably was, but she was so afraid of Roman, of what he could do, that she couldn't put Shawn at risk.

He took a step toward her, and the next thing Maggie knew, she was in his arms. Her nose was buried in his neck as she latched onto him as tightly as she could. It was still shocking, how good the touch of another human felt. She understood now why newborn babies needed their mother's touch, or that of a warm human body. There was something so elemental about being held as if you were the most important thing in another person's life.

"I've got you. You're all right," Shawn murmured as one hand tangled in her hair and the other spanned across her upper back. She felt cocooned by him. Safe.

But he was wrong. She wasn't all right. Not in the least.

Maggie felt Shawn shuffling them backward, toward her couch. He sat them both down but didn't let go of her, which was the exact thing Maggie needed right now.

How long they sat on the couch with his arms around her, Maggie clutching him as tightly as she could, she had no idea. But after a while, she leaned back. Shawn still didn't let go, but he let her put some space between them.

"Okay," he told her.

Maggie frowned. "Okay what?"

"I'll back off. Give you time to truly believe that I'm on your side. That I can have your back. I'm not afraid of your ex, Maggie. He's a bully, and bullies never win."

Maggie wasn't so sure about that.

"My friends and I can help you, but I understand that you need more time to let that sink in. We know people. People who can prevent that asshole from fucking with your life any more than he already has. Not only that, but they can look into what it might take to get your conviction overturned."

He couldn't have shocked her more if he'd stood up and took off all his clothes and began to dance around the room like a male stripper. "What?" she whispered.

"I don't know if that can be done, but our connections will do whatever they can to at least see if it's possible."

The urge to blurt out all her troubles to this man was strong. But a small part of her was still skeptical. Though she did trust him enough to ask, "Can you teach me how to record calls on my phone?"

"Yes." The answer was immediate and heartfelt.

Just knowing she'd be able to record Roman's threats in the future, and maybe catch him incriminating himself, made her feel better. Stronger.

"Thank you."

"You don't have to thank me for doing what any decent person would do."

She did. He didn't understand how little kindness and decency she'd experienced recently. Adina letting her stay in her apartment had literally been it, before Shawn came into her life.

Taking a deep breath, Maggie straightened, and Shawn's arms finally fell away from her. The pang of regret was surprising but she pushed it down. "You wanted to talk?" she forced herself to ask.

Shawn stared at her for a moment. "I did. You don't. So we won't."

It struck her then—he'd wanted to talk about her ex. He wasn't planning on ending their friendship. Relief swam in her veins.

"But when you're ready, no matter when that is, what time of day, how long from now...I'll listen. Okay?"

Maggie nodded.

"You hungry?"

As if her stomach heard his words, it growled.

He grinned.

Lord, this man was good-looking. Boyish at times, almost scary in his intensity at others. But carefree and handsome as an actor at the moment.

"Come on. And fair warning?"

Maggie waited for him to continue.

"I didn't plan on everyone showing up to join us. But I mentioned to Kevlar that I was bringing you to Aces tonight and the next thing I knew, Remi was texting me to find out what time we'd be there. Then the guys decided they hadn't played pool in a while. And someone called Julie, who called Caroline and Fiona and Summer. Jessyka, who owns the bar, found out...and now it's a freaking party or something. So if you want to go to McDonald's, or even stay here and order in, we can."

Maggie was genuinely shocked. A bunch of random people never wanted to hang out at the same place as her, just because she was there. Granted, none of what Shawn had just said actually indicated it was all about *her*.

Then his next words blew that thought out of the water.

"Although if we go to McDonald's, everyone will probably just shift their plans and follow us there. They're determined to meet you and make you feel welcome."

Feeling like the Grinch when his heart grew three sizes with the kindness of the Whos from Whoville, Maggie swallowed hard.

"Is the food at Aces good?" she managed to ask.

"The best."

"Then we can go there."

"You sure? There's nothing I want more than for you to join the ranks of my Navy family, but not at the expense of you feeling uncomfortable or unsure."

"As long as none of your friends is my ex, then I'll be fine."

He blinked, then frowned. "They aren't your ex," he said firmly. "First of all, no one I hang out with would be douchebag enough to get a woman thrown in prison for two years over drugs. Second, most of my friends are either married, or dating a woman they want to eventually marry. And third—fuck him. Your ex."

Maggie couldn't help but smile at those words.

"I love that. Seeing you smile. You don't do it enough," Shawn said quietly. He licked his lips, and his gaze locked on her mouth.

Her breaths sped up and her belly clenched, but not with hunger this time. It had been ages since she'd felt desire. She'd been too consumed with protecting herself. But now? Sitting this close to Shawn, smelling his clean scent, seeing how obsessed he seemed to be with her lips... Maggie felt her nipples tighten, and she resisted the urge to squirm, to press her thighs together to try to ease the ache between her legs.

Mimicking him by licking her own lips, Maggie leaned forward an inch.

That encouragement was all Shawn needed. His hand came up and rested on her cheek as his gaze finally moved upward to meet hers. "May I?" he whispered.

Shawn asking for her consent for something as innocent as a kiss did something to Maggie. The shields she'd been desperately holding on to shattered into a million pieces.

Instead of answering him verbally, she leaned in, closing the distance between them.

Their lips met, and any thought of innocence in regard to kissing this man flew out the window. It felt as if she'd touched a live electrical wire. If she thought Shawn being a virgin would mean he didn't know how to kiss, she'd been wrong.

His hand shifted from her cheek back into her hair and his head tilted. He licked her lips, and Maggie opened for him.

A moan escaped as he devoured her. He licked, sucked, and nipped at her, making her lose all sense of time and place. He tasted like mint, as if he'd brushed his teeth recently, and she needed more.

His hand held her still as they kissed, and Maggie had never felt more feminine in her life. She was a pile of mush, and she found herself melting against him.

He pulled back way before she was ready, and the way he was panting reassured her that he was just as affected by their kiss as she'd been.

Licking her lips, she tasted him there. Instantly, his gaze went back to her mouth, and he ran his thumb along her bottom lip reverently. Some women might think the move was calculated, something he did to seduce. But Maggie could see the awe in Shawn's eyes.

"Thank you," he whispered after a moment.

"For what?" she asked, struggling to get her equilibrium back after that kiss had rocked her world.

"For trusting me with yourself."

Was that what she'd done? To Maggie's surprise, she realized she had. Usually for the first kiss with a man, she held back. But there'd been no holding back with Shawn. She'd shown him her desire, her wants and needs, and he hadn't broken that trust by putting her on her back on the couch and pushing for more.

"I thought you were a virgin," she blurted. "That didn't feel like a virgin's kiss."

Shawn chuckled. "I am," he said. "And while I've kissed women in the past, that was the first time it's ever felt like *that*."

She knew what he meant without having to ask. Knew what *that* was. It was a deep-seated feeling that she was finally with the right person.

"And for the record, while we're on the subject. I may not have ever had intercourse with a woman, but I *have* shared orgasms with one."

Maggie blushed but asked, "What does that mean?"

"Let's just say I'm a big fan of oral."

She felt her cheeks heat even more at that. "Oh."

"Yeah. Oh. I just want to make sure you don't think I'm going to be like a fifteen-year-old kid, fumbling around and not knowing what I'm doing in bed."

"I think that kiss told me everything I needed to know." Maggie didn't comment on the fact that his words definitely implied they'd eventually end up in bed together. She was surprised to realize she wanted that. Almost desperately.

This man had changed her life in such a short amount of time. It should've scared the shit out of her, but instead it felt...right. For a second, she wished she'd met him in her before life. But then again, since she wasn't the same woman she was back then, she probably wouldn't have recognized how special he was two years ago.

"I'm not going to fuck this up," Shawn said, more to himself than to her.

"I probably *will* do something that will fuck this up," she couldn't help but say.

"Then I'll make sure I'm the voice of reason for us both. Now, come on. My phone's been vibrating in my pocket for the last few minutes, I'm sure it's everyone at Aces, wondering where we are. You sure you want to do this?"

"I'm sure." And she was. Suddenly, Maggie couldn't wait to hang out with Shawn's friends. "And I'm even going to let the comment about your vibrating pocket go."

He burst out laughing and stood, grabbing her hand and hauling her to her feet in the process. "Appreciate that." Then he leaned down and kissed her hard and fast, before turning and heading for the door.

Her lips had still been tingling from their *last* kiss, and that nonchalant smooch, just because he felt like it, almost put Maggie over the edge. "Wait! My purse. Do you still have my phone?"

He waited patiently as Maggie got herself situated and ready to leave.

They walked out the door, her hand in his, as if it was the most normal thing in the world. And for once in her life, it felt as if it was.

CHAPTER SEVEN

Glancing around the room, Preacher scowled. Usually he loved hanging out with his friends, but tonight they'd been hogging Maggie, and he was a little annoyed. He'd been looking forward to seeing her talk, laugh, come out of her shell a little more.

And she was doing all that and more—except it wasn't *him* bringing it out of her. It was his friends.

A hand clapped his shoulder as he was standing by the pool table, waiting for his turn to shoot. Glancing over, Preacher saw Dude standing beside him. He was a retired SEAL who'd gotten close to Preacher and the rest of his team. Wolf, Abe, Benny, Cookie, and even Julie's husband, that team's former commander, was there tonight. Along with their wives. It was a full house, and the building overflowed with happiness and friendship.

"It's hard, isn't it?"

For a horrified moment, Preacher thought Dude was commenting on the state of his dick. He'd been half erect all night, ever since that amazing kiss he'd shared with Maggie on her couch.

Dude chuckled as if he knew *exactly* what Preacher was thinking. "It's difficult letting everyone commandeer her."

Inwardly sagging in relief, he nodded.

"She needs this," Duke continued.

He didn't need his friend to tell him that. He'd noticed it for himself. Maggie had come alive at Aces. Smiling, laughing, acting as if she'd known the other women all her life. She'd been nervous at first, but it hadn't taken her long to loosen up. And it hadn't escaped Preacher's notice that it didn't take any alcohol either.

She'd politely declined any drinks, instead asking Jessyka, who was helping behind the bar, for a glass of sparkling water with a lime. She'd been sipping on that single drink all evening, and when Preacher had taken her aside to check in with her a while ago, make sure she was good, he'd commented on it. She'd sheepishly told him that if she carried something that looked like an alcoholic drink, no one gave her a hard time. Then added that it was against her probation to drink alcohol or use drugs, admitting that she was drug tested on a regular basis.

Preacher understood...and he kicked himself for not thinking about that. When all the important people in his life had glommed on to his date, he should've changed the venue to somewhere other than a bar. He wasn't much of a drinker himself, and he often used the same trick as

Maggie, finding that if he nursed a bottle of beer all night, people were less likely to press more alcohol on him.

"Preacher?"

Turning to Dude, he realized he'd zoned out. "Sorry. I know. She's outgoing."

"Everything okay with her? The situation with her ex?"

Preacher wasn't surprised Dude knew about Maggie. The SEAL community was tight...and gossip typically spread like wildfire through the ranks as well. It didn't matter that Dude and the other men from his team were retired. They were still obviously very much in the know.

"Honestly? I don't think so," Preacher told his friend. "He's been calling her. She hasn't told me what he's saying, or even who he is, but I know it's eating at her. She's stressed that if she's caught doing anything wrong, she could go right back to prison."

"And since her ex got her in trouble in the first place, he could plant more drugs on her or do something else that would cause her probation to be revoked."

"Exactly," he said with a nod.

"You need to find out who her ex is."

Preacher huffed out a frustrated breath. "Do you think I don't know that? It's not as easy as just asking, Dude. We talked about it tonight, and she's terrified of him. Like, she broke down even *thinking* about talking about him. I promised that I'd give her some time. Time to realize that I'm really on her side. To trust me. I also let her know that my friends and I would do what we could to look into the situation that put her in jail in the first place, and if there's a way to get her conviction overturned, we'd find it."

"She was caught with a pretty large amount of drugs in her car. Even if they weren't hers, there's no doubt that she was driving and the car belonged to her," Dude said.

"I know."

"And it's likely the only reason she got as short a sentence as she did was because she had no criminal history whatsoever."

"I know that too," Preacher said. "But if we can prove that her boyfriend was involved in drug trafficking, and find out who his connection might have been in Los Angeles, it could go a long way toward proving her innocence." He wasn't so sure about that, because Dude was right. There was no denying that the drugs had been in Maggie's car. But he hoped there might be video from the officer's body camera showing her genuine surprise, and that, along with anything else Tex or one of his computer friends could dig up, might just help her case.

"I think the more pressing issue is making sure the asshole leaves her alone," Dude said.

He wasn't wrong.

"Yeah," Preacher agreed.

Both men were silent for a moment, then Dude said, "You need anything, you call me. Not Wolf. Not Kevlar. *Me.* I'll take care of it for you. Whatever it is. It enrages me when men abuse women. Especially the ones important to us. And since Maggie's important to you, she's important to me. Our women should be protected at all costs.

Not because they're weak or can't look after themselves, but because they're the most precious things in our lives.

"My team and I have been where you are. Where it seems bad things keep happening to the ones we love. It's frustrating and infuriating. You've all been through enough. With Howler, Remi, Blink, Josie, Wren, *everyone*. So I'm taking what happened to your woman personally. It's bad enough that someone lied and caused her to have to spend two years behind bars, but to continue harassing her after she's out, to be causing her so much worry when all she should be thinking about is getting back on her feet...it's *wrong*. Offensive."

Preacher wasn't sure what to say. So he simply nodded once.

Dude returned the gesture, then headed across the room to where his wife, Cheyenne, was standing with Caroline, Remi, Wren, Josie, and Maggie. He wrapped an arm around her waist and leaned down to say something in her ear.

Cheyenne practically melted into her man's arms. She turned and looked up at him with so much love, it almost made Preacher uncomfortable. She nodded at him, and he stepped away, heading toward Benny, Flash, and Mozart.

Preacher decided he'd given Maggie enough space to get to know the women and men who'd come to meet her. Now his need to be near her was almost overwhelming. He followed in Dude's footsteps, stopping at her side.

The smile she gave him when he put his hand on the small of her back was almost blinding.

"Hi!" she chirped.

"Hi," he returned with a small smile.

"You know Cheyenne and Caroline, right?" she asked.

Preacher chuckled. "Yeah."

"Right, sorry. Of course you do. We were all just talking about how crazy a SEAL's job is. How one day you could be sent to help with a natural disaster, and the next, you're having to jump out of a plane miles and miles above the ground so you can infiltrate a hostile country holding hostages, to get them out."

She wasn't wrong. "Doesn't sound like a very interesting conversation to me," Preacher said, taking a risk and putting his arm around Maggie's waist. He was thrilled when she leaned against him.

"Are you kidding? It's fascinating. And I know you can't talk about your missions, deployments, whatever they're called, but for the record, I'm so proud of you. What you do is amazing, even if no one knows about it. It's even more amazing *because* of that."

Her words meant the world to Preacher. He'd been thanked before. People thanked him for his service all the time. But somehow the words coming from this woman carried so much more weight.

"And Caroline is a chemist. And Cheyenne's a nine-one-one operator. Isn't that cool?"

Her enthusiasm was contagious, and everyone around her had huge smiles on their faces.

The rest of the evening, Preacher stuck by Maggie's side as she made the rounds to different groups of people.

She fit in perfectly with all his friends and was a great conversationalist. She complimented people, listened with all her attention to whoever was speaking, and genuinely seemed interested in whatever was being discussed.

Preacher was comfortable staying on the sidelines, and not only because as a SEAL, he was used to blending into the background. He wasn't the best in social situations. But with Maggie, he didn't need to be. He was content to let her take the lead, and he simply stood by her side as she won over every single person in the bar.

She even spoke to some people Preacher didn't know. She was in her element, and he loved seeing her come out of her shell.

When last call was made, Maggie was still going strong. Most of the SEALs had left, along with their significant others. The only holdouts were Smiley, Summer, and Mozart. The five of them were sitting around a table, chatting amicably.

He was surprised that Smiley had stayed behind after the rest of their teammates left. Even more surprising, he'd just finished opening up to all of them about the woman he'd briefly met in Las Vegas while extricating Josie from the clutches of the bitches who'd kidnapped and attempted to sell her into sexual slavery.

"Let me get this straight," Maggie said, with the most serious look Preacher had seen on her face all night. "This woman, Bree, had been sold to this asshole by her ex, and while you guys were making sure Josie was safe, she just disappeared?"

Smiley nodded.

"Where did she go? She couldn't have disappeared into thin air. Did her ex get to her? Did the asshole guy have an accomplice? Was she simply too scared to stay in the truck and wait for you to get back?" Maggie asked.

"I don't know," Smiley said with a shrug. "But it's eating at me. What if she *did* get caught by the traffickers again? Is anyone other than me looking for her? Does anyone even know she's gone? The wondering sucks."

"Wow. I bet she's scared," Summer said.

"What can we do to help?" Maggie asked, putting a hand over Smiley's.

"Nothing," he said without hesitation. "There's not much *to* do."

"But you said that you've been going to Vegas on the weekends trying to find her. Maybe we can come help with that," she insisted.

Smiley shook his head. "I've been going to Vegas every weekend I can spare, but it honestly feels pretty hopeless. It's not as if she's still going to be hiding in the bushes in that neighborhood or anything. I was able to track down the apartment where she was living, and it's empty. Cleaned out."

"What? Really? By her?" Summer asked.

"No clue. But that was a dead end. She hasn't been back to her job either. She's literally just disappeared."

Preacher frowned. He'd had no idea Smiley was so invested in finding the mysterious Bree woman. Of course, he and the rest of the team knew he'd been going back to

Vegas frequently, but not that he'd actually tracked down her address or where she worked. He'd never seen Smiley so...worried about anyone. Especially a woman. It wasn't as if he was unfeeling, more that he always had a tight rein on his emotions.

"Well, shit," Maggie said. "If there *is* anything we can do, you'll tell us, right?"

"Yeah, most of us women know what it's like to feel completely alone," Summer added.

"Thanks, ladies," Smiley said. "I'm sure she's fine. I just don't like not knowing."

"It's like those crime shows that end without telling the viewers who did it," Summer said.

"Or the ones about missing people where you watch for the entire hour and at the end...they're still missing. I hate that," Maggie agreed.

Preacher was right there with the women. He hated that too, which was one of the reasons he didn't watch a lot of crime TV. He saw enough of death and hatred in his job. He didn't need to see it on his time off as well. He was a sports kind of guy. Football, basketball, soccer, and diving. Preferably the stuff off the high platforms. Or cliff diving. He could get lost for hours watching YouTube videos of athletes leaping off insanely high platforms.

"...to go."

Preacher had missed most of what Mozart had said, but figured he was calling it a night by the way he stood up and helped his wife to her feet.

Maggie stood and hugged her new friend, promising to

keep in touch. Smiley said his goodbyes as well, and then it was only Preacher and Maggie at the table.

"You look happy," he told her.

"I am," she said without hesitation. "I love your friends. They're all so nice."

They were. "I didn't know you were a night person. Or an extrovert."

Maggie laughed. "Does it make a difference?"

"Not at all. It just makes me realize anew how hard a time you must've had in the last two years."

She sobered. "Yeah," she agreed. "I kept to myself because I was terrified of saying the wrong thing to the wrong person. And it wasn't as if I had a choice to stay up late or not, lights went out at the same time for everyone."

"I shouldn't have brought you to a bar tonight. I'm sorry," Preacher told her.

"It's okay. I've never been much of a drinker, so it's not as if I was tempted."

"Still. It wasn't cool. I'll make sure we have our get-togethers somewhere else from now on. Or at least until your probation is over."

Maggie stared at him for a long moment. "You're almost too nice to be true."

"I'm not nice," Preacher countered.

She rolled her eyes.

"Okay, I'm nice to you, but I don't think I go out of my way to be nice to anyone else."

"Whatever, Shawn. Every single person I talked to tonight had nothing but great things to say about you."

He didn't want to talk about himself. He'd much rather take care of her. "You ready to head out?" he asked.

"Yeah. I didn't mean to keep you up so late. You have PT in the morning...well, later today, right?"

"Won't be the first time I don't get a lot of sleep before having to work out. It's fine," Preacher said.

"See? Nice," Maggie said under her breath as she stood.

Preacher found himself grinning. He gave the bartender a chin lift as he steered Maggie toward the door. He led her to his car, keeping an eye on their surroundings. It was extremely late, or early, and nothing good usually happened after midnight. But it was quiet, and they arrived at his car without any issues. Preacher got Maggie settled in the passenger seat and he went around to the driver's side.

"It's a beautiful night," Maggie said as he pulled out of the parking lot. Her head was tilted back and she was looking out the side window. "It was weird going so long without seeing stars. Or the moon."

Making a split-second decision, Preacher turned his car toward the naval base.

"Where are we going?" Maggie asked.

"You have your ID on you, right?" he asked without answering her question.

"Of course."

"Good. Get it out. Please."

She did as he asked and was silent the rest of the way to the base. They went through the gates, and Preacher showed both his military ID and Maggie's driver's license to the guard. Once they were waved through, she asked again. "Shawn? Where are we going?"

Except this time she sounded nervous, which he hated.

"There's a spot I want to show you. I swear you're safe with me. I have nothing nefarious planned. I just think you'll love this place as much as I do. I sometimes come here when we get home after an especially gnarly mission."

It didn't take long to get to the stretch of beach he had in mind. Preacher parked on the side of the road; there wasn't even a real parking lot. He shut off the engine and by the time he'd walked around the car, Maggie was waiting for him. He held out his hand, relieved and thrilled when she took it.

He followed an almost nonexistent trail through some bushes and tall grasses to the small strip of sand. This wasn't a good swimming beach, which was why it wasn't well known or popular. There were a lot of jagged rocks along the shore and the waves broke over them almost nonstop. It was actually kind of loud on the sand, but that had never bothered Preacher.

He stopped and turned to Maggie. "Sit with me?"

She nodded, and they both sat on the soft sand. Preacher wished he'd thought to bring along a blanket or something, but it was too late, and the trip had been too spontaneous for that. But Maggie didn't seem to mind.

"It's beautiful. I love the sound of the waves hitting the rocks."

"Look up," Preacher told her.

He smiled as a small gasp left her lips. "Oh my," she whispered.

Preacher didn't need to look up to know what she was seeing. The stars out here, away from a lot of the light pollution from the city, were amazing. They seemed to go on forever.

Instead of looking at the stars, he kept his gaze on Maggie. Her mouth was open in awe and he would swear as he watched, he saw her muscles relax. This was why he wanted to bring her here.

"It's...wow. It makes me feel so small," she whispered.

"Yeah. Coming here reminds me that I'm just a tiny little cog in this thing called life."

Her gaze moved to him. "That sounds like song lyrics."

He chuckled. "I don't know about that. All I know is that hearing the water and seeing the stars...it settles me."

"Yeah," Maggie agreed, looking back up at the sky.

After a moment, Preacher tugged at her hand, the one she hadn't pulled out of his grip. He urged her to lie back. It would be easier on her neck muscles. She went willingly.

They lay there on the sand, staring up at the sky for several minutes without a word.

"Thank you," Maggie said after a while. "I needed this."

"You're welcome." They were both going to have sand in their hair, he'd be exhausted at PT tomorrow, but it was worth it. At least in his eyes.

"You know what the worst thing about being in prison was?" she said after another few minutes had gone by.

He could think of a lot of things that would suck about being locked away. But instead, he asked, "What?"

"Knowing he was out *here*. Free. Living his life. Knowing people were looking up to him. Thinking he was this great guy. That makes me petty as hell, but I can't help it. I thought the same thing once. But then I started to see him for who he really was. I was distancing myself from him. Was going to break up with him. But I waited too long." She sighed.

Preacher desperately wanted to know the name of the asshole she was talking about. But he refrained from asking. Hopefully she'd tell him when she was ready. Then he'd see what he could do about ruining the guy's life, just as he'd done to Maggie's.

"He'll get his," Preacher told her. "I firmly believe that those who do bad things to others will pay for their wrong-doings in the long run."

"I don't like having such hate in my heart for a person. It doesn't feel right. But I can't help it."

"You're human," Preacher told her with a squeeze of his hand. "And he did you wrong in a huge way."

"Yeah," she agreed. She fell silent then. After another few minutes went by, she asked, "What time is it?"

"Does it matter?"

She laughed a little. "It does if you miss PT because we're sitting out here on the sand."

Preacher chuckled. "Even if I did miss it, it'd be okay. I mean, yeah, I'm supposed to be there, but Kevlar isn't going to report me AWOL if I'm not."

"He seems like a good man."

"He is."

"I really like Remi, Wren, and Josie. They were all so nice to me. I feel as if I've known them forever. It's hard to believe all that stuff really happened to them. I'm glad they're okay."

"Me too."

"Shawn?"

"Yeah, Maggie?"

"This is great. Thank you."

"You're welcome."

She took a deep breath, then sat up. "You need to get home."

"You want to stay and look at the stars longer?" Preacher countered.

She considered his question, then shook her head. "No, I think I'm good. But I wouldn't protest coming back here sometime."

"Done."

Preacher got to his feet then helped Maggie stand. He wiped as much sand off himself as he could and helped get some out of Maggie's hair. To his surprise, she returned the favor, and the feel of her hand in his hair made goose bumps break out on his arms.

Then she grabbed his hand and led the way back through the small break in the bushes and grass to his car.

The ride to her apartment was done in a comfortable silence. He walked her to her door and couldn't stop himself from putting his hand on her cheek. "I had a good time tonight. A *great* time."

"Me too."

Preacher felt tongue-tied. There was so much he wanted to say and do, but he couldn't get his thoughts in order.

Maggie didn't seem to have the same problem. She went up on her tiptoes and lifted her chin. Preacher didn't hesitate to lean down.

The kiss they shared in front of her door was just as passionate and intimate as the one they'd had earlier. Except this time, Maggie pressed her body against his, and he could feel her along every inch of his body. She felt at home there. As if she was made for him.

As corny as the thought was, it felt right. Preacher wrapped his arm around her waist, holding her against him, even as his other hand went to her nape. Her own arms clung to him just as tightly.

They were both breathing hard when she finally pulled back.

"You sure you'll be okay to go to PT in..." She pulled her wrist around and looked at her watch. "Three hours?"

"I'm sure," Preacher said. Working out would suck, but he didn't care. He wouldn't have traded tonight for anything. Especially sleep.

"Will I talk to you tomorrow?"

"Of course. You working at the store?"

"Yeah. Noon to five."

"You want to have lunch together? I can come by around eleven with sandwiches or something."

"I'd love that," Maggie said with a big smile.

"Sleep well," Preacher told her, forcing himself to let go of her and step back.

"You too."

Maggie turned around and unlocked her door. She stepped into the apartment and turned back to him. "Shawn?"

"Yeah?"

"I *want* to tell you. I...I'm just not there yet. The last thing I want is to put you in his crosshairs."

Preacher knew exactly who and what she was talking about. As much as he hated her words, they also made hope flare. She'd said *yet.* And she wanted to trust him, she just needed more time. He could give her that. Maybe. "He can't hurt me," he said.

"I think he could. And I can't risk it."

"Let me help you, Maggie," Preacher said. "You don't have to deal with this alone anymore."

She gave him a sad smile. "Good night, Shawn."

"Night, Maggie. I'll see you tomorrow."

"Bye."

Preacher stood in the hall until he heard her lock the door, and only then did he turn and head toward the stairs. Frustration swam through his veins. Not sexual frustration, although he felt that too, but frustration over the situation Maggie was in. He hated that someone was still out there threatening her. She needed help, but until she gave him the information he needed, he was on the outside looking in. And he absolutely hated that, but he wanted her trust more than he wanted to pry. Wanted her to open up about her ex of her own free will, without him having to go behind her back to find out who the guy was.

In the meantime, the only thing he could do was be there for her. Make her feel safe. Then, and only then, would she hopefully open up to him.

* * *

As he sat behind his desk at the naval base before his day got started, Roman Robertson studied the picture he'd been sent and grinned. It was exactly what he needed to blackmail Maggie. To continue to torment her. He wasn't doing it because he wanted her back or had any kind of ridiculous thought about if he couldn't have her, no one could.

It was exactly as he'd told her—because it was fun.

He'd had no idea she'd get pulled over when he'd put the drugs in her car to take north to his contact. But when she was, he'd felt a huge rush of power knowing that no matter *what* she said, she'd take the fall for something he'd done.

Roman loved having people at his mercy. That was why his job as an officer in the Navy was so perfect. He loved being saluted, being treated with respect, having millions of the government's money at his disposal. And since he'd put in his time, he didn't have to worry about being deployed or being put in harm's way. He could order others to do the difficult shit.

And thanks to the picture on his phone—taken by one of the many people who would do whatever he asked without question because of the power he held over them —Roman knew exactly who he was going to fuck with next.

He'd warned Maggie. Told her that if she did anything that made him question for a second whether or not she was even thinking about ratting him out, she'd regret it. This felt like a perfect time to both mess with her head *and* fuck with men who thought they were untouchable.

Roman had hated SEALs ever since he'd failed to make it through BUD/S himself.

Fuck her.

Fuck him.

It would be fun to mess with them both.

Let the games begin.

CHAPTER EIGHT

"What?" Maggie asked in disbelief.

The last week had been quiet. Almost too quiet. She hadn't gotten any threatening calls from Roman, work had been smooth, and she'd loved getting to know Shawn better and better. And his kisses made her knees weak and her lips tingle. She wanted more but wasn't exactly sure how to proceed, since he was a virgin. She didn't mind that he was inexperienced, but she wasn't sure if she should take the lead. He was an alpha, that was clear. Would he be turned off if she made the first move?

It looked like it was a moot point for the time being.

"We're being deployed today," Shawn said in her ear. It was just before lunchtime, and Maggie had thought he was calling to ask what she wanted him to bring her to eat, but instead he'd dropped a hell of a bomb.

"Deployed? For how long?"

"Shit," Shawn muttered. Then he sighed. "We haven't talked about this part of my job, but unfortunately, I can't tell you much of anything. That's the nature of being a SEAL. Many times we don't even know ourselves how long we'll be gone. But our missions aren't like your friend Adina's deployments. They typically don't last for months."

The panic Maggie felt was a surprise. She hadn't known Shawn, or his friends, for that long, but the thought of not being able to talk to him every night like she'd been doing, or see him, felt wrong.

She'd learned a lot from Remi and the other women, however. This was what it was like being with a military guy. Besides, it wasn't as if she wasn't used to being alone.

As if Shawn could read her mind, he said, "Remi, Wren, and Josie will be here for you. And Caroline, Summer, and the other women too. And their husbands. You aren't alone, Maggie. I promise."

"I know," she whispered. And she did. The way everyone had embraced her had been nothing short of a miracle. She'd never had so many friends before. And it felt great.

"I wanted to be able to tell you in person, but the orders came down and we have to leave almost immediately."

"You'll...be careful?" It sounded stupid, but suddenly Maggie was afraid for Shawn.

"I'm always careful. And now I've got something, someone, to come home to, so I'll be even more vigilant."

Wow. That was... Maggie wasn't sure what that was. But

his words made her toes curl and for the first time in years, she felt as if she really mattered. "Shawn," she whispered.

"I know, this sucks. But it's what I do. Usually we have more prep time, but sometimes this happens. I'll be back before you know it. Again, if anything comes up, call Dude, Cheyenne's husband. He'll be able to help you."

Maggie wanted to ask what he thought might come up, but she knew what he was referring to. Her ex. She'd told him the other day that she hadn't heard from him in a week, and while she was relieved, it also made her worry that he might be planning something. Of course, that admission didn't make Shawn happy. At all.

For the first time since they'd met, Maggie wondered why she was working so hard to keep her ex's name a secret from Shawn. Yes, she was scared of what Roman could do, but if people knew about him, who he was, then if anything happened to Maggie, maybe Roman would be considered just a little more seriously.

"When you get back, we should talk," Maggie blurted. Now that Roman's last threats weren't so recent, she felt braver about telling Shawn who he was.

"We will," he told her. "I need to go, we have a lot to do to get ready since this mission came about so unexpectedly. Be safe while I'm gone. Maggie?"

"Yeah?"

"I'm going to miss you. I've really enjoyed the talks we've had every night."

Maggie sagged. "Me too," she admitted.

"I'll call as soon as we're back on base. Okay?"

"Okay."

"Take care."

"You too."

Maggie reluctantly clicked off the phone and sighed. Already she felt more alone than she'd been since the day she'd met Shawn and his friends.

By the time she got to My Sister's Closet for her shift, word had obviously gotten out that Shawn and his team had been sent on a mission.

"How're you holding up?" Julie asked.

"Honestly? I'm not sure how to feel," Maggie said.

"If it's any consolation, it gets easier. Not your man willingly going into danger when everyone else is running away from it, but him leaving. And I'm not really one to talk, as my husband was a commander and by the time we got together, he was thinking about retiring, but that's what Caroline, Fiona, and the others say. Wait, we should call them. No! I know! Let's have a sleepover!"

Maggie blinked at the other woman. "A sleepover?" she asked incredulously.

"Yeah! They're really fun. Caroline usually has them at her place. She has a basement that's pretty big and lots of comfy furniture we can crash on. We can invite Remi, Josie, and Wren too. I'll call her now!"

Maggie wanted to protest. Tell her that at thirty-five, she was way too old for sleepovers, but the other women had to be at least ten years older than she was. And the more she thought about it, the more the idea of hanging with the women she'd met at Aces in a more intimate setting sounded fun.

When was the last time she'd really *had* fun? Probably a week ago, when she'd met all Shawn's friends at the bar.

To her amazement, the sleepover was planned before the end of the day. The group text Maggie was in had been active with Wren and the others asking a million questions, and she'd even heard from Caroline about how excited she was to host the get-together.

It was planned for the following weekend, and Maggie was looking forward to the outing with more enthusiasm than she'd had in a very long time.

* * *

A week later, Maggie found herself sitting cross-legged on a queen-size bed in Caroline Steel's basement, surrounded by ten other women. For dinner, Caroline had made four huge charcuterie boards and everyone was stuffing their faces with finger foods.

Maggie had needed this. She'd started falling back on old habits during the last week...sticking to herself and getting too deep into her own head. The texts from her new girlfriends and the occasional phone calls from Remi, Wren, or Josie had kept her from going out of her mind. And her job at the clothing store at least got her out of the apartment.

Shawn being gone made her realize how much she needed human interaction. The two years behind bars had almost broken her. Yes, there were plenty of chances to interact with others, but most of her fellow inmates weren't trustworthy. And that made all the difference in the world. Maggie realized that she could trust not only Shawn, but his friends as well.

And these women? Maggie had never known the value of true friendship until meeting them. How having someone to talk to could make the difference between having a shitty day, and one that was merely annoying.

She chuckled to herself. She was becoming quite the philosopher. It was ridiculous.

"What's so funny?" Cheyenne asked.

"Nothing. I was just thinking about how different my life is now than even a few months ago."

"Girl, that part of your life is done. Gone. You aren't going back," Wren said firmly.

Everyone else agreed immediately.

Maggie loved them for it...but that wasn't quite true. She was one mistake away from standing before a judge and possibly being sent right back to prison. But she wasn't going to get into how all it would take was for Roman to decide he wanted to follow through with his threats and she'd be incarcerated again. "Thanks, guys."

"Can I ask a question?" Remi asked.

"I think you just did," Summer said with a giggle.

"I mean another one," Remi said with a roll of her eyes.

That set everyone off, and it took a moment for the room to quiet enough for Remi to actually ask her question.

Maggie braced, figuring she was going to ask her something about prison. No one had really come out and asked about all the things most people took for granted. Like using the bathroom, showering, how meals worked, and what she *did* all day.

But instead of turning to Maggie, Remi looked at the older women, the SEAL wives who'd been involved with the Navy for years. "Does it get easier? The deployments?"

"I got this," Caroline told the other women, before meeting Remi's gaze. "I would love to sit here and say that yes, it does. But at least in my case, the opposite was true. Each time Matthew left, I found it harder and harder. Maybe because I had a better idea than most of the situations he and his teammates were heading into. Maybe because I loved him harder and deeper with every day that we were together. Maybe I was just sick of him leaving me alone. I don't know. But no, they don't get easier. That's not to say that I wasn't more proud of him every time he left. And grateful that he and the others were out there doing what needed to be done. If not him, then who?"

"I was thinking about this the other day, when I saw that three hostages in the South Pacific—I forget which island—were rescued. They'd been taken from the hotel where they were staying and held for ransom. What would happen if men like ours weren't willing to do what needed to be done? To put their lives on the line to help others?" Cheyenne said.

"What would *I* have done?" Josie asked. "No one was looking for me. And Nate could've escaped, but instead he went through more torture because he wouldn't leave without me. I'm in awe of him and his friends."

"I think the question is...can *you* handle what Kevlar does?" Jessyka asked Remi gently. "Because sometimes, being a SEAL wife or girlfriend sucks. But most of the time it's like any other relationship. You have fights, you're glad to see each other after a long day's work, you worry about money, and you love each other for who you are."

"I just...this latest mission...it feels...*weird*," Remi said.

"I agree," Wren said. "I mean, I haven't been with Bo for very long, but in the past when they got a mission, they usually had longer to plan. It makes me worry that they went into a situation they weren't ready for."

"They didn't get at least twenty-four hours?" Alabama asked.

"No," Wren said. "Bo called from work and said they were leaving in like two hours. He didn't even get to come home to say goodbye."

"Hmmm, that does sound unusual," Summer agreed.

"It *is* odd," Julie said. "Look, I don't have all the answers just because I'm with a former commander. But generally the leaders try to give their people time to talk to their families. To say goodbye. Two hours either means something major is happening somewhere, and there was no time for anything other than debriefing and getting them on a plane...or someone fucked up."

The room was silent for a moment. Then Caroline grabbed her phone and started scrolling.

"What's up, Caroline?" Fiona asked.

"I'm just looking at the news. Seeing if something happened somewhere."

Everyone waited and watched as Caroline stared at her screen. Finally, she lifted her head and shrugged. "Just because I can't find anything major doesn't mean it isn't happening."

The others all started talking at once, trying to figure out why the team might've been sent out so quickly, while also reassuring Wren, Josie, Remi, and Maggie that the guys were fine and would be back soon.

But Wren's question made the hair on the back of Maggie's neck stand up. What if...

No, it was a crazy thought. He wouldn't...would he?

Yeah, he would.

The question was, did Roman *really* have the clout and power to send a team of Navy SEALs off on a mission they weren't fully prepared for? It was terrifying to even think about.

Instinctively, she looked down at her own phone. She hadn't gotten any calls from Roman in almost two weeks now. She'd hoped that meant he'd grown tired of messing with her. But what if he hadn't? What if this was his way of telling her that she and everyone she cared about would *always* be under his control? That she'd always have to look over her shoulder and wonder if he was there, waiting, lurking, preparing to fuck her life in any way he wanted.

She shuddered.

"Maggie? What do you think?"

Jerking her head up, she looked at Cheyenne. "I'm sorry, I wasn't listening. What do I think about what?"

The other woman gave her a sympathetic smile. "About not talking shop anymore and making hot chocolate and watching a movie."

Maggie agreed wholeheartedly. The thought that seven men might have been put in danger because of her made her nauseous. If anything happened...

She couldn't go there. Shawn and the others were very good at what they did. Even if—and it was a big if—Roman had something to do with them being deployed, they'd be able to handle it. Maggie had heard enough stories about the men in action from Remi, Wren, and Josie to know that down to her bones.

But still, she couldn't stop wondering about Roman. Would he really use his power to get the guys sent off to some foreign country?

She'd have to be extra careful. On alert. Maybe he'd sent Shawn away so he could more easily get to her. The thought of him planting drugs in her car again, or in her apartment, or spiking a drink so she'd fail a drug test... there were lots of ways he could screw with her so she'd break one of her rules of probation. The thought made her want to hide under her covers in her apartment and never come out again.

Following behind as all the women headed upstairs to the kitchen to make hot chocolate, Maggie shivered. What if Roman came after one of *them*? It was bad enough that she'd spent as much time behind bars as she had. What if he did something to get one of her friends sent away?

She wouldn't be able to handle that.

It was time. Time to talk to Shawn. She'd already decided to tell him who her ex was, but she needed to tell him *everything*. As soon as possible. She had no idea if he and his friends would be able to do anything to keep her safe, but at least they'd know. Maybe, just maybe, Shawn would be able to do something to stop Roman from ruining someone else's life.

But on the flip side...Roman could ruin *Shawn's* life.

No. She had to believe Shawn when he said he could take care of himself and that he had friends who'd be able to help her. Because anything else was straight out of her worst nightmares.

CHAPTER NINE

"Seriously, what the fuck is this?" Smiley asked as they gathered in the bunk room they'd been assigned on the nuclear-powered aircraft carrier currently stationed in the Mediterranean Sea.

Preacher had the same question, and obviously so did his teammates. They'd been questioning this mission one-on-one with each other for the last week, but this was the first time they'd discussed it as a group.

"Why the hell are we here?" Flash asked. "There's no imminent threat from anyone and there're already two SEAL teams aboard this ship."

Kevlar frowned. "I talked to our commander today, and he's trying to figure out what's going on. He thinks someone messed up and wires got crossed. He thought we were coming over here as support for the other teams, but since all we've done is sit here, he started asking questions.

It seems the mission we were supposed to support got canceled—but no one informed the commander. Bottom line, we *shouldn't* be here."

"So when are we going home?" Safe asked.

"That's the thing...I'm not sure," Kevlar explained.

"Fuck," Blink swore.

"This is bullshit," Preacher added.

"I know. And the commander's working on it. But you guys know how shit works. It could be tomorrow or a month from now before heads get out of asses and we're sent home."

"It better not be a fucking month," Safe growled.

"Can't we call Tex? Surely he can do something to get this FUBAR'd situation fixed. I have a meeting with a detective in Vegas that I don't want to miss in a couple weeks," Smiley said.

"I'm on it," MacGyver said, his thumbs moving lightning quick over the keyboard of his phone screen.

"I don't think we should bring Tex into this," Kevlar said. "I'm sure the Navy will get it figured out."

Smiley snorted. "Yeah, right, like they *figured* they should send us here when we definitely aren't needed?"

"Okay, you have a point," Kevlar conceded. "Let me know what he says, MacGyver."

"He says he's on it."

"Wait, *what*? You already got a hold of Tex, explained the situation, and he's working on it?" Flash asked.

"Yup," MacGyver said with a grin.

"Hot damn! Maybe we should pack," Safe suggested.

Preacher wasn't so sure about that, but anything the computer genius could do to fix this fucked-up situation would be welcome. They'd been on this ship for too damn long.

He'd sent a few emails to Maggie since he'd been gone, and even though she said she was fine, he sensed that something was off with her. He wasn't sure what, longed to be able to talk to her in person because he could read her pretty well when they were face-to-face.

"So I guess the sleepover went well," Kevlar said, changing the subject.

"What I would've done to be a fly on the wall for *that*," Flash said, laughing.

Safe threw a pillow at his friend. "I don't know what you think goes on at those things, but I'm completely sure it's not what's in your head right now."

"You mean they aren't all wearing skimpy little negligées and having pillow fights?" MacGyver asked, trying to sound innocent but failing.

"Don't ever think about Wren in a negligée again," Safe threatened.

Everyone laughed. "Remi said they talked about being SEAL wives and girlfriends, about how much they missed us, and then drank too much sugary hot chocolate and watched movies. Preacher, apparently Maggie won the contest on who could stay up the latest."

He smirked. He had no doubt about that. His Maggie was a night owl. "Did you hear what she did while the others were all sleeping?" he asked.

"Hands in warm water to make them pee? Put plastic spiders all over the house to give the girls a heart attack when they woke up? Set alarms on everyone's phones?" MacGyver asked.

Everyone chuckled.

"That's a little juvenile, isn't it?" Flash asked.

"She took their bras, soaked them in water, and put them all in the freezer," Preacher said.

Kevlar, Safe, and Blink grinned, having obviously heard about the prank already from their women, but the other three men's mouths dropped open.

"Seriously?"

"Holy crap, I think I love her."

Smiley lived up to his nickname and grinned maniacally. "Knew I liked that girl."

"It sounds like they all had a good time," Blink said.

"Any word about her ex?" Safe asked.

Preacher sighed. "No. But she's getting closer to talking. I can tell."

"So...she told you he was a high-ranking Navy member...Any chance this mysterious asshole could've had something to do with all of us sitting on our asses, twiddling our thumbs on this ship, while our women are back home missing us?" Kevlar asked quietly.

"There's no way," Preacher said. But the question made him uneasy all the same.

"That would be impossible, right?" Safe questioned.

"No clue. If her ex is someone high enough in the chain of command, maybe," Flash said.

"He would have to be a captain or higher," Smiley said.

"Most likely an admiral," MacGyver agreed.

"But would an admiral really be involved in selling drugs and tormenting an ex? Would he really go to the lengths Maggie's ex did to get her put in prison? And for what? Why would he do something like that?" Flash asked.

Preacher had the same questions.

"No clue," Kevlar said. "But either some huge glitch happened to get us here, or we have to at least consider maybe Maggie's ex has way more clout than we expected. Unless someone knows something about an imminent declaration of war that we don't know about yet, which is unlikely."

Talk turned to the unstable conditions of many of the countries in the area. Preacher let his friends' words go in one ear and out the other. He couldn't stop thinking about who might've messed up enough to get their SEAL team sent to this ship on such short notice. Or the fact that maybe it wasn't a mistake at all. And if it wasn't…what were the odds it was actually connected to Maggie? Did her ex really have *that* much power in the Navy?

If he did, they could both be in danger.

It was a crazy idea. As far as he knew, her ex didn't even know about him. Shouldn't even know he and Maggie were seeing each other. Hell, what they'd been doing could barely even be called dating.

But as soon as he had the thought, Preacher knew he was lying to himself.

The kisses, the phone calls, the dinners, holding hands.

They were definitely dating. And if her ex found out, why would he even care?

He had too many questions and no answers...and it was maddening. And now that Kevlar had brought up the possibility of Maggie's ex being involved in this fuck-up of a mission they didn't even need to be sent on, Preacher couldn't stop thinking about it. The thought made him more anxious to get back to Southern California. To Maggie.

* * *

Maggie's phone rang around ten at night a few days after the sleepover, and for one moment, she had the thought that maybe it was Shawn. Maybe he was back. She missed him terribly. In a way she hadn't missed anything in her life before now. Even when she was in prison and was missing Del Taco, or having spices on her food, that was *nothing* like the pit in her stomach from missing Shawn.

But when she looked at her phone, her muscles clenched with anxiety at seeing the dreaded word—unknown.

"Hello?" she said tentatively as she answered.

"Hi, Mags. How are you?"

She closed her eyes. She'd honestly thought Roman had given up. That he'd finally moved on. But of course she'd been wrong.

"Don't hang up," he ordered, right when she was about to do just that. "I'm calling to let you know that if you don't want your boyfriend sent to worse places than a ship in the middle of the ocean, you'll continue to keep your mouth shut."

Her worst fear had just been realized.

"Why...?" she whispered.

"Because I can," Roman said, clearly amused. "This time, I just sent them on a fool's mission. But next time it could be Iran. You think Blink might like to revisit that cell where he and his girlfriend were guests? Or maybe North Korea...how do you think the guys would like that? I think they'd stick out like sore thumbs, huh? Maybe get captured and thrown in work camps. Or I hear Russia's nice this time of year."

"Seriously, Roman, *why*? You've already fucked up my life! Why are you doing this?"

"I already told you—because it's fun. And to make sure you don't screw up. I have pictures of you, bitch. Making out with that pansy-ass SEAL in his car. I have eyes and ears *everywhere*. Nothing you do is a secret to me. I know all about you working in that fucking clothing shop, your little sleepover at Caroline Steel's house, the visit to that apartment building on Third Street. If I hear *anything* about that SEAL and his team looking into me, they're as good as dead. You hear me? I'll have them shipped out so fast your head will spin, and I'll do whatever it takes to make sure they never come back."

"I won't say anything! Just leave them alone!" Maggie pleaded.

"Or maybe I'll get your ass put back in prison. It was so

much fun the first time, watching you go down. I could have a chat with your probation officer. Or it wouldn't be hard to put *another* stash in your car, maybe break into your apartment and sprinkle some paraphernalia around. Enough to get your probation revoked and add time to your sentence. Don't fuck with me, Maggie. Now that I've proven what I can do, be smart for once in your life."

She wasn't sure what else to say.

"What's the draw, anyway?" Roman asked.

Maggie wanted to hang up, but she couldn't. She needed to keep him talking, let him keep incriminating himself.

"Everyone knows SEALs are shit in bed. They only care about getting themselves off. Their egos are too fucking big to think about anything other than racing to the finish line. But you know what? On second thought, it makes perfect sense that you're with him. I mean, it's not as if *you* were any good in bed either. The worst I've had—and I've had a lot. You just laid there like a dead fish."

Okay, maybe she didn't need to hear what else he had to say.

"You gave the worst blowjobs that I've—"

Maggie clicked off the connection and immediately blocked the number he'd called from. Then she went to the app that she'd installed and made sure the conversation had recorded.

She had plenty of material to have Roman put in jail, but she was scared to death to bring it to anyone. Because she had no doubt he wouldn't immediately be arrested.

There would have to be an investigation. They'd ask him about the call. Probably play it for him. But if he wasn't put behind bars right then and there, she was screwed. He'd do *anything* to make her pay. She wouldn't be safe. Not even close.

Carefully, Maggie saved the message into a folder on her phone and emailed it to herself as well. Later, she'd save it on her computer. If something *did* happen to her, if she disappeared without a trace, there would be some record of who had it out for her. The *why* was another story. Even she didn't understand exactly why Roman was determined to ruin her life. She'd thought she was a good girlfriend. But she'd obviously done something to piss him off. Or maybe he enjoyed having power over others.

She didn't want to believe it was just like he said. This was simply fun for him.

Whatever the reason, it didn't really matter anymore. All that mattered was the clear fact that he had no problem messing with Shawn and his team, putting their lives in danger, just to screw with her.

Feeling guilty as hell, Maggie sat on the couch in Adina's apartment and stared into space. Then some of the other things Roman said began to sink in. Someone had taken pictures of her and Shawn, making out in his car. That had to be in the parking lot of My Sister's Closet, a few days before his deployment. A happy memory that was now tainted, knowing that they'd been watched.

They'd also followed her to an apartment she'd thought

about renting. They knew she'd gone to Caroline's house with her friends.

She was putting *so many* people's lives in danger.

Then something surprising happened—anger began to grow deep inside her.

She'd done nothing wrong. *Nothing*. Even though the judge believed the drugs were hers. Even though she'd made her share of mistakes in the past. That didn't mean she deserved what was happening now. And Shawn and his friends *certainly* didn't.

The only way to stop this was to do exactly what she feared most. Tell someone about what was going on. Who Roman was, and all about his threats.

And the one person she trusted enough to tell was Shawn. Which was hard, because telling him would put him in immediate danger. But he was a SEAL. He wasn't some random man with no connections. He'd said it himself, he knew people. People who could hopefully not only keep *her* safe, but everyone else too.

If she didn't say anything, Roman wouldn't stop. He'd probably send Shawn and his friends to one of those awful places he threatened anyway, just because he could. It wouldn't matter that Maggie hadn't told anyone who he was. At least if she said something, if she exposed Roman for the criminal that he was, others would be prepared for whatever he might try next.

At this point, she was willing to do whatever it took to keep her new friends safe, even if it meant she wasn't. She'd face whatever consequences her actions brought, as long as they were on *her*.

She was terrified of Roman and what he could do, but she was even more scared of what he could do to others. And that was what made up her mind.

The ironic thing was that if Roman hadn't threatened Shawn, if someone hadn't followed her to Caroline's house, she would've done exactly what he wanted. Kept her mouth shut.

But now that he'd brought others into it, innocent people who didn't deserve for some psychopath to ruin their lives, Maggie had found her backbone. Roman Robertson wouldn't hurt someone else the way he'd hurt her. She'd do whatever it took to make sure everyone knew what a scumbag he was. Or die trying...which was definitely a possibility.

CHAPTER TEN

It had taken another week, but finally they were home. Preacher wasn't sure what had actually happened, but one day they were just called to the admiral's office on the ship and told they were leaving the next morning. At that point, it didn't matter if it was Tex's doing or if someone in the chain of command realized what a waste of resources it was to have three SEAL teams on that ship, not doing anything...but they'd been sent home.

It was four-thirty in the morning, and even though Maggie would be sleeping—hell, she'd probably gone to bed only a couple hours ago—Preacher didn't hesitate to call. Kevlar, Safe, and Blink had already called their women as well.

"'Lo?" Maggie said sleepily when she answered.

"Hey, it's me," Preacher said with a small smile at how out of it and adorable she sounded.

"Shawn?"

"Yeah. We're home."

"You are?" She definitely sounded awake now.

"Yup."

"Are you coming over? Do you want me to come to your place? Are you okay? Is everyone else all right? What do you need me to do?"

Preacher chuckled, and he couldn't believe how touched he was by her eagerness and concern. He'd never had this. Had envied his teammates when they called their women after returning from previous missions, but hadn't expected how much joy he'd get out of the emotion he heard in Maggie's voice.

"If it's okay, I'll come to you."

"It's okay!" she practically shouted. "Do you want me to make breakfast?"

"No. I want you to stay in bed, all warm and sleepy. And what I *really* want is to join you there when I arrive. Just to sleep. I can never get any rest on a plane."

"Okay. I'll get up and unlock the door. Shawn?"

"Yeah?"

"I'm so glad you're home. I have a lot I want to tell you."

"Me too. I'll be there in about fifteen minutes, okay?"

"Okay. See you soon."

"Yes, you will."

Preacher hung up and knew he had a sappy smile on his face. He was exhausted, he hadn't lied about that. He could think of nothing better than snuggling up behind Maggie and falling asleep with her in his arms. He'd dreamed about it. About her.

It took thirteen minutes to get to her apartment, since there wasn't much traffic out this early in the morning. Her door was unlocked, as promised, and while he wanted to scold Maggie for being unsafe, he was too eager to see her.

Making sure to lock the door behind him, Preacher dropped his duffle bag on the floor of the foyer and made his way to the bedroom. Taking a deep breath, he pushed open the door—and the sight that greeted him took his breath away.

It was one of his fantasies come to life. Maggie had turned on a light next to the bed, giving the room a soft glow. She was awake, lying in the middle of the queen-size bed with the covers up to her chest. She sat up and smiled at him when he entered. "Welcome home."

Preacher stepped toward her. He leaned over the mattress and, to his delight, she tipped her chin up to him, offering her lips. He took them.

At first their kiss was soft and sweet. But it quickly morphed into more. The next thing he knew, Maggie was tugging at his shirt, trying to get it over his head. And he wasn't much better. He pulled the comforter down, then he had Maggie's head in his hands, holding her still as he kissed her hard, long, and deep. All thoughts of sleep went out the window.

Preacher had thought about this moment a lot over the years, what he'd be feeling when it came time to lose his virginity. He'd fantasized about how it might go. What he'd say and do, the emotions he might experience. But nothing he'd considered in the past came close to being with Maggie.

Before he knew it, they were both naked as the day they were born. Preacher's cock was dripping precome, but the only thing he could think about was making sure Maggie was ready to take him. He might be a virgin, but even Preacher knew his dick was bigger than average. He was long and thick, and the last thing he wanted to do was hurt this woman.

Maggie lay on her back under him, her nails digging into his skin as she clung, desperately trying to pull him closer. They'd only stopped kissing long enough to get their clothes off. As much as Preacher wanted to continue to kiss her, he needed to see her, all of her, even more.

Lifting his head, he looked down at the woman sprawled on the bed. Her black hair was fanned over the pillow, she had a small mark on one cheek from where she'd been sleeping earlier, and as he stared down at her, she licked her pink, puffy lips.

"You are the best homecoming I've ever had," Preacher told her reverently. His gaze slowly slid down her body, memorizing the moment. She was perfection. Not in the strictest sense of the word. She had a scar near her collarbone, a smattering of freckles across her upper chest, a few beauty spots here and there, but all he could see was smooth, gorgeous skin.

His hand moved to her tit as if he'd done it a million times. He squeezed gently and loved how she squirmed under him. Then he ran his thumb over her nipple, grinning when it immediately tightened under his touch. He took hold of it with his thumb and pointer finger and pinched lightly, loving the surprised noise that left Maggie's mouth, the way she arched into him.

She was so responsive. He wanted to play with her tits all night, but there was no way that was happening this time. He needed to be inside her too badly.

Reluctantly letting go of her nipple, he ran his hand down the small pooch of her belly to the neatly trimmed hair between her legs. "Spread for me," he urged in a tone he didn't recognize.

She immediately relaxed her thigh muscles and opened her legs wider. Preacher's gaze was glued to her pussy. He wanted to move. To get between her legs and examine her more closely. To taste her. To run his tongue between her folds and watch her fall apart under the ministrations of his mouth and fingers.

But he was too impatient.

Thankfully, she seemed to be as well.

She moved one of her hands between her legs and began to stroke herself. Preacher's gaze flew up to meet hers.

"I want you," she told him boldly. "But I need to be wetter. It's...been a while for me."

He loved that she wasn't afraid to say what she needed. He turned his attention back between her legs and watched as she pleasured herself, making mental notes about what she liked.

He placed his hand over her own as her finger began to move faster on her clit. When her hips began to undulate, he roughly pushed her hand out of the way and took over.

Once again, a surprised squeak left her lips, and Preacher could only grin at the sound.

"Yes...harder, Shawn. More!"

The little nubbin between her legs was hard under his thumb, and he eased his pinky into her body as far as it would go as he stroked her.

She was so damn hot. And wet. He could feel her slickness drench his pinky, and his dick throbbed with impatience.

"Oh!" Maggie exclaimed, as she lifted her ass off the mattress and seemed to freeze. Then she broke, shaking almost uncontrollably against him. Preacher had seen women orgasm before, but it was nothing like this. If Maggie hadn't reached down to grab him, to hold him against her, he might've thought she was in pain.

She'd never know the gift she'd just given him.

Her hips lowered back to the bed and when she subtly flinched away from his touch on her clit, he got the message. Easing his hand farther down between her legs, it was Preacher's turn to moan. She was soaked. He eased one finger inside her body, then two. He gently finger fucked her as she came down from her orgasm. Her juices coated his fingers and he pulled them out of her body and brought them to his cock.

He was hard as steel, and her juices combined with his

precome was more than enough lubrication to make sure he didn't hurt her when he entered.

Then he froze. *Fuck.*

"What? What's wrong?" Maggie asked, obviously feeling him tense up.

"I don't have a condom," he admitted. This was his moment. His chance to lose his virginity with the woman of his dreams—and like an idiot, he didn't have anything to protect her with.

"It's okay," she said.

"No, it's not."

"Shawn, you're a virgin. And I haven't had sex in over two years because I was in jail."

"Pregnancy," he reminded her.

He could see her cheeks turn pink. "It's not the right time. And I know that sounds like a line, but it's not."

Preacher hesitated. He should stop this right now...

Maggie made the decision for them both when she reached down and took his cock in her hand.

He grunted and couldn't stop himself from pushing into her grip. She smiled up at him.

"It's all right, Shawn. I promise. Please. I need you. I *want* you. I want to be your first."

Moving without hesitation, Preacher settled between her legs, pushing them wider with his knees. Her folds were sparkling in the low light. He couldn't resist touching her again, feeling how hot and wet she was.

"Are you really sure?" he managed to ask.

"Positive."

"If there are any consequences, I'm going to do what's right. I want to be in my child's life. I will *not* be an absentee father."

He felt her pussy clench against the fingers he hadn't been able to resist easing back inside her.

"Okay."

"Last chance, Maggie. If you say yes, I'm going to fuck you. There's no going back." Preacher could barely think. His gaze was glued to her pussy. He wanted this. And not just sex. But sex with *her*. This wasn't just about losing his virginity. It was about being as close as he could get to Maggie.

"Yes," she said firmly.

Preacher eased his fingers out of her body and wrapped his hand around his cock once more, using the lubrication to coat himself again. Then he scooted closer, pushing her legs even farther apart. Looking down, he almost came when he saw the head of his dick touching her mound. He could feel her pubic hair against the sensitive tip. Could smell the musky scent of sex. Hear her breathing, hard and fast. See the way her belly rippled with anticipation.

Every one of his senses was engaged. This moment was imprinted on his brain forever...and he hadn't even gotten started.

He notched the head of his cock at her entrance and pushed.

* * *

Maggie held her breath as Shawn entered her. For a moment, the pinch of pain was almost overwhelming. It had been so very long since she'd made love. But the discomfort dissipated almost immediately.

Her gaze had been glued between her legs, watching as Shawn's surprisingly long and thick cock disappeared into her body. But a strange noise coming from Shawn had her gaze whipping up to his face.

The reverence she saw there made this moment extra special. This was his first time, and she'd never felt more powerful and sexy than she did right that moment.

"Fuck," he muttered. He inched closer, pushing his fat cock even deeper inside her. Then he didn't move. He simply stayed planted as far as he could go.

"Shawn?" Maggie asked, getting concerned.

He made a noise somewhere between a yes and a grunt. She grinned and deliberately tightened her inner muscles around his dick.

His gaze had been locked on where they were joined, but he looked up when he felt her clench around him. "Do that again," he ordered.

She did.

"Holy shit, that feels amazing!" he breathed.

"You can move," she whispered.

Shawn simply shook his head. His pupils were so big, she could barely see any of the green color of his eyes.

"Am I hurting you?" he asked.

"No."

"Good. Because I think I might never leave. You're so hot. And so damn wet. I've never...this is...*fuck*."

Maggie couldn't stop smiling. "Wait until you start thrusting," she told him.

To her surprise, he pushed against her—then his face contorted. She felt his hips thrust once more.

"Did you...did you just come?" she asked.

"Yes," he said without embarrassment. "You feel too amazing. So damn good!"

She was thrilled that he'd found his pleasure. She was a little disappointed too, but this *was* his first time. He'd get the hang of making love in no time, she was sure.

He leaned down and kissed her gently. When he pulled away, there was a glint of...*something*...in his eyes. "Now that *that's* out of the way, you ready?"

"For what?" Maggie asked.

"To get fucked."

She couldn't help it. She laughed. "Yes."

To her amazement, when he pulled out of her body all the way to the head of his cock, she realized he was still hard. He plunged back into her with one long thrust.

"Oh!" she exclaimed, loving how he felt as he bottomed out inside her. She was even wetter now after his orgasm, and he slid easily into her body.

Her belly clenched as he began to move in a slow and steady rhythm. His cock touched places inside her that no man had ever reached. Before long, he was thrusting harder and harder. One hand braced on the mattress next to her shoulder, the other clutching her thigh, keeping her open wide.

With every thrust, her tits rippled and bounced on her chest, and seeing the pleasure in Shawn's gaze as he took her in was almost as exciting as what he was doing to her body. Almost.

Then his hand moved between them. Still thrusting, he lifted his hips a bit to make some room for his hand to touch her clit.

"Shawn!" she exclaimed as he began to strum her.

"That's it. Come on my cock. I want to feel it. You felt amazing gripping my finger, and I bet you'll fucking strangle my dick. Oh! I can feel you rippling. That's fanfuckingtastic!"

She never would've pegged Shawn as a dirty talker, but Maggie loved it.

He lifted her hip as her orgasm neared. All she could do was hold onto Shawn as he fingered her like a freaking maestro. It was hard to believe this was his first time. He was the best lover she'd ever had. He'd ruined her for anyone else. Period.

By the time she flew over the edge, Shawn was panting and grimacing as if he was being tortured. She heard him groan, "Thank fuck," while she was orgasming, then both hands were holding her hips, trying to keep her writhing body still as he fucked her in earnest.

It didn't take long for him to stop moving altogether as he yanked her against him so hard, Maggie had a feeling she'd have bruises. Then he grunted once more and came.

She actually felt his cock twitching as he emptied inside her.

"Holy shit," he said in awe as his hands slowly relaxed their iron grip around her hips. Then he fell forward, thankfully not squishing her under him. He buried his nose into her neck and panted against her as he tried to regain control of his body.

Maggie couldn't stop smiling. Her hands ran up and down his slightly damp back as she did her best to soothe him until he could recover from his second orgasm of the night.

When he eased himself up far enough to look her in the eyes, he was still lodged deep inside her body.

"Hi," she said a little self-consciously.

"Thank you," he responded.

Maggie frowned. "For what?"

"Are you seriously asking that?" he asked a little peevishly.

Maggie giggled.

A strange look came across his face. "I felt that," he informed her. "You laughing. Felt it on my cock. I liked it."

She couldn't help but laugh again.

This time a small smile formed on his face. "I have a confession."

When he didn't continue, Maggie asked, "Yeah? What's that?"

"I like sex. With you. And I think you've created a monster."

She smiled up at him. "I like it too. With you. Are you

sure you haven't done this before? Because you are *very* good at it."

"I'm sure. And I was inspired."

Maggie hadn't felt this happy in a long time. Her life had been shit for quite a while now. And there were a lot of things that were still shit, but right now, in this moment in time, she was as content as she'd ever been. "You're okay? Your mission went okay?" she asked.

"I'm fine. The mission was a shitshow. A nonentity. We were sent out there and we weren't needed. Like, at all. We sat on our asses, waiting for our commander to get his shit together and get us back home."

"Oh," Maggie said, not completely surprised. Roman had basically said as much. But it was also a little scary because she'd hoped against hope that he'd been lying to her. That he hadn't had anything to do with their deployment.

"I don't want to talk about work right now," Shawn said.

Maggie was completely all right with that. She didn't want to think about Roman, his threats, or anything other than the man who was still lodged deep inside her body. "You don't? Whatever should we do then? Sleep?"

"Hmmmmm, maybe. Or maybe we could think of better things," he said.

Somehow, without pulling out of her, he flipped them until Maggie was straddling him. "Oh!" she exclaimed in surprise. "You're hard again."

"I have a feeling around you, that's going to be my

normal state. There are a lot of positions I want to try. I mean, I *am* a virgin, after all."

"Were," Maggie said with a grin. "You *were* a virgin."

"True. Show me how this works, Maggie. You fuck *me* this time."

Twenty minutes later, Maggie wasn't sure who'd fucked who. Shawn had let her take the lead for a while, then he'd held her still as he took her from below. Thrusting into her over and over again while he ordered her to finger her clit so she could come around his cock once more.

She fell on top of him, boneless, when he'd finally orgasmed. They were both sweaty now, and she'd never felt more satisfied. He'd pulled out of her, and she could feel his come seeping out from between her legs. "I should get up and shower."

"Don't," he ordered. "I want the full experience."

Maggie rolled her eyes but didn't make a move to climb off him. The truth was, she was comfortable right where she was. Using Shawn as a pillow.

"Okay, but don't blame me when you're sticky and uncomfortable in the morning."

"It's already morning," Shawn said with a small laugh.

Maggie felt it move through her body, since she was draped all over him. It felt...intimate. Nice.

"Do you work tomorrow...er...today?" he asked after a moment.

"I'm supposed to. But I can call later and ask Julie if it's okay if I take the day off. I'm sure she'll understand. She already told me I could have the day off when you guys got home."

"Okay. I have the day off as well," Shawn told her.

"Good."

"Yeah. Good. Sleep, Maggie."

* * *

Preacher was exhausted. It had been a long trip home from the Middle East and his body had no idea what time it was. But he couldn't sleep. He held Maggie against him and closed his eyes.

Sex with Maggie had been...life changing. He'd known she was different, special, but the connection they'd just shared had proven him more than right. He'd never felt this way with anyone before. And while he'd never gone all the way with another woman, he'd done enough to know what he and Maggie had just shared went deeper than anything he'd ever experienced...or expected.

He wanted to spend the rest of his life with her. Coming home from deployments to her in his bed, welcoming him just as she had tonight. Laughing about the antics of their kids, figuring out their schedules around their kids' activities. He wanted it all. With Maggie.

The thought of kids with this woman had his dick twitching once more. But while he had no doubt she'd enjoyed what they'd just done, he wasn't sure she was on the same page as he was.

Maggie had slid off his chest to rest on the mattress

next to him, and she was cuddled up to his side, using his shoulder as a pillow. He'd covered them with a sheet, but he could see the tent in the material that his dick was making as he thought about filling Maggie up once more with his come.

"Slow your roll," he whispered to himself. He couldn't fuck this up. He needed to slow the hell down. Maggie wasn't ready to have babies. Her ex was still out there trying to mess with her, and the threat of her going back to prison was forefront in her mind. Not to mention she'd told him more than once that she wanted to get the hell out of California.

Sighing, Preacher did his best to push his worries to the back of his mind. To enjoy the present. Maggie's warm breath against his shoulder wasn't something he'd experienced before. He'd never slept with a woman. In any sense of the word. It was nice.

As he lay there, holding Maggie tightly, Preacher closed his eyes and relived the moment he'd first entered her hot, wet pussy. He understood now why men did stupid things in regard to sex. The feel of her body holding him in a vise grip was indescribable. He should be embarrassed by how fast he'd come that first time, but he wasn't. The pleasure had been overwhelming. Thankfully he hadn't gone soft and was able to fuck her properly after that.

Thinking about what they'd done, and how good it felt, had Preacher's cock at full mast once again. He tried to ignore it. Maggie was probably sore, and she needed her rest.

But the more he tried to ignore his dick, the more it throbbed. He wanted her again. Needed her.

He refused to do anything while Maggie was sleeping.

He had no idea how long he lay there with his cock throbbing with the need to be inside Maggie once again, but the second she stirred against him, he moved.

He urged Maggie to her stomach, then grabbed a pillow and put it under her hips. He then crouched behind her and used his fingers to stimulate her.

"Shawn?" she asked sleepily.

"Can you take me again?" he asked, not recognizing his own voice.

In response, she lifted her hips.

"Lay still. I'll do all the work," he told her.

Seeing her displayed in front of him, her ass round and welcoming, her pussy still wet from all the come he'd pumped into her earlier, Preacher thanked the stars above for putting her in his life.

He scooted closer and pushed inside her pussy with one long, slow thrust.

They both groaned.

Knowing he needed to keep this slow and easy, Preacher made love to his woman with nothing but her pleasure in mind.

Before long, she was squirming under him. "Let me get to my knees."

Preacher helped her, and he had to agree this position was even better. He eased a hand under her and found her clit and stroked it as he took her from behind.

"I like this," he declared.

He felt Maggie chuckle. "Figures you're a doggy-style man," she said in time with his thrusts.

"I'm a Maggie man," he corrected.

He'd meant to keep this lovemaking session gentle, but when Maggie began to thrust back against him, smacking her soft ass against his thighs, Preacher lost his iron control.

He held her hips still as he fucked her hard from behind. The sound of their skin slapping together just added to the carnality of the moment. And when he looked down and saw his cock disappearing in and out of her pussy, it made him all the more excited. Her tits swayed with his every thrust, and the moans leaving her throat told him all he needed to know about how much she was enjoying this.

Her orgasm approached fast, and she was shaking with its arrival much sooner than Preacher had expected. But her pleasure triggered his own. Without thinking about what he was doing, he pulled out and sprayed come all over her gorgeous ass. Before he was done, Preacher plunged back inside her pussy, finishing deep inside her once more.

Then his hands moved to massage her ass, spreading his seed all over her body. Marking her as his woman.

"Holy shit, Shawn," she breathed.

He couldn't agree more.

CHAPTER ELEVEN

By the time she and Shawn got up and showered and were making breakfast, it was almost noon. Maggie was sore, but in the best way possible. She would've never pegged Shawn as a sex fiend, but she couldn't say she was upset about it. Not when he'd made sure she'd orgasmed every time before he did.

Every derogatory thing Roman had said about their sex life had been blown out of the water in one session with Shawn. The lackluster sex she'd had with her ex had nothing to do with *her*, obviously.

And now that they'd been intimate, Shawn couldn't keep his hands off her. He touched the small of her back, ran his hand over her arm, brushed against her in the kitchen, and Maggie loved every second. This was what she'd always dreamed about in a relationship. This closeness. This desperate need to be around each other. It

162

wouldn't always be this way, she knew that, but this was a hell of a good start.

She hadn't expected to even get into a relationship with anyone ever again. Not after Roman's unbelievable betrayal. But Shawn had taken her by surprise. His earnestness and openness had won her over. It wasn't as if they were getting married tomorrow or anything, but she could definitely see herself in a long-term relationship with him.

"You didn't sleep much, are you sure you're okay?" she asked when they were sitting at the table eating the muffins and sausage casserole they'd made for brunch.

"You saying you want to go back to bed?" he asked with a grin.

Maggie rolled her eyes. "No. I'm sore. I was being serious. You didn't get much rest."

The lightness in his expression disappeared in a heartbeat. "I hurt you?" he asked.

"No. Not at all. But I told you it's been a while for me. Obviously. And you're not a small man."

The frown didn't leave his face. "I'm sorry."

"Shawn," Maggie said, leaning closer to him and putting a hand over his. "I'm not complaining. I'm just saying that a few hours' break for me wouldn't be a bad thing."

"Right. Tonight, you can teach me what you like when I go down on you. Then maybe I'll masturbate and come on your pussy and belly. That should give you a decent break."

Maggie felt herself blushing. "Holy crap, Shawn. I had no idea such a dirty talker lurked inside you."

"Neither did I. You bring it out in me," he said with a smirk.

Maggie couldn't help but return his smile. And she couldn't stop the image of him kneeling between her legs, stroking himself, from flashing through her brain.

"What do you want to do today?" Shawn asked, smiling as if he knew exactly what she was thinking about. "I need to do some laundry, got a duffle bag full of dirty shit that would probably stand up and walk by itself if it got a chance."

And just like that, Maggie's mellow mood vanished. "We need to talk," she blurted.

Shawn turned to her. "Okay. You know I'm always here for you. Last night...rather, this morning...it meant something to me. *You* mean something to me. I'm not a man who hops into bed with women, which you already know. I want to be exclusive, Maggie. I want to be your boyfriend, your man. I'll do everything in my power to stand by your side, support you, and be your sounding post when you need one."

He was killing her. Because she wanted that too. All of it. But there was a very real stumbling block to them becoming an official couple. And she wanted to talk to him about it. Tell him about Roman. "I want that too," she said. "I want to be your girlfriend, and being exclusive goes without saying."

"If you don't want to have my baby immediately, one of us will need to do something about birth control," he added as nonchalantly as if they were talking about what the weather was going to be that week. He met her gaze and continued. "Because I have a feeling I'm going to want to be inside you as much as you'll let me. I'll wear condoms if you want. Though it's probably ridiculous of me to admit how much I enjoy coming inside *and* on you. Okay, that was weird, wasn't it? I can tell by the look on your face that it was weird."

Maggie couldn't help but giggle. "A little. But if you're weird, so am I, because I like it when I can feel your come dripping down my thighs when I stand up. And I appreciate you offering to cover the birth control. Not every man will do that. They'd simply expect me to take care of it."

"If you get pregnant, it affects both of us," Shawn said firmly. "And it shouldn't only be up to the woman. You tell me what you want. I'll do what you decide."

"I can go on the pill. Or get a shot."

"Okay. If that doesn't work out, we'll figure something else out. In the meantime, I'll get condoms so we don't have to abstain while we wait for you to get an appointment with a doctor."

This man. How'd she get so lucky?

Wait...she wasn't lucky. Not at all. She'd spent two years behind bars because of how *unlucky* she was. Especially in love. That thought sobered her.

"Are you done?" she asked, gesturing to his plate.

Shawn nodded, and Maggie immediately stood and grabbed his plate. The food she'd eaten suddenly sat like a lump in her belly. She needed to get this discussion out of the way. The sooner Shawn found out who her ex was, the sooner he could get with his connections to see what he might be able to do about mitigating the threats. And he needed to know who was behind his team being sent on that worthless mission. Know that the possibility of them being sent to really horrible places was on the horizon, simply because Roman was a vindictive asshole.

She put their dishes in the sink and turned to go back to Shawn—and gasped when she ran into him. He'd followed and was standing right behind her.

"Oh!" she exclaimed. "I didn't hear you."

"I *am* a SEAL," Shawn said with a smile that didn't reach his eyes. "Come on. I don't like how stressed you look all of a sudden." He grabbed her hand and led her toward the couch. He sat and pulled her down next to him. They were touching from knee to hip, and he had his arm around her, his hand resting on her opposite hip.

Maggie would've preferred some space between them for this conversation, but at the same time, she loved being so close to him. She was a mess, and all she wanted to do was get this done so they could move on.

"I'm ready to tell you about my ex," she blurted.

"Okay. I'm ready to listen without judgement," Shawn said calmly.

Taking a deep breath, praying this wasn't going to backfire, Maggie started to speak.

"I thought he was great at first. He was so gentlemanly. Taking me out to eat at the fanciest places. Wining and dining me. He honestly made me believe he cared about me. He'd show up at the pharmacy where I worked with lunch. He complimented me all the time. Thinking back, I realize now that it was over the top. Too much, too soon... and I can't believe I fell for it. But I did.

"The next thing I knew, I was sleeping at his place—he never came to mine—and we were a couple. Or so I'd thought. He was super possessive, always wanting to know where I was and when I'd be home. At the time, I mistook it for protectiveness. I didn't realize he was intentionally separating me from the few friends I had when he started telling me they were bad news, or how he thought they were talking about me behind my back. I was old enough to know better, to not fall for his shit, but...I really wanted to be in a relationship. Wanted to be loved.

"By the time I mentioned I was going to LA for my job four months later, to visit another pharmacy up there, and he asked if I would take something to a friend of his, I didn't think twice. Not even when he wouldn't tell me what was in the bag...or when, instead of putting it in the back-seat with my suitcase, he shoved it under the passenger seat.

"I was a total idiot. But again, it never once occurred to me that with his position in the Navy, he'd ever have anything to do with *drugs*. It absolutely never crossed my mind that when I was *caught* with his drugs, he'd deny everything. That he'd tell the police I was an addict. Insinuate that I was stealing pills from the pharmacy.

"He destroyed not only my belief in myself—the belief that I was a competent, independent woman—but my professional reputation and my entire life. And when he looked me right in the eye as he testified against me in court, and lied to my face and everyone in the courtroom, I knew he had no soul. Everything he'd said to me, everything he'd done to get me into bed, had been part of his plan to use me all along. It was just bad luck that I'd been stopped for speeding the first time he'd tricked me into delivering drugs for him. I think he was planning some sort of long-term transport thing, using me as his unknowing mule."

"Who is he, Maggie? I need a name," Shawn said.

Maggie was as tense as she could ever remember being. Shawn wasn't much better. He was sitting straight up, his gaze boring into hers. But his hand at her hip was gentle. A finger rhythmically brushed against her over and over again. Soothing. Letting her know that he would be there for her no matter what.

"Roman Robertson."

Shawn blinked. "What?"

"Roman Robertson. That's who my ex is. Do you know him?"

"*Rear Admiral* Robertson?"

Maggie shifted next to him. She couldn't read his tone. "Yeah. I guess. He told me his rank once, and I looked it up, but I'm not familiar with the Navy and ranks and stuff, so I don't really remember."

"Fuck," Shawn said.

Then he stood up and begin to pace.

Maggie stilled.

"That can't be right. There has to be another Roman Robertson. Or he's impersonating the *real* Rear Admiral Robertson. Did you ever see his military ID? Did he bring you on base at all?"

Maggie swallowed hard. This wasn't going how she'd thought it would.

No, that wasn't right. Unfortunately, this discussion was going *exactly* how she'd feared...before she'd been intimate with Shawn. This was the reason she hadn't wanted to tell him who her ex was. Because she was afraid he wouldn't believe her. And now her nightmare was coming true. "No. And no."

"I bet this asshole read about the rear admiral's name in the paper or something. Maggie, honey, the man you know as your ex has to be impersonating the real Roman Robertson."

"No, he's not. He told me that he was the reason why you and your team were sent on that mission so fast. Because he made it happen. And that next time, he's going to send you somewhere horrible, like North Korea or Russia, just because he can. He doesn't want you to make it home, Shawn. He *told* me."

"Honey, we're SEALs. We get sent to places like that all the time. And we also get deployed with little to no notice frequently, as well."

Maggie stared at him—and she suddenly felt cold. So damn cold.

Shawn didn't believe her.

It had taken everything within her to tell him the name of her ex—and he was dismissing her out of hand.

It hurt. A lot.

She lowered her gaze and instantly felt herself shutting down. Putting up the shields she'd hidden behind anytime her life went to shit. It happened more than she cared to remember. It happened when she was caught with those drugs, and the officer refused to believe they belonged to *Rear Admiral* Roman Robertson.

But this was different. She hadn't felt this kind of hurt since the night she'd overheard her adoptive parents arguing, when she was sixteen. Fighting over Maggie and the trouble she'd been getting into recently. It was just typical teenage stuff...she'd snuck out one night and gotten caught. Started coming home after curfew. Was talking back. Even at the time, she knew it was stupid, but the peer pressure she'd felt at school to fit in, to be "cool," had made her act in ways she wasn't proud of. But instead of sitting her down and talking about it, her parents began blaming each other.

Then her mom had actually admitted to her dad that they'd made a mistake in adopting her all those years ago. Saying they'd done it for the wrong reason, to try to help their marriage, and it hadn't worked.

They'd both admitted to each other that they *regretted* adopting her.

Those words still haunted her. They'd flipped everything she thought she knew about family and trust upside down. Of course, she'd known her parents weren't happy. They argued all the time. But hearing them flat-out say they didn't enjoy being parents and wished she wasn't around was devastating.

It changed who she was as a person. Maggie became more withdrawn. Cautious when it came to opening up to others. As soon as she graduated, she moved out and didn't look back. It was telling that neither of her parents had ever made more than a cursory attempt to keep in touch with her after she left.

By the time Roman came along, she was desperate for love. And look how that turned out? But even after everything Roman had put her through, after being in *prison*, Shawn still managed to completely destroy the walls she'd used for years. She'd trusted him, quickly and completely. Had truly believed that maybe, just maybe, she was worthy of being loved after all.

Instead...with his instant denial of her story...she felt as alone right now as she had the day she realized her parents didn't want her around.

Last night should've meant *everything*. It had to her. But now, hearing Shawn's complete disbelief that her ex could be the rear admiral, she realized it meant nothing. She was just the first notch on his bedpost. He'd decided it was time to get rid of his pesky virginity and she happened to be there.

It was a crushing blow.

She thought of the recording she'd made. It might prove to him that she wasn't lying. That he was wrong, and her ex really was this rear admiral he obviously knew. For a moment, she wanted to do whatever it took in order to make him believe her, to fight for their relationship.

But she shouldn't *have* to. He should believe her...right? Should trust and want her unconditionally.

Then again, why would he? Her parents didn't.

Anger filled her at the fact that Roman was ruining her life *again*. And she knew he wouldn't stop there.

She didn't want him to dupe another innocent victim the way he had her. He'd pulled the wool over everyone's eyes. The Navy, the people who worked for him, the people he interacted with.

No. She needed to let Shawn hear the phone call. The threats.

And she would. But not right this moment. She was too raw. Too disappointed in him. She needed to wait until she'd had time to shore up her shields once more. That way, if he still didn't believe her, even though she had solid proof of Roman's asshole-ness, it wouldn't be *quite* as devastating as it was right now.

"Maggie?" Shawn questioned.

She had no idea what he might've said while she was stuck in her thoughts. So she simply uttered, "Okay." Refusing to look up, she studied the pattern on the carpet under Shawn's feet.

"Honey, look at me," he said.

She didn't want to. *Really* didn't want to, but Maggie lifted her head anyway.

"Rear Admiral Robertson was never a SEAL, but he's still highly decorated. He was a medic and has been on some extremely harrowing missions alongside not only SEALs, but other special forces teams as well. He's well-respected, and he was specifically asked to come to Riverton to help manage the teams."

"Okay," Maggie echoed woodenly.

"Can you tell me more about this guy? What does he look like? Wait, you said you stayed at his place, can you remember the address? I can have my connections see what they can find out. Figure out who this guy *really* is. Get him to stop harassing you."

Suddenly exhausted, she wished he'd just leave. She couldn't take much more of him trying to convince her that she was wrong.

"I'll need to think about it for a while. I don't really remember," she muttered, trying to make the lie sound convincing. She needed Shawn *gone* so she could lick her wounds. She'd say whatever was necessary to make that happen, because she was holding on to her emotions by a thread. "Besides, he's probably moved since I was last there. I *was* gone for two years."

"Shit, yeah, that's a good point. Okay, we'll figure something out. We won't let this guy continue to harass you. And trust me, he can't do anything to me or my team. There's no way he can infiltrate the Navy system. He just told you those things to make you think he has power over us that he doesn't."

Shawn was wrong. But at the moment, Maggie was too devastated to try to convince him. Later, when she felt stronger, when she was no longer so...emotionally involved, she'd sit him down again and pull out all the stops to make him understand that she wasn't lying. That the Roman Robertson who was threatening her, threatening *him*, was the same person he held in such high esteem.

"Okay," she repeated yet again. "You know, I just remembered. I have an appointment with my probation officer today. In an hour, in fact. I need to get ready."

"Oh...all right. I can go home and start my laundry. We'll meet up later?"

"Sure," Maggie said. Anything to get him to leave. She needed to be alone. To strengthen her shields once more. Shawn had obliterated them, and now when she needed them most, they were totally gone.

He stepped closer to where Maggie was still sitting on the couch and knelt in front of her. "We'll figure this out, honey. I swear."

It took every ounce of control Maggie had not to burst into tears and scream at him and tell him that there was nothing to figure out. The Roman she knew was the same man *he* knew. Even if he didn't want to admit it. "Okay." She felt like a robot, saying the same word over and over, but that was all her brain could manage to get out at the moment.

Shawn leaned forward and kissed her briefly, then stood and headed for the door. Maggie got up and let him kiss her once more, before shutting and locking the door behind him. She sank to her butt right there against it, lowering her head to her knees.

* * *

Preacher frowned as he drove back to his apartment. He wasn't in the mood to chat with the older lady who owned the house where he rented a room, so he was relieved when her car wasn't in the driveway. He went up to his room and started a load of laundry, then sat on the edge of his bed and stared into space as he went over everything Maggie had told him.

Anger filled him at the thought of someone impersonating Rear Admiral Robertson. The man was a legend. Had been to hell and back and now helped run the SEAL program as a high-ranking officer. There was no way he was involved in drug smuggling or dealing, and he couldn't imagine the man treating anyone, especially a woman he was dating, the way Maggie's ex had treated her.

For a split second, Preacher wondered if *anything* Maggie had told him was true. Yes, Adina had vouched for her...but was she telling the truth about the drugs found in her car not really being hers?

Almost as soon as he had the thought, Preacher dismissed it. Maggie wasn't lying. He'd bet his SEAL career on that. Whoever her ex was, he was obviously smart. Knew how to masterfully impersonate others. How to manipulate.

He needed to call Kevlar. And maybe Wolf. No...Dude. The former SEAL had asked him to call if he needed assistance. And the older man knew the rear admiral, sometimes worked with him to arrange training sessions with the newer SEALs.

Maybe Preacher would even call Tex.

Between all of them, they'd get to the bottom of this. Figure out who was gaslighting Maggie and put an end to it once and for all.

* * *

Maggie was sitting on her couch, knees drawn up to her chest, stewing about what had happened earlier that day. She'd lied about the meeting with her probation officer—but that was *all* she'd lied about. She knew in her bones that the Roman Robertson she'd dated was the same person Shawn knew. She just had to prove it.

Analyzing their conversation again and again, she reluctantly admitted she'd reacted emotionally instead of rationally. She shouldn't have kicked Shawn out so fast. She should've done more right then to make him believe her. In her defense, she'd been so blindsided by his immediate denial that they weren't talking about the same person. But he was an honorable man—Shawn, not Roman. Of course it would be hard for him to believe something so horrible about someone he admired and looked up to. If someone had told her that Roman was as much a dick as he was when they were dating, she probably wouldn't have believed them either.

The man had everyone snowed, which was how he'd gotten away with everything he'd done for so long. He wasn't stupid, he knew how to work the system. But he also felt he was untouchable, and sooner or later, he'd screw up. Maggie just had to hope it happened before he landed her back in prison.

Sitting up, she reached for her phone. She needed to apologize to Shawn. Admit that she'd lied about the meeting and ask him to come back over, or offer to meet him somewhere. She'd be calmer the next time they spoke. She'd share the phone recording. Let him hear the threats. Maybe he'd recognize the man's voice. She'd do whatever it took to convince him that Rear Admiral Roman Robertson wasn't a man to be looked up to.

Pressing on Shawn's number in her contacts, Maggie waited impatiently for him to answer. Disappointment filled her when it went to voicemail. Taking a deep breath, she left him a message.

"Hi, Shawn. It's me. Maggie. I wanted to apologize, because I lied about having a meeting with my probation officer today. I needed some space after it was obvious you didn't believe me about my ex. But I understand. I know it's hard to believe. Trust me, it was a surprise to me too that such a highly respected man could be such a heartless animal. I have a phone recording of his threats...against me, and against you and your team. I can give you the address he had two years ago, and I'll even go online and show you pictures of him. It's him, Shawn, and I'm worried about you. And myself, now that I've told you. He said that if I ever told anyone about

him, that I'd pay. Please. Call me back. Thanks...um...I'll talk to you later. Bye."

Maggie's stomach rolled as she hung up. She'd been about to tell him how much she loved him...but that would be crazy, right? It was too soon. Way too soon. Look what happened with Roman. She'd leaped into that relationship and ended up a convicted felon as a result. Thankfully, she'd caught herself in time, but the worry in her gut didn't dissipate as she waited for Shawn to call her back. She had to convince him...for both their sakes.

CHAPTER TWELVE

Preacher felt nauseous. He hadn't felt this way since the first day of BUD/S. He'd talked to Kevlar. Then Dude. And finally Tex. Now he was pacing one of the conference rooms on base, waiting for the rest of his team to arrive. It probably wasn't the best place to meet, especially if Maggie's ex really *was* Rear Admiral Roman Robertson, but the room was secure. It had to be, considering the missions that were planned in there.

Everyone he'd talked to had been utterly shocked to hear that Rear Admiral Robertson was the man Maggie claimed was her ex. The man who'd thrown her under the proverbial bus. Who was currently threatening her with a return to prison.

Preacher didn't want to believe it. *Couldn't* believe it. And yet, even though all his friends had agreed with his skepticism...a niggling doubt lingered.

Maggie had sounded so sure. And he couldn't shake the look of betrayal and sheer disappointment in her eyes when he'd said she was wrong. When he'd instead suggested her ex was actually impersonating the rear admiral.

What if she was right and *he* was wrong?

It would be a huge scandal for the Navy...and every mission the SEALs had been sent on—all of them, not just *his* team—would be scrutinized to make sure they were legit. The ramifications of the rear admiral possibly sending SEAL teams out on missions for his own agenda would be far-reaching and long-lasting.

Not to mention the drugs and the threats against Maggie. If it was true, if he *was* Maggie's ex, there was no telling how many other women he'd conned, or was *currently* conning. Leading on. Using.

Hence the nauseous feeling in Preacher's gut.

The door opened and Kevlar entered, followed by the rest of his team.

Smiley didn't beat around the bush. "Is it true? Is Rear Admiral Robertson Maggie's ex?"

"That's what she says," Preacher answered.

"Fuck," Blink muttered.

"This isn't good," MacGyver added.

"Not good at all," Safe agreed.

"Everyone take a breath. There's a chance someone out there is impersonating the rear admiral," Kevlar said.

"How much of a chance?" Flash asked.

Kevlar sighed. "Twenty percent?"

"*Fuck*," Blink said again.

Twenty percent.

Preacher pressed his lips together. He'd fucked up. Big time. Maggie was never going to trust him again. He'd just gotten to the point where he felt good about how much she'd lowered her shields around him. And after this morning...he'd never felt as close to another human being in his life. And he'd gone and ruined it.

"Have you talked to Tex?" Safe asked.

"I called him. He's looking into it," Preacher told his friends. "I also called Dude and got his opinion on this entire fucked-up situation."

"And?" Smiley asked.

"He was stunned. At first said there was no way. But I guess after we hung up, he thought about the situation some more. Rang me back and said now he thought there was a possibility it could be true," Preacher said with a sigh.

"What convinced him?" Smiley asked.

"I have no idea. He mentioned making a few calls, then said that he didn't think Maggie would lie about something as serious as this. Especially since it would be easy to prove or disprove who her ex was."

"So now what?" MacGyver asked.

"I think I need to talk to Maggie again. Get as much intel from her as possible. Then we go to the top brass here on base. And NCIS. Get an inquiry started," Preacher answered.

"The second Robertson finds out he's being looked into, she'll be in danger," Blink said.

"She'll need to have someone on her twenty-four seven," Flash agreed.

"And her probation officer will need to be informed of what's going on. In case Robertson retaliates by trying to set her up again," Safe agreed.

Preacher loved these men. Loved that their first thoughts were about Maggie. Not about how fucked up it was that they'd been sent on missions that might have been bullshit. A thought struck him then. "Blink, that mission where your team was ambushed...do you think...was that..." He couldn't even finish the thought.

Blink stared at him, living up to his nickname by not blinking even once. "If he was behind that FUBAR'd mission, I'll fucking kill him."

Preacher wouldn't blame the man. He'd lost some very good friends in that clusterfuck of a mission. Not to mention how he'd been sent back to Iran with another SEAL team...was someone trying to get rid of him too? The only other witness to everything that had gone wrong on the earlier mission?

"I think this solidifies our guess that we were likely sent to that fucking ship when we weren't needed on purpose, huh?" Smiley asked no one in particular.

"I need to call Maggie," Preacher said, having an almost desperate need to talk to her. They'd left each other on a not-so-great note that morning. Pulling out his phone, he was surprised to find a message from her, forgetting that he'd put his phone on do-not-disturb for this meeting. Blocking out his friends' heated discussion on whether or not Rear Admiral Robertson was responsible for their last mission, Preacher brought his cell up to his ear.

He didn't smile as he listened to Maggie's message, but he *was* relieved. He liked that, even though they'd had a disagreement, she hadn't hesitated to apologize for lying to get him to leave. He needed to do the same. Her need to be rid of him was mostly his fault. If he'd been a little more open to the possibility of who her ex was, things wouldn't have escalated to the point where she'd felt she needed some space.

Knowing she'd recorded her ex's phone call made him extraordinarily proud. And he wasn't sure why *he* hadn't thought about having her ID her ex in photos.

He immediately clicked on her name, needing to tell her right that second that he was sorry for how things went down too, and he and his team would keep her safe while an investigation was opened into Robertson. But his call immediately went to voicemail. Which was odd. In all the time he'd known her, which admittingly wasn't *that* long, her phone had always been on.

Looking at his watch, Preacher wondered if she'd decided to go into My Sister's Closet for a few hours, after all. He was about to call Julie and ask if Maggie was there, and if he could speak to her, when Kevlar asked about Maggie's message. He told his team about her recording a phone call from her ex, and that she was willing to give him the address where he'd lived before she was incarcerated.

Then Preacher's phone rang. Glancing at it anxiously, he saw it wasn't Maggie calling, much to his disappointment. Tex's name flashed on his screen instead.

"Tex, hey," Preacher said.

"I'm guessing your woman isn't lying," Tex said, not beating around the bush. "I admit I was highly skeptical at first. I mean, a rear admiral isn't exactly someone I'd suspect of being a drug dealer or sending an innocent woman to prison. But the deeper I looked into the man, the more I dug up."

"Hang on a sec," Preacher said, putting his phone on speaker and telling his team what was going on. "Okay, go ahead. We're all listening," he told the computer genius.

"Right, so it took a bit of serious work—some of this stuff was buried *deep*—but I found that the esteemed rear admiral definitely has some skeletons in his closet. For instance, Roman Robertson isn't his real name."

"Holy shit, seriously?" Kevlar asked.

"Seriously," Tex confirmed. "He didn't go to college right after high school either. Instead, he spent time in Chicago...and he was married."

"Really?" Flash asked, frowning. "From what I've heard, he's a die-hard bachelor. Always has been."

"Can we go back to what his real fucking name is?!" Kevlar protested.

"He was married for two years. Before his wife disappeared," Tex said, ignoring Kevlar as he dropped the next bomb on them.

Preacher sucked in a breath.

"What the fuck?" Blink said what they were all thinking.

Tex went on. "Records state they had an argument, and the next morning, Robertson woke up and she wasn't in their apartment. There was no sign of her. Her car was in the parking lot, her purse, keys, money, it was all still in the apartment. The door was unlocked and there was no sign of any kind of altercation inside. Robertson was considered a suspect but was never charged because there was no evidence of foul play. There was no evidence he was involved in her disappearance at all.

"After that, he moved to the East Coast and went to college," Tex continued. "I compared the prints the cops had on record when his wife went missing, and from the Navy when he joined, and low and behold...they matched. Bartholomew Jones became Roman Robertson."

"Hell, I'd change my name if it was Bartholomew," Smiley said snarkily under his breath.

"What else?" Safe asked.

"You're assuming there's more?" Tex said.

"A man doesn't go from a grieving husband—assuming he was even worried about his wife's disappearance—to where he is now without a whole lot between the two," Safe said confidently.

"You're right. I tracked his naval career, and everywhere he was stationed, there were drug charges against men working under him. Every time, he came out smelling like a rose. I tried to look for money trails, to see if he'd paid people off, but too much time has passed to know for sure.

Not to mention, he's probably smart enough to use cash, not write a fucking check or electronically transfer money to someone for any evil shit he wants done."

"Anything on Maggie's situation?" Preacher asked.

"Nothing concrete, but one of the officers who pulled her over did a stint in the Navy. And guess who his commanding officer was..."

"Fuck," Blink growled.

Preacher normally would've grinned at the stoic SEAL using his favorite curse word over and over, but there was nothing remotely funny about this situation.

"I'm guessing he's been using subordinates as mules. To move his drugs from one place to another while he rakes in the profits. He fucked up with Maggie though. He got personally involved, used one of his girlfriends as a courier, and she got caught. He probably thinks she's the only person who can bring him down. Military subordinates have as much to lose as he would, so they'll keep their mouths shut. But Maggie has no reason to stay silent. Hell, she tried to tell everyone the drugs weren't hers. Robertson probably assumes she's going to keep trying to get someone to believe her...and eventually she'll succeed. He doesn't want that to happen under any circumstances."

"What next?" Preacher asked. Guilt filled him. Maggie had tried to get *him* to believe her—and he'd failed her. And he was at a loss as to what he, or anyone, could do to help Maggie, now that it seemed certain Robertson was indeed her ex. He couldn't be by her side every minute of every day, and he had a sick feeling that anyone who tried to help her would find themselves in the crosshairs of the very powerful rear admiral. And there was no way Preacher wanted to put Wolf or any of his team, along with their wives and families, on Robertson's radar.

Any more than they might be already.

Before Tex could respond, Kevlar's phone rang. Then Safe's, Smiley's, and the rest of the teams' cells. Looking down, Preacher could see an incoming call on his own screen, as well.

"Fuck!"

That time it was Kevlar who swore.

"What's happening?" Tex barked through the speaker.

Kevlar had answered his phone, and they all heard him as he responded in clipped tones to whoever was on the other end of the line. "Yes, Sir. I understand. Right now? Do we have time to go home and talk to our families? Right. Thirty minutes. They're here, I'll let them know. Aye-aye, Sir. Out.

"We're being deployed," he announced as soon as he hung up, not making anyone ask what the hell was going on. "Right now."

"It's him," Preacher said, feeling sick.

"We don't know that," Kevlar argued, but the uneasiness was clear in his tone.

"The hell we don't," Preacher retorted, raising his voice.

"I'm on this," Tex said. "If this is a bullshit deployment, I'll get it rescinded. And if I can't do that before you head out, I'll get you home as soon as I can."

"I need someone to have Maggie's back," Preacher told the older man.

"I'm on that too," he promised.

But Preacher wasn't reassured. He felt helpless. And pissed off at the world. "I need to call her."

"Understood. Do *not* lose your focus," Tex warned. "Keep your mind on your mission. That might be the toughest thing you've ever done, under the circumstances, but if you don't, I can't bring you back from the grave."

Preacher took a deep breath. Safe, Blink, and Kevlar were on their phones, probably talking to Wren, Josie, and Remi. His other three teammates were staring at him, arms crossed, scowling.

"Right. I know."

"I'm on this," Tex repeated. "If Robertson is sending your team on bogus missions, he's fucking *done*. If he was behind Maggie's incarceration, he's going down. I'm going to dig so hard and deep, he'll definitely feel like he's been fucked."

Normally, Preacher would've at least chuckled at the innuendo coming from the usually serious Tex, but he didn't have it in him at the moment.

"Call her. Tell her to stay on her toes. And let her know that I'll be calling and that I'm going to want a copy of that phone call she recorded," Tex ordered. "Stay safe. I'll be in touch."

The second Tex hung up, Preacher clicked on Maggie's name and brought his phone to his ear. Once more, the call went straight to voicemail. Dread made bile rise in his throat as he hung up.

"She's not answering?" Smiley asked with a frown.

"No."

"Call back and leave her a message," MacGyver ordered.

Preacher nodded, but he had a bad feeling about this entire situation.

"Maggie, it's Shawn. I...fuck. Shit is fucked up here. We're being sent out again. Now. And you aren't answering. I hope like hell you're all right. I'm so sorry about this morning. I should've listened to you more. I believe you. I've got people on this. Someone named Tex is going to get a hold of you. He's literally the smartest man I know, and if anyone can help us, it's him. He's going to want that recording you told me about. It's okay to send it to him, I swear. Be safe, okay? I have a bad feeling in my gut, and when a SEAL says that, it's never good. I'm going to keep trying to get a hold of you, please answer. Even if you're still mad at me, I need to know you're okay. It's too soon for this, but fuck it. I'm falling in love with you, Maggie. And if anything ever happened to you... Right. Okay, I have to go. But as soon as I get back, I'm locking us in a room—yours, mine, doesn't matter—and we're going to figure this out."

He clicked off the message, not wanting to say goodbye.

That felt too final. Too much like some sort of damn fore-shadowing.

He hadn't noticed that everyone else had left the room to gather their gear for deployment, except for Smiley.

"If this is him, he won't get away with it," the other man promised.

Preacher wanted to nod. Wanted to agree with his friend. But he was afraid he was wrong. Robertson was getting away with it already...whatever *this* was. The rear admiral was separating Maggie from her support network —him and the rest of the SEALs. Yes, she still had Wolf's team, but she didn't know them as well as she knew Kevlar, Safe, and the rest of the others. Preacher wasn't sure she'd call Dude or Wolf if something happened.

"He's underestimating us," Smiley said. "He's going to find out what happens when he gets an entire community of badass Navy SEALs riled up. When we get back, we're going to shake the trees...make sure every SEAL, active duty or retired, gets involved. Like Tex said, he's going down, Preacher. Mark my words."

Of that, Preacher had no doubt. He just hoped it was before he managed to ruin any more lives than he had already. Namely, Maggie's.

* * *

Maggie groaned as she tried to turn over—and realized almost immediately that she couldn't really move. She was lying on her side and her hands were restrained behind her, making it extremely uncomfortable to lie the way she was, and there was something wrapped around her head, over her mouth. She worked her jaw back and forth...Tape. It was tape, pulling at her skin. Worse, she was in the dark. She could see tiny bits of light coming through what was obviously slats, making it clear she was in a box of some kind. But otherwise, it was pitch black.

It was also weirdly silent.

Tipping her head against her shoulder, Maggie felt something in her ear. Shit...had someone put *earplugs* in her ears? Panicking now, she frantically tried to rub her ears against her shoulders, the boards beneath her...anything to remove whatever had been stuffed inside. But it was no use.

She was essentially blind, deaf, and mute.

Whatever was happening wasn't good. Not at all.

Furrowing her brow, her head pounding, Maggie tried to remember how the hell she'd ended up in a *box*. She'd been in her apartment when someone had knocked on the door. She'd thought it was Shawn, coming over to talk some more. Assumed that he'd gotten the message she'd left for him and had come straight over.

Instead, it was a stranger. A man she'd never seen before. He was big. Way taller and heavier than she was. He'd grabbed her around the neck the second she'd opened the door. She'd had no time to react, to kick him in the balls. The only thing she'd been able to do was grab his hands, trying to get some air into her lungs. But she failed.

She must've passed out...and now she was here...wherever *here* was.

All of a sudden, the box she was in began to sway. Maggie was almost hyperventilating now. It was hard to only breathe through her nose with the tape over her mouth. She couldn't really see through the slats, and she couldn't hear anything going on around her.

The box swayed for several minutes, until the movement suddenly stopped. Then the box felt as if it was dropped none too gently. The pain in her hip reverberated throughout her body. She groaned, but the sound only echoed in her head because of the noise-canceling plugs stuffed in her ears.

The box shook as what she could only guess was more containers were placed on and around it. The reality of her situation began to seep in. She was as good as dead. She couldn't move, she couldn't eat, she couldn't call out for help. There was no place to use the bathroom. After three days without water, she'd simply fade away.

Would Roman go this far to shut her up? Probably. He definitely had the connections. He didn't even have to get his own hands dirty. He just ordered someone to kidnap her and stuff her in this box. There was no telling where she'd end up at the end of her journey.

Shawn's face popped into her head then, and sorrow hit Maggie hard. He'd never know how much he meant to her. Their last words were said in anger and frustration...at least on her part. He was literally the best thing that had ever happened to her, and she'd never get a chance to tell him.

PROTECTING MAGGIE

Tears filled her eyes and dripped onto the wooden planks beneath her. This was it. She was going to be just another missing woman. People might wonder where she'd gone. Her probation officer would think she ran off, maybe to Mexico. There would be warrants for her arrest, but she'd never be found.

Shawn would probably think that since he hadn't believed her about Roman, she'd left him and gone into hiding.

Well...maybe, maybe not. She *had* left him that message. Maybe he'd find her computer and the recording of the call with Roman. Maybe there'd be a huge investigation and he'd eventually be found guilty. There would be a special *48 Hours* TV show on everything that happened... and it would end on a fucking cliffhanger, because while Roman might be convicted, which would be tough without her body, she'd still be missing.

Wanting to laugh hysterically at the ridiculous thoughts running through her head, Maggie closed her eyes. Whatever Roman had in store for her, it probably wasn't a slow, relatively painless death from dehydration. No, whatever he had up his sleeve would be hell.

Trying to ignore the pain coursing through her body—her neck where Gigantor had strangled her, her hip, her shoulders from her arms being wrenched behind her for so long, her hair and face because they were both being pulled from the duct tape, and several other places where she was sure she'd have bruises from being manhandled—Maggie closed her eyes.

Maybe if she slept, she'd wake up and this nightmare would be over.

CHAPTER THIRTEEN

"This is a joke, right?" MacGyver asked no one in particular.

The "mission" they'd been sent on was to fly to the other side of the world, go up in helicopters, and drop crates of weapons in strategic places so Ukrainian forces could gather them up and use them against the Russian forces attempting to occupy their country.

It wasn't as if the SEALs hadn't done this kind of thing before, but usually they'd been tasked to do so in the middle of a war zone. Dropping weapons and ammunition to fellow American soldiers who'd been pinned down and needed reinforcements. From what Preacher understood, the Russian army was miles away from this particular DZ, and wouldn't be anywhere near it for at least a day or two.

The bottom line was, this drop wasn't particularly dangerous. Any platoon could've done what they were doing. It made no sense. And things that didn't make sense made every SEAL's "oh shit" meter go crazy.

Something had to be wrong. Preacher would normally assume their intel was faulty and they were flying into an ambush. In theory, they had plenty of time to make the drop. The small city not too far from the drop zone had already been pretty heavily bombed. Most civilians had fled the area, and their intel said the Russian troops sent to flush out any remaining stragglers were in no rush. Which was the alleged reason they were dropping weapons here. The area should be safe for Ukrainian soldiers to get in and out before the enemy arrived.

Maybe the Russian forces were closer than they'd been told. Maybe that was the feeling churning in Preacher's gut.

"This is a red herring," Smiley muttered. "We're being tasked to do this bullshit drop to distract us from something else."

"Yeah. To get us out of the fucking country so Robertson can get to Maggie."

He glanced at MacGyver. His friend sounded just as pissed as Preacher. It made it hard to swallow through the lump of emotion in his throat. The team had talked a lot while on the plane, and they all agreed that Maggie was in danger. They hated that they'd had to leave so suddenly, and everyone was extremely worried about the fact that Preacher hadn't been able to get a hold of her before they'd gone wheels up.

And now, hearing the concern and anger on Maggie's

behalf coming from MacGyver made Preacher truly understand the meaning of friendship. Yes, he'd felt the same way when shit had happened to Remi, Josie, and Wren, but this was different. Because he was on the other side. It was *his* woman possibly in danger—and he couldn't do a damn thing about it.

"So we drop these crates then get the fuck back to California," Smiley said firmly.

Preacher wanted that more than he wanted to breathe, but it wasn't so easy. They were at the mercy of their government. They went where they were told and did what they were ordered. They couldn't decide to disobey an order and just get on a plane, a plane owned by the United States, and fly back to California.

"Arriving at the DZ in sixty seconds."

The voice of one of the pilots in his ear made Preacher flinch. Looking out the open door of the chopper, he scanned the ground, surveilling the area where they were dropping the crates. Smiley and MacGyver were in the helicopter with him, and Safe, Blink, and Flash were in a second chopper. Kevlar was on the ground, monitoring the mission from their safe point in western Ukraine.

Preacher did his best to turn his mind to the task at hand. Anger bubbled just below the surface, but remembering Tex's warning to keep his head in the game helped him concentrate on what needed to be done right that moment.

They had six crates that needed to be offloaded. The plan was for the chopper to hover about five feet off the ground while the SEALs pushed the crates out the door onto the deserted farmlands just outside the city. The goal was to avoid them breaking apart when they landed to protect the supplies inside. Ukrainian soldiers in the area would come and collect the weapons, then disappear into the city to get ready for the Russians.

Nothing about this felt right, but at this point, Preacher simply wanted to get it done and get back across the border. The sooner they finished, the sooner he could try to get a hold of Maggie again.

"Thirty seconds."

Smiley and MacGyver were busy with the crates, pushing them closer to the open door, readying them to be released.

"Fifteen seconds."

The chopper began to lower closer to the ground at a high rate of speed. Just because hostile forces weren't immediately visible didn't mean the pilots wanted to stick around any longer than necessary.

"Go, go go!" the pilot said.

Without hesitation, Preacher moved to the side and helped MacGyver push the first crate out the door. It landed and bounced once on the grassy surface. Smiley was already pushing the next crate forward, and Preacher repeated his actions.

They quickly got five crates out the door and were on the last one.

"This one is way lighter than the others," MacGyver

commented over the headset as he pushed it toward the open door.

Preacher didn't care. All he wanted was to be done with this asinine assignment and get back to fucking Southern California.

The pilots had moved the chopper forward several feet after each crate had dropped, so they didn't land on each other. Preacher watched with detachment as the last crate landed in the long weeds below. The helicopter had begun to rise back into the air as soon as the crate had left the cargo area.

Instead of bouncing or rolling a few feet to a stop, the last crate cracked open upon impact. And what Preacher saw had his blood running cold.

He didn't have time to say anything to the pilots. He ripped off his headset, grabbed the safety line that had been prepared earlier just in case they needed to evacuate the chopper at a moment's notice, and leapt through the door, fast-roping to the ground below.

He felt more than saw the helicopter stop its ascension, but all Preacher's concentration was focused on that last crate. He couldn't have been more shocked by what was inside if someone had told him he'd won the lottery...when he didn't even play.

Maggie.

He'd recognize her anywhere, and not only because she was wearing the same thing she'd had on the morning they'd argued, when he'd left the country on this fucking mission.

It was impossible. Yet, his eyes weren't deceiving him.

Maggie had been in that last crate. And she was currently lying motionless in the tall grasses and dirt.

Preacher felt as if he was running through molasses. He couldn't get to her fast enough. His heart was thumping hard in his chest, and adrenaline was making him shaky. Was she dead? Had Robertson killed her, and this was how he was going to dispose of her body? By making Preacher and his team do the dirty deed? The thought made him want to puke.

He had to get to her. Nothing else was in his mind. Not hostiles who might be incoming. Not the chopper hovering over his head. Not even the sound of MacGyver, yelling his name behind him.

Maggie was all that mattered.

* * *

Maggie groaned. She was so confused. She'd been through hell in the last two days. At least...she thought it had been two days. In the dark box, though, she'd had no real way of telling time. She'd been moved a few times, and even with the earplugs still in her fucking ears, she'd been able to hear the loud, unmistakable sound of a helicopter.

She had no idea what was happening or where she was, but when the box she was in suddenly became weightless for a few brief seconds, she'd let out a startled scream behind the tape.

The pain from landing was intense, and for a moment,

she'd blacked out. But when she opened her eyes, Maggie was surprised that she could see. The box she'd been in had broken open.

Hands grabbed at her, and her self-preservation kicked in. Even though her own hands were still bound behind her, she fought. Using her legs to kick at whoever was hovering over her, turning her onto her side, kneeling...

The sudden light after days of darkness almost blinded her, but Maggie forced herself to look at whatever horror she'd suddenly been thrown into now—and froze.

She couldn't be seeing what she thought she was seeing. *Who* she was seeing.

Shawn.

"What the fuck?"

She didn't hear him, but she could read his lips. He began to tug at the tape around her mouth, which yanked at her hair, so she tried to pull away from him.

Then another set of hands was on her. Looking to her side as best she could, Maggie saw MacGyver. She had no idea where they were, or how Shawn and his friend had found her, but she was eternally grateful.

But panic quickly sank in. This was probably all part of Roman's plan! Whatever he had up his sleeve couldn't be good. Shawn was in danger. Because of *her*. She tried to tell him to get away from her. To leave her and go, but the damn tape was still over her mouth.

MacGyver had already managed to remove what turned out to be zip-ties around her wrists, and the relief she felt at being free was almost as overwhelming as it was painful.

The blood flowing freely down her arms was like the sensation of hitting her funny bone. Hard.

Shawn's mouth was moving as if he was talking to her, but the damn earplugs made anything he was saying impossible to hear. Turning onto her back, and groaning at how good it felt, she reached a hand up to her ear. She removed one earplug, then the other.

"What the fuck?" MacGyver said, mimicking Shawn.

"Earplugs," Maggie said behind the tape, even though he could clearly see for himself what they were.

"Maggie! Are you all right? How the hell are you here?"

She shook her head at the same time she said, "I'm not okay yet. But I will be if you give me a minute or two to get my bearings." That was what she *tried* to say, but the tape over her mouth prevented the words from being understandable.

"Here," MacGyver said, handing something to Shawn.

It was a knife. A wicked-looking one with serrated edges. Anyone else who came at her face with that thing would've gotten a foot to the groin, but it was Shawn holding the deadly weapon. Maggie closed her eyes, letting him do what needed to be done.

She felt the tape loosen around her face, then Shawn said, "This is going to hurt."

Maggie nodded but didn't open her eyes. She'd done what she could over the last couple days to try to dampen the tape, to loosen it around her lips, but that wouldn't help the adhesive that was stuck tight to her cheeks.

Shawn did his best to move fast, but he hadn't been

wrong. Peeling the tape off her face still hurt like a son-of-a-bitch.

"Maggie?" he asked fearfully.

"Shawn," she whispered. Her mouth was dry, she felt kind of sick from lack of water or food. But she was alive. That was all that mattered.

"Fuck!" he said. He was breathing hard, his eyes were huge, and his hands actually shook as he took her face in his hand.

Then his lips were on hers. It was a gentle kiss, but a life-affirming one.

He pulled back and immediately reached for something on his belt. "Here, drink this."

Water.

Maggie would never take it for granted again. She tried not to gulp it down, but she could feel it leaking out the corners of her mouth as she desperately took in the life-saving liquid faster than she should.

"Easy," Shawn warned, pulling the canteen away from her.

Maggie made a small sound of protest in the back of her throat.

"I know. I'll give you more in a second. You need to let that settle first."

"Preacher, we have incoming," MacGyver said.

Glancing at him, Maggie saw him gesture over their heads. Looking past Shawn for the first time, she saw a helicopter in the distance—coming at them fast. A second chopper, one much closer that seemed to be hovering nearby, suddenly banked hard to the left, gaining height and speed as it took off in the opposite direction.

"What the hell? Thought they weren't coming for a couple days," Shawn said.

"Guess our intel was wrong. Not that I'm surprised. We need to get going," MacGyver said.

"Can you stand?" Shawn asked Maggie.

"Yes," she told him, not knowing if that was true or not. But if the look MacGyver was giving Shawn was any indication, she didn't have a choice. She'd fucking cartwheel her way out of here, wherever *here* was, if she had to.

A loud *crack* echoed around them, and both Shawn and MacGyver flinched and hunched over, as if trying to duck below whatever had made that sound.

"We need to get away from the crates," MacGyver said, sounding almost calm now, when moments before he'd definitely seemed anxious.

"Hostiles or friendlies?" Shawn asked.

"Don't know. But I'm thinking the farther away from these crates we can get, the better. I'd rather not get between two dogs and the bone they both want."

"The Russians were supposed to be days away," Shawn repeated.

Her head swung back and forth between the two men as if she were at a tennis match. Then what Shawn said sank in.

Russians? What the hell?

"We'll hole up," Shawn added. "The team'll come back when things quiet down."

"Smiley and the others are gonna be pissed that we've been left here," MacGyver said, sounding as if he was merely discussing where to go out for lunch.

"They'll be back as soon as they can. They can't risk an international incident, and they know we can take care of ourselves," Shawn said. He looked down at Maggie. "Come on, we need to get you up and moving."

Maggie tried to stand, and immediately found that she was extremely weak and shaky. If it wasn't for Shawn's arm around her waist, she would've fallen on her face.

"Russians?" she asked, as she prayed to get some strength back in her body.

"Yeah. We're in Ukraine. Come on, take a few steps, see if that helps."

Maggie's eyes nearly bugged out of her head. "How... what... I don't understand."

"We'll talk after we're safe. Because we are definitely *not* safe right now."

The loud cracking sound happened again, and this time Shawn put his hand on the back of her head and urged her to duck down with him and MacGyver.

"You'll have to carry her," MacGyver said.

"Yep." Shawn turned around. "Climb on," he told her.

Maggie blinked. Things were moving way too quickly. She didn't understand anything that was happening. She was in Ukraine? The *country*?

MacGyver didn't give her time to further process anything, he simply picked her up under the arms and placed her on Shawn's back as if she were a kid. Instinctively, she tightened her legs around his waist and her arms around his neck. One of Shawn's hands went under her ass to hold her up.

"Go!" he said urgently to MacGyver.

The other man took off, with Shawn and Maggie at his heels.

The cracking sounds, which she now understood to be gunfire, echoed around them more and more. It felt as if they ran forever, and Maggie had to close her eyes as she was jostled and bumped on Shawn's back. The water she'd guzzled threatened to come back up, but she refused to puke all over Shawn's shoulder and chest.

The sounds of gunfire eventually faded as they continued to run. Maggie opened her eyes and saw they were nearing what seemed to be a city. Well, what *used* to be a city. Now it was mostly a pile of rubble. Everywhere she looked, there were destroyed houses and buildings on the outskirts. Burnt-out cars sat in the middle of what were once roads. The smell of death and destruction was thick in the air.

Once they entered the city proper, they didn't stop, although they weren't running anymore. MacGyver led them over piles of rock and debris as they picked their way farther and farther into the heart of whatever city this used to be.

Every now and then, Maggie could swear she saw a person duck behind a broken window of a dilapidated building or scoot around a crumbled wall, but she couldn't be sure. No one approached them, but maybe more importantly, no one threatened them in any way.

She was just about to beg to be put down—her feet were numb and she still thought she might throw up—when MacGyver approached what looked like just another pile of rocks.

"Wait here," he told Shawn, before ducking under a huge piece of plywood and disappearing.

Shawn slowly lowered Maggie to her feet, and she could've gone to her knees and kissed the ground right then and there, but he turned, wrapped an arm around her waist, and pulled her against his chest. She buried her nose into the space between his shoulder and head and hung on, as tightly as he was holding onto her.

One hand was at the back of her head, and the other was an iron band around her waist.

"Fuck, Maggie. *Fuck.*"

"You sound like Blink," she muttered against him.

She felt more than heard him snort. Then he pulled back. "I'm sorry. I should've believed you without question."

Maggie shook her head. She'd had lots of time to think about what had happened back in California. "No, you had plenty of reasons to doubt what I was saying."

"Well, suffice it to say, I believe you now. We all do."

"Are we really in Ukraine?"

"Yes."

"I'm still confused about what's happening."

"Me too. But we'll talk and figure it out, as soon as MacGyver finds us a safe place to hole up."

"Okay."

"Here, drink some more water," Shawn urged. He took the hand from behind her head and held out the canteen once more.

Maggie wanted to gulp it down again, but something occurred to her. Looking around, she realized there wasn't going to be a handy faucet to deliver more clean water once the canteen was empty. And Shawn would need to drink too. Probably needed more than she would, since she was definitely out of her league right now. This was Shawn's world, and she hadn't ever been more grateful for someone at her side than she was right that moment. She had no idea how the hell he was there, but she wasn't going to question her luck.

After taking a long sip, which didn't come close to satisfying her thirst, she tried to hand it back to him.

"No, finish it," he told her with a shake of his head, trying to bring the canteen back up to her lips.

"But you need to drink too," she said.

"I will. After you're taken care of."

Maggie looked around exaggeratedly. "I'm not seeing any water fountains around here to refill the canteen," she told him sarcastically.

To her surprise, he grinned. Then got serious quickly. "God, I could've lost this. Lost *You*."

Maggie swallowed hard. She wanted nothing more than to burst into tears to let out some of the stress that had built up over the last couple of days, but she needed to stay strong. "Seriously, Shawn, I'm not going to drink all our water and not leave you any. Out of the two of us, I need *you* to stay strong the most. I'm completely useless here."

"No, you aren't. And we aren't going to be here long. Kevlar and the others will arrange to come get us. Also, we can find water. I have purification tablets in my vest. We're okay. Drink."

With a sigh, she did as he ordered. She was thirsty, desperately so. And if he thought they would be rescued quickly, she'd believe him.

Just as she was finishing up the water, MacGyver reappeared, scaring Maggie so badly, she would've fallen on her ass if Shawn's arm hadn't still been around her.

"Easy, it's just MacGyver."

"It's clean. Come on," he told them.

Maggie was still shaky on her feet, but with Shawn's help she was able to step over debris and crawl behind MacGyver until they'd reached a small pocket of safety between the crumbled ruins of a building.

"It's not the Ritz, but it'll do," MacGyver announced. "Scrounged some stuff while I was finding this place too." He gestured to a pile of odds and ends in the corner.

Shawn chuckled and turned to Maggie. "That's why he's called MacGyver. Because he somehow manages to create the most amazing tools out of nothing. Here, sit. Then we'll talk."

Once upon a time, those three words would've struck fear in Maggie's heart. But now? She *wanted* to talk.

Needed to. Had to find answers as to how the hell she'd ended up in freaking Ukraine in the middle of a conflict she'd only read about in the papers.

But deep down, she already knew. Roman Robertson. He'd done exactly what he'd threatened—fucked her and Shawn at the same time. She could only hope this time, things would be different. That she and the man she was definitely starting to think she was in love with wouldn't fall prey to an evil man's manipulations and immoral, evil plans.

CHAPTER FOURTEEN

Preacher couldn't stop touching Maggie. He kept staring at her, unable to believe she was actually with him. When he'd seen her unmoving body fall out of that crate, he'd almost had a heart attack. He'd acted without thinking, something Tex and his team would chew his ass out for later. But there was no way he was letting that helicopter fly away with him on it while leaving Maggie lying in the dirt.

For a split second, he'd thought she was dead. That Robertson had gotten the ultimate revenge on his ex. But then she'd moved, and a whole new fear had nearly overwhelmed him. If Robertson had the power to do *this*—to kidnap Maggie, ship her across the world, and get her new boyfriend to unwittingly dispose of her body—what else could he do?

But that was a question for another time. Right now,

they needed to get out of this FUBAR'd situation. Then he and the others would tackle the Rear Admiral Robertson problem.

The duct tape that had been used to silence her was still hanging from either side of her head, stuck fast in her hair. The sight of it was offensive, making Preacher feel sick to his stomach. But he did his best to ignore that for now. She was alive, that was all that mattered.

How? He had no idea. She'd been strangled—he saw the clear finger-shaped bruises on her throat—restrained, thrown into a crate, gagged, had earplugs put in her ears so she couldn't hear anything going on around her, and then pushed out of a fucking helicopter. She should've died. But she didn't. She was way tougher than Robertson ever dreamed. Not only for surviving two years behind bars for a crime she didn't commit, but for inexplicitly making it through his sick plan to dump her in the middle of a goddamn war zone.

Roman Robertson was going to suffer. Preacher made a mental vow to do whatever it took to make it happen. Even if it meant ruining his own reputation and getting kicked off the SEAL teams and out of the Navy. Robertson would pay for what he'd been doing—ruining people's lives simply because he could.

"You feel okay?" MacGyver asked Maggie gently.

They'd given her some protein bars, and she'd had more water. There was color in her cheeks now, and even though she had to be exhausted, she was still too quiet for Preacher's liking.

"Yeah. I'm okay," she said.

Preacher wanted to snort. He had a feeling she'd say that if one of her arms was hanging on by a tendon. She and him...they were a lot alike.

"What happened, Maggie?" MacGyver asked, leaning forward a little, keeping his voice low just in case there were people around who might hear them. At this point, they had no idea if anyone still in the area was friend or foe. It was best to lay low and not draw attention to themselves.

Preacher felt her take a deep breath—she was plastered against his side, and every movement she made transferred to him—then she spoke.

"I was sitting on my couch, feeling sorry for myself. Kicking my own ass for being such a baby about the disagreement I'd had with Shawn, when there was a knock on the door. I thought it was you," she said, looking up at him. "I ran to the door and opened it without looking. Which was stupid."

"You had no reason to think it was anyone but me."

"I guess. The guy grabbed me around the throat, and I passed out. It was that simple, really."

She sounded disgusted with herself.

"I don't understand how Roman knew that I'd talked to you about him. I mean, it had only been a few hours. And while he said some stuff in that call I recorded that made me think he had people watching me, following me, could he have somehow bugged my place too?"

"Maybe," Preacher said, feeling sick. "But I think it's probably my fault."

"You?" she asked.

"Yeah. I made a bunch of calls after I left. I think he could've found out because of that."

"You think Dude or Tex somehow notified Robertson?" MacGyver asked.

"No. They'd never do that. But even if Dude was discrete in any inquiries he made, word gets out," Preacher said.

Maggie sighed again. "I guess it doesn't really matter. Eventually, he was going to find out regardless."

Preacher didn't agree. Robertson would've found himself in a world of hurt when the Navy started investigating him, but if Preacher had been a little smarter about Maggie's safety, the man never would've gotten his hands on her so quickly.

"Anyway, I woke up in that box. I couldn't yell out for anyone to help me because of the tape, or hear if anyone was around because of the earplugs. I had no idea where I was or what was happening."

"Until that box broke," MacGyver said. "Thank God it did. Otherwise, we would've left."

Preacher shuddered in revulsion. "That's exactly what he wanted. No one ever would've discovered what he'd done either. Maggie would've been just another missing woman. And Robertson would get some sick, twisted enjoyment out of knowing I'd done his dirty work for him."

He felt Maggie's hand squeeze his arm, but Preacher wasn't ready to be comforted. "So, what now?" she asked.

Both men looked at her.

"I mean, his plan failed. I'm alive, and you guys figured it out. You realize he's an extreme asshole and totally evil. So...what now?"

"We wait for our team to pick us up, then we get the hell back to the States and get his ass fired," MacGyver said heatedly.

To Preacher's surprise, Maggie chuckled. "Right. You make it sound so easy."

"It won't be," MacGyver told her in a somber tone. "It's going to suck. I'm guessing there might even be some Witness Protection involved for you."

Preacher expected Maggie to freak out at hearing that. He himself wasn't feeling all that level-headed about it at the moment.

But to his surprise, she just said, "I'm guessing that won't be approved by my probation officer."

It took a moment, but MacGyver burst into laughter. Quiet chuckles, but he was definitely amused.

Maggie smiled at him, then turned her head to look at Preacher. "I'll do whatever it takes to make him pay for what he's done. Not for getting me locked up. I did my time, and I can't go back and *undo* it, so the damage is done. But for what he's doing to the Navy. How many other SEAL teams has he sent to places they shouldn't have been in? Or without the support they needed? His power trips know no bounds. I was child's play for him, but manipulating people who signed up to serve their country? To give their lives if necessary? That's not right. He's not playing Risk, for God's sake. He's messing with real people, real lives. He needs to be stopped."

She wasn't wrong. But Preacher wanted Robertson to pay for the time Maggie had done behind bars. She hadn't knowingly transported those drugs, and she certainly hadn't planned on selling them. She'd lost her career, her friends, her apartment, her car, and two years of her life— for what? For Robertson's amusement? That wasn't acceptable. No fucking way in hell.

"I agree," Preacher told her a little belatedly.

"Me too," MacGyver said.

Maggie yawned then, sagging heavily against him.

"Why don't you sleep?" he suggested.

"Are we safe?" she asked, looking around the room with tired eyes.

"As safe as we can be at the moment," MacGyver told her.

"I'm not sure that's very reassuring, but I'm too tired to care," she said dryly. It didn't take her long to go completely boneless against him.

Preacher looked up at MacGyver and said quietly, "Tell me you have your radio on you."

"Nope. We had no plans to put boots on the ground. No need for it."

"Damn," he swore.

"Doesn't matter. They'll find us," MacGyver said. "If I have to, I'll find the parts to make a fucking radio."

That made Preacher smile. He didn't doubt his friend could do just that.

"Besides, I have a tracker. Tex'll lead 'em right to us."

Relief swam through Preacher's veins. He'd forgotten about the trackers. "I don't have mine because we didn't get to go home and pack." After what happened to Blink, he'd concealed one of his trackers in the waistband of a pair of briefs. Not that bad guys couldn't strip him completely bare, but Blink was a perfect example of how that usually didn't happen. Of course, that underwear was sitting at home in a drawer, useless.

"I've started wearing one of mine every goddamn day," MacGyver said with a shrug. "Paranoid? Yes. But I'm damn glad now."

"Me too," Preacher agreed.

Several minutes of silence stretched between them, before MacGyver broke it by saying, "He's insane."

Preacher didn't have to ask who he was talking about.

"Putting her in that box and arranging for us to drop it? For *you* to drop it? He's fucking sick."

"He's going down," Preacher growled between clenched teeth.

"I know some guys. They live in Indiana. They run a completely legitimate business but do contract work on the side. If needed, I'll get a hold of them. They'll take care of Robertson once and for all."

The thought of an assassin taking out the trash was appealing, but Preacher wasn't a man who worked outside the law. None of them were. There were rules for what they did. And hiring someone to put a bullet in Robertson's head was way outside what he was comfortable with.

Preacher looked down at a sleeping Maggie, and once more saw the duct tape hanging from her hair. It would most likely have to be cut out.

His conviction wavered.

Taking a deep breath, he said, "I think this stunt will be his undoing. He thought he was so smart, getting rid of Maggie in a way he didn't think anyone would ever find out about. But he was too cocky. Sending us on this asinine mission will be the nail in his coffin. He thought Maggie would die, and he probably hoped the Russians would take care of us as well. But she didn't. And he'll get his, MacGyver."

"Okay. But if anything starts going sideways, and it looks like he's going to get off with some bullshit punishment, I'm calling Silverstone."

"Deal," Preacher said without hesitation. Personal moral code or not, deep down he knew the very idea of a man like Roman Robertson wandering around, free to fuck with other people's lives, was abhorrent. Not to mention it would put Maggie's life in extreme danger. The fact that she'd survived what he'd planned for her was reason enough for him to do everything he could to take her out. Until the man was stopped, he'd always be a threat.

Silence fell between the two men once more. Preacher didn't feel the least bit sleepy. The creaks and groans of the dilapidated building over their heads didn't exactly make him feel all that safe. But all they needed to do was wait things out. Kevlar and the others would hopefully be there soon.

All of a sudden, there was a scraping sound from the direction of where they'd entered the small room.

Preacher sat up straighter, and MacGyver did the same.

Moving Maggie so she was lying down instead of using him as a pillow, he took note of how she didn't even flinch. Getting pissed all over again at how exhausted she had to be, Preacher pulled his KA-BAR knife out of the sheath at his side. MacGyver had done the same thing as they prepared to face whoever was about to enter the room. They moved silently to either side of the entrance, ready to subdue whatever threat might appear.

To their surprise, three children crawled through the makeshift door.

Preacher grabbed the biggest, putting an arm around the kid's chest and lifting him off his feet. MacGyver did the same to the next largest intruder, and they hauled them into the middle of the small room.

Chaos immediately broke out. The kids struggled, the third one—the child who hadn't been grabbed, and who couldn't have been older than around five—didn't hesitate to run up to Preacher, kicking and hitting him.

The extremely odd thing about the entire situation was how it was all done silently. These kids obviously knew not to announce their location to anyone else who might be nearby.

"Calm down," Preacher ordered firmly but quietly—and amazingly, they did. Moving slowly, he put down the boy he'd grabbed, and MacGyver did the same. The little girl who'd so violently attempted to protect the boys ran to them, and they immediately hugged her, then shoved her behind them as they glared at the two men.

Preacher re-sheathed his knife at the same time as MacGyver, then crouched down on the balls of his feet. "Hello," he said, wondering how much English the kids understood.

"Why you here?" the largest boy asked. His English was accented, and a little stilted, but Preacher was impressed that he was speaking it all the same.

"We came to rest and to hide from the bad guys."

"This is *our* place," the other boy said.

"I'm sorry, we didn't realize. Can we share?" Preacher asked.

The older boy looked from him to MacGyver, then back to him. His eyes filled with tears, but the boy angrily wiped them away with his arm. "No. We go."

"Wait!" Preacher exclaimed. Now that he'd gotten a better look at the trio, he couldn't in good conscience let them simply leave. All three were filthy, covered in dirt and grime. Their clothes were ripped and torn, and the shoes on their feet were nothing but basically slippers. They all had the hollow eyes of hardened soldiers who'd seen too much hate and death. It tugged at his heartstrings.

"Stay," MacGyver said. "I promise we won't hurt you."

The younger boy looked over at Maggie. "You hurt girl."

"What? No. She isn't hurt. She's sleeping," MacGyver protested.

Preacher hated that these kids thought they'd hurt Maggie, but he wasn't that surprised. War had devastated the city, and these kids had seen things they never should've had to see. He stepped over to Maggie and gently shook her shoulder. "Maggie? Wake up, sweetheart."

Her eyes popped open in an instant, as if she was used to coming awake at a moment's notice, and he supposed she probably was. Letting down your guard behind bars was probably a dangerous thing to do. Even while sleeping.

"What? What's wrong?"

"Nothing. We have guests," Preacher told her.

Her eyes focused on the three children. "Oh!" she whispered.

"See? She's okay. Not hurt," MacGyver said. He'd moved so he was sitting on his butt on the ground, and he was holding up his hands as if to show he was unarmed. "We don't have any food, but we have some water. It's clean. Do you want some?"

The boys looked skeptical, but the little girl tugged on the older kid's shirt and said something in Ukrainian. He nodded once.

MacGyver smiled and leaned forward, placing his canteen on the floor in front of the children, then sat back.

The smaller boy took one step and snatched the water up so fast, if Preacher hadn't been watching, he would've missed it. Instead of drinking the water himself, he handed it to the girl. She smiled at him as if he was her whole world and brought the canteen to her lips.

"What are your names?" MacGyver asked softly.

"Where did they come from?" Maggie whispered to Preacher.

"Don't know. They just appeared."

"My name is MacGyver. Well, my real name is Ricardo. Some people call me Ricky."

"Three names?" the smaller boy asked.

MacGyver smiled. "Yeah, I guess. But you can choose which one you like best."

"Ricky," the little girl said.

He beamed. "Ricky it is. And what's your name?" he asked her.

"Yana."

The oldest boy said something in harsh tones to the girl, and she immediately frowned and ducked her head.

"It's okay," MacGyver said. "I'm not going to hurt you. Any of you. Yana is a beautiful name."

Preacher remained silent as MacGyver did his best to win the trust of the three very skittish kids.

"How old are you, Yana?"

She held up four fingers, then looked at the boys as if wanting reassurance that she'd either gotten her age right, or it was okay to still be interacting with MacGyver.

"She four. I am eight. My brother is seven."

"And what should I call you?" MacGyver asked him.

For a moment, the boy frowned. Then he said, "I am Artem. My brother is Borysko."

"It's nice to meet you both. As I said, I'm Ricky, and my friends over there are Maggie and Preacher... um...Shawn."

Three sets of eyes swung toward Preacher and Maggie.

"Oh my God, they're adorable," she whispered.

"Your English is very good," MacGyver praised. "Where did you learn it?"

"School," Artem said, not hiding his derision at what he obviously thought was a stupid question.

"Right," MacGyver said with a small chuckle.

"This is our place," Borysko told MacGyver again.

"I'm very sorry to have come here without asking if it's okay. But we were afraid of the guns. And Maggie needed a place to rest. She was hurt. We'll leave if you want us to... but can we share for a while?"

Preacher had never seen this side of his teammate. He was speaking soft and low and all his attention remained on the children.

Artem's gaze went from MacGyver, to where Preacher and Maggie were sitting, then back to MacGyver. "Did Russians hurt her?"

"No. It's complicated."

Both boys' brows furrowed in confusion.

"Sorry, um...it's hard to explain," MacGyver said, trying to use words that the children might understand.

Yana tugged at Borysko's shirt and said something in Ukrainian.

Her brother translated. "Her English is not good. She

had not started school when the bombs came. We are trying to learn her."

"That's good," MacGyver praised. "Where are your parents? Mom and Dad?"

Both boys frowned again.

"Dead," Artem said woodenly. "Bomb came and made the house flat."

"Oh no," Maggie whispered.

Preacher had been watching the entire exchange, and something about the matter-of-fact way Artem had said the word "dead" made his heart break. War was hell, he knew that better than most people. But he was an adult. He'd signed up for what he did. But these kids, and the other innocent civilians caught in the crossfire of wars around the world during whatever power struggle was happening, they were innocent. These three siblings were the epitome of the consequences of man's greed and need for control and power.

"I'm so sorry. My mom and dad are still alive. They live about an hour from where I live now. I have two brothers and two sisters," MacGyver told the kids. "I'm in the middle, but I did my best to protect my sisters when I was around your age."

He kept talking, telling stories about when he was young, saying anything he could to keep the children calm. It seemed to work. Preacher could see their muscles beginning to relax. Their shoulders were no longer hunched up around their heads, and they seemed to be leaning toward MacGyver rather than away.

"This is breaking my heart," Maggie said quietly. "What will happen to them when we're gone?"

Preacher swallowed hard. "Hopefully there are people around here who will take them in."

"But wouldn't they have done that already if they were going to?" she asked.

"I don't know. War does strange things to people. It makes them more...selfish. That's not really the best word, but when food gets scarce, when shelter is iffy, it's human nature to hoard what you have and not let others in."

"But they're kids," Maggie whispered fiercely. "That little girl is only four! How could someone *not* help them?"

"I'm not condoning anyone's behavior, just trying to explain it," Preacher said calmly.

Maggie nodded and snuggled up against him. "I know," she muttered into his chest. "I just hate this for them."

"Me too," Preacher told her. And he wasn't lying. There was something about these kids that hit him hard. The older boys had obviously taken their job of protecting their little sister seriously. And the way they'd fought silently, so they didn't bring any attention to themselves, it was... wrong. On all levels.

"Can we take them with us?" Maggie asked.

Preacher's stomach clenched. He wanted to, but he knew that wasn't something they could do. There were many times when he and his team had wanted to save the children they came across on their missions. They'd done what they could, left food and water, but taking them back to the US was definitely against military policy. And something that could result in severe punishment.

"I'm sure they'll be all right," Preacher said. The words sounded lame to his own ears, but he had no good answer to make Maggie feel better.

He heard a strange sound, and he looked over at MacGyver and the kids. Somehow his friend had gotten all three children to sit around him, and they were now playing tic-tac-toe in the dirt. There were three games going at the same time, and MacGyver was doing his best to keep up with all three.

The sound Preacher heard was little Yana giggling.

These kids had suffered, were *still* suffering, and yet they'd managed to lower their guard enough to play a simple game with a foreigner in the dirt, in a bombed-out building, in the city they'd probably grown up in that was now nothing but rubble. Their parents were dead, and who knew how many other adults they'd known had been killed as well.

This was why feuds never really ended. This *war* would end, as they all did, but the things these kids had seen and done would stay with them. Hatred would fester, and in a decade or more, tensions would rise again, and it was likely Artem and Borysko, and possibly even Yana, would be some of the first ones to sign up to fight.

It sucked.

"Want to play tic-tac-toe?" Preacher asked Maggie, desperately needing to help shine some light in the kids' world, even if it was just playing the simple game for a while.

"Yes," she said, looking up at him sadly. Preacher wasn't surprised she was on the same wavelength. She'd just been through hell, and yet, all her concern and attention was on these kids, not her own situation. She impressed him, and he wanted to spend the rest of his life with her by his side.

They shuffled over to where the kids and MacGyver were playing and asked if they could join. The boys looked wary, but eventually relaxed enough to let them play.

After half an hour or so of playing the game over and over again, Preacher took a break, glancing over at Maggie. At some point, Yana had crawled into her lap and fallen asleep. Maggie was leaning against a slab of concrete, also out cold. Yana's head was against her breast, her body curled into a tight little ball.

A thought flashed through his brain right then. Of Maggie holding their own little girl the exact same way. The vision was so real, it took his breath away. He wanted that. So damn bad.

The sound of Borysko's stomach growling had both MacGyver and Preacher looking at the little boy. The kid didn't acknowledge his hunger in any way, obviously used to it.

Which was just another thing that upset Preacher.

MacGyver obviously felt the same way. He asked, "What do you eat here?"

Artem looked at him. The boy had lived a thousand years since his parents had died, it was obvious. He'd assumed the role of protector over his siblings, and it was taking a toll on him. How could it not?

"What we can find," he said simply.

"Show me?" MacGyver asked.

Preacher opened his mouth to protest. To tell his friend it wasn't smart to be wandering around the ruined city right now, especially since the sound of gunfire hadn't really abated since they'd taken refuge in the rubble of the building.

Artem studied MacGyver, then nodded. He turned to his brother and said something in Ukrainian. Borysko shook his head, and they had a small argument. But Artem obviously won, because he stood up and told MacGyver, "You after me."

"I'll follow you," he agreed.

The two slipped out of the room, and Preacher hoped they hadn't just made a huge mistake. Artem could be a spy for the Russian army. Or he could be leading MacGyver into a trap. But he shook his head. The kid was eight. And he wouldn't do anything that might put his brother and sister in danger. He knew that as well as he knew his name. MacGyver would be all right. He'd find something for all of them to eat, and by then, hopefully Tex would have done his thing and sent their SEAL team to pick them up.

Looking over at Maggie and Yana sleeping soundly made his heart clench again. For the first time in his career, Preacher wasn't sure he *wanted* to be rescued. Going back to California meant dealing with Robertson, which was going to be a special kind of hell. As much as he now believed everything Maggie said about the man, prosecuting him wouldn't be easy. And while they waited for the hands of justice to spin, Robertson would be a danger to all of them. He'd managed to kidnap Maggie and ship her across the fucking world; there was no telling what he'd do when he found out his plans had been thwarted.

Then there were these kids. They'd obviously done all right on their own, but the thought of leaving them in this destroyed part of the country with no adults to look after them...it hit Preacher hard.

Scooting over, he sidled up next to Maggie and put his arm around her, pulling her against him, so she was using him rather than the hard concrete as a pillow.

Borysko eyed the three of them for a moment, before lying down in the dirt next to them, one hand under his head, the other draped over his sister's foot. Obviously wanting to keep a connection with her even in sleep.

Even after closing his eyes to get some rest himself, Preacher still couldn't stop seeing Borysko's dirty little hand reaching for his sister.

Somehow, someway, he'd do something for this little family.

CHAPTER FIFTEEN

Maggie looked around at their little group and shook her head in amazement. How long she'd slept while MacGyver and Artem had been gone, she had no idea. But when Shawn woke her up, the two were back, and they had their hands full of food. Two dented cans and two MREs. She'd asked where in the world they'd found everything, but MacGyver had shaken his head, making it clear he wasn't going to talk about it...at least not in front of the kids.

Artem had frowned at Maggie and woken up Yana, taking her by the hand and leading her to the other side of the room. It was clear he wasn't especially happy at how quickly she'd trusted the Americans. The three kids knelt over an MRE, and if the way they shoved food in their mouths was any indication, they'd been very hungry.

Seeing their desperation and enjoyment of the meal made Maggie's hunger disappear in a flash.

"I know," Shawn told her in a low voice. "But you have to eat, Maggie. You need the nutrients. You've been deprived too."

She knew that, but it was still really hard to eat when she felt as if she was literally stealing food from the mouths of babes.

Even though Yana had fallen asleep in her lap, it was obvious the children were drawn to MacGyver more than her and Shawn. The SEAL was amazing with the kids. Didn't talk down to them and asked for their thoughts on subjects ranging anywhere from the situation with the Russians to their favorite foods.

And despite Artem still being distrustful and wary, clearly something happened when he and MacGyver had gone foraging for food. They'd bonded in a way that was obvious to Maggie. Artem seemed more relaxed around the man, and his gaze was glued to the SEAL anytime one of his siblings wasn't talking.

Suddenly, a loud explosion sounded way too close to where they were holed up.

Artem was on his feet instantly, his sister's hand in his own and Borysko on her other side.

MacGyver quickly gathered up the uneaten food and shoved it into the pockets of his cargo pants.

"We gotta go," Shawn said unnecessarily. "Maggie, you take Yana. MacGyver, you're in the lead. Artem behind him, then Maggie, Borysko, and I'll bring up the rear."

Maggie wanted to protest, but the SEALs were the experts here. She knew nothing about evading incoming bombs or defeating any unexpected bad guys they came across.

To her surprise, Artem nodded in agreement, towing Yana over to where she was standing next to Shawn. He said something to the little girl, and she nodded and held up her arms to Maggie.

Once again, Maggie's heart melted. It wasn't that the little girl was coming to her for protection; she'd done it because her big brother told her to. And yet, she was still in awe of the trust Yana was showing.

MacGyver turned to Artem and held out his KA-BAR knife. In any other situation, Maggie would've protested giving such a lethal weapon to a child, but this wasn't suburbia United States.

Artem took the knife and nodded at the SEAL. He held it in his small hand, and Maggie had a feeling he wouldn't hesitate to use it, which made her feel queasy all over again. No child should feel as if he had to use violence to protect himself or his family.

They made their way out of the hidden room that had somehow felt safe, which it obviously was not, if the sound of the explosions coming closer and closer were any indication.

It was eerie how they didn't come across anyone as they crept out of the rubble and through the streets of the small city. Every now and then the sound of gunfire echoed around them, making Maggie flinch every time.

This was scary. She could admit it. And even though MacGyver and Shawn were there, they couldn't stop a bullet. Not from hitting her or going through their own bodies. At that moment, she hated Roman a little more, and she already hated him with every fiber of her being. *He'd* done this. He was evil to his core. He had to know it was likely she wouldn't die in that crate. So his plan was to dump her here, in the middle of a war zone, alive, bound, and unable to protect herself in any way.

If she'd been found, she could've been sexually assaulted, beaten, sold, killed on the spot...the possibilities were endless. She wanted to be rescued so damn badly, but at the same time, she didn't want to go back to California. Because Roman would be more determined than ever to torture her once he realized she was still alive. He'd have to get rid of her once and for all. She was as good as dead the second she set foot back in Riverton.

She began to shake with fear. Of the current situation *and* what awaited her back home. She literally couldn't win. Maybe she should ask if Shawn could drop her off in Turkmenistan or something. Somewhere no one would find her. Not that she wanted to live abroad or be away from Shawn, now that she'd finally met a man who she felt as if she could spend the rest of her life with. But she didn't want to die either.

"Mag okay?" Yana whispered, patting Maggie's cheek as they walked.

Meeting the little girl's gaze, Maggie took a deep breath. "I'm okay," she echoed, not feeling okay in the least, but for this child, she had to be. "Yana okay?" she asked.

Yana nodded. The serious look on her face was tragic. This child should be laughing and smiling, not being carried through streets of rubble, dodging gunfire.

All of a sudden, those streets were full of Russian soldiers. They spotted their little group immediately and pointed their rifles, yelling something Maggie couldn't understand but assumed was something like "stop."

"Run!" Shawn yelled—and then they were all literally running for their lives.

It was difficult to run with little Yana in her arms, but she knew if she didn't, they'd all end up dead or captured, because neither of her brothers would leave Yana, and Shawn sure as hell wouldn't, and it was obvious that MacGyver had bonded with the little family and wouldn't leave *any* of the siblings behind. So it felt as if she was the only one keeping them out of the Russians' hands...which was almost a joke. Out of everyone in their little group, she was the least equipped to handle what was happening.

But she did her best.

She almost tripped over a piece of debris in the street, but thankfully Shawn was suddenly at her side, her elbow in his grip, helping her stay on her feet as they fled.

Just when she thought they were going to get away from the men chasing them, they went down a street that was completely blocked by the rubble of a building that had been bombed sometime in the past. There was no way around it, and they couldn't go back the way they came because they could still hear the soldiers yelling.

"Up!" MacGyver ordered, turning and grabbing

Borysko by the waist and heaving him upward, toward a little shelf of concrete about eight feet above the ground.

Shawn took little Yana out of Maggie's arms without a word and held her up to her brother. Before Maggie could blink, MacGyver had lifted Artem up to join his siblings.

"Your turn," Shawn told Maggie, leaning over and clasping his hands together. "Step here, I'll help you up."

She wanted to argue that this was crazy, but time was of an essence. There was no room for hesitation. Putting a hand on Shawn's shoulder for balance, she stepped into his hands—and practically flew into the air. Before she knew how it had happened, she was standing on the ledge with the kids.

She had only seconds to wonder how Shawn and MacGyver were going to get up there with them before the soldiers appeared at the end of the street. They shouted something, then began to run toward the two men.

"Shawn!" Maggie screamed—but it was too late. The soldiers were there, hitting the SEALs with their rifles, yelling at them.

"Go!" Shawn managed to shout, before someone hit him in the face with the butt of a rifle. He went down, hard...and then didn't move.

Maggie stood frozen in shock and horror. MacGyver was fighting for all he was worth, but eight against one wasn't a fair fight, and it was obvious he was going to go down like Shawn at any moment.

"Come!" Artem said urgently, tugging at Maggie's hand. The ledge they were standing on was part of a wall that had fallen, which sloped downward into the darkness on the other side. She could just make out a tangle of steel and concrete that had obviously once been some sort of residence.

She didn't want to go. Wanted to stay where she was to see if Shawn got back up. But then one of the soldiers looked right at her. When he realized she was a woman, she could see the rage in his expression turn to lust in a heartbeat. He said something to the other men, and they all looked up at her.

She turned and ducked out of sight. Nothing good would come out of her being captured. As much as every molecule in her body was screaming at her to help Shawn, she knew she stood no chance against eight men. Self-preservation kicked in.

Yana was surprisingly quick for someone her age, and the small spaces they had to squeeze through were easy for the kids but more difficult for Maggie. Her body was getting scraped up as she forced her way under rebar and around obstacles all around them. But Artem seemed to know what he was doing and where he was going. He'd either been here before, or he had an innate sense of how to get out of the rubble.

Maggie didn't know how long they'd ducked, squatted, crawled, and shimmied through the destroyed building, but before she knew it, they were standing once more on a debris-littered street.

"Come," Artem said again, reaching down and picking

up his little sister. He and Borysko started walking, not looking back to see if Maggie was following them.

Maggie's breath hitched, and she realized that at some point she'd started crying. She had no idea when, only that her face was soaked with her tears and it felt as if her heart had been torn in two.

"Shawn," she whispered, not able to move her feet. She was as frozen now as she'd been when she'd seen the soldiers first start to beat Shawn and MacGyver. It had been horrible. Violent and full of hate. She'd seen fights when she'd been incarcerated, but nothing like what she'd just witnessed.

She kind of thought the siblings might disappear into the streets of the city without her. But to her surprise, Artem had a short conversation with Borysko, and the younger boy walked back to where she was standing and took her hand in his. "Come," he said, repeating his brother's simple instructions.

"Shawn," Maggie said. "Ricky." She used the name the children called MacGyver.

"We get. But first safe."

Two words. That was all it took to get Maggie's muscles working again. *We get.* She had no idea what three kids and a woman clearly out of her element could do to save two Navy SEALs from a roving band of Russian soldiers, but she so badly wanted to have faith in the boy, she allowed him to pull her forward as they made their way toward another hiding spot.

CHAPTER SIXTEEN

"Fuck," Preacher moaned as he rolled over.

"You really do sound like Blink," MacGyver said from next to him.

Opening his eyes—no, his eye; one was swollen shut—Preacher saw his teammate lying in the dirt next to him. They were in a room much like the one they'd holed up in. It was obviously a bombed-out building, but this room was less protected from the elements. He could see two Russian soldiers standing outside the walls with their rifles at the ready.

"Maggie? The kids?" Preacher asked. The last thing he remembered was seeing Maggie standing at the top of the concrete ledge he'd hoisted her up to, staring down at them in horror.

"As far as I know, they got away," MacGyver said.

Relief swamped through Preacher. That was followed

by determination and anger. This was no place for three kids or Maggie to be wandering around. It would also be more difficult for them to stay hidden with Russian troops roaming the city.

He wondered if the crates of weapons they'd offloaded had really been for the Ukrainians, as they'd all thought, or if Robertson had been paid to leave the weapons for the Russians. If so, it would add treason to all of his other crimes.

At the moment, that didn't matter. He and MacGyver needed to get the hell out of there. The last thing they wanted was to be transported over the border into Russia. Special forces units weren't fighting in this conflict. Yes, the US was helping in other ways, by supplying weapons and training for Ukrainian soldiers, but if word got out to the media that there were Navy SEALs on the ground, things could get ugly for everyone involved.

"What's the plan?" Preacher asked.

The other man chuckled, but the sound changed to a moan almost immediately. "Shit, I was hoping *you* had a plan," MacGyver told him.

"Still got that tracker?" he asked.

"Yeah. Skivvies still on. Check."

"Right, so Tex, and thus the team, still know where we are."

"But not where Maggie is."

Preacher frowned. He was right. She could literally be anywhere, and there wasn't a chance in hell that he was leaving Maggie behind. Their separation made things more difficult, but when rescue came, maybe enough of a ruckus would be made that she'd somehow be drawn to it, and they could get the hell out of here.

"The kids," MacGyver said in a low, desolate tone.

Preacher closed his eyes. Their situation upset him too, but obviously they'd made a bigger impact on the taciturn MacGyver.

"We can't leave them."

"We can't *take* them," Preacher countered. "They're not US citizens. It would be akin to kidnapping."

"You saw them," MacGyver said. "How skinny they are. They don't have anyone to look after them."

"We can get Tex to reach out to one of his contacts, make sure they're found and brought to safety."

But MacGyver snorted. "Then what? They go into the system? *What* system? Look around, Preacher, this country is being torn apart. And who are the people suffering the most? The kids. No one is going to adopt them. Especially not all three. Besides, I have a feeling Artem would rather be on his own, living in the rubble of burned-out buildings, than be separated from his brother and sister."

"What do you want me to say? That we'll take them with us? You know that won't go down well. We can't just be stealing kids from the countries we're sent to."

"I don't want to steal them. I just want them to be safe. To have food in their bellies. For Artem not to have to be a grownup when he's only eight. I want Yana to be able to play without fear."

Preacher pressed his lips together. He wanted the same

things. But they were in an impossible situation. They weren't even supposed to be here right now. Their job was to deliver the crates then retreat back to western Ukraine and get the hell out of the country. Then again, their mission was most likely bullshit from the start, a way for Robertson to get rid of his ex-girlfriend and use the SEAL team to do his dirty work.

"If we brought them with us, what would your plan be going forward?" Preacher asked.

A full two minutes of silence passed, and Preacher thought that maybe his friend had fallen asleep or hadn't heard him. But then MacGyver spoke.

"I want them," he said in a voice so low, it was almost a whisper. "I know it's stupid. No one's gonna give a thirty-three-year-old bachelor, a special forces operative at that, custody of three orphans. But there's something about them that I just can't shake."

He wasn't wrong. The odds of the three siblings being placed with MacGyver were probably a million to one. And that was *if* they even got to the US. It was likely they'd be taken away when they arrived in Germany to switch planes.

"I'd have to find a nanny. Someone who could help me with them while I'm at work. Maybe I'll do one of those fake marriage things...you know, to grease the wheels. Find someone who needs health insurance or something and marry her. She gets the benefits from the Navy, and I get someone to help me with the kids."

"That sounds like a terrible plan," Preacher said with a

small chuckle. But when his friend didn't laugh, he realized he wasn't kidding.

"I can't think of any other way," MacGyver said. "Besides, it's not as if women are beating down my door otherwise. I'm too...geeky."

Preacher couldn't help but laugh at that. "You're a SEAL. You aren't a geek."

"I am. And I'm okay with that. You haven't been to my place in a while, but it's kind of a mess. With parts and wires from computers and other electrical crap I bought online and at yard sales. I love taking shit apart and putting it back together. Hell, Preacher, you know I got my nickname because of the crap I can manufacture when we need it."

"All right, but there's nothing wrong with that," Preacher told his friend.

"I know. And I like who I am...but apparently it's not what women want."

Preacher snorted, then groaned. "You want to know what women want?" he asked. "They want to be loved. They want to know the man they're with is trustworthy. That he'll be there when she needs him. That's it. Everything else is gravy."

"Who went and made you an expert on women?" MacGyver asked.

"Maggie," Preacher said with conviction. "Look. I'm the last person to preach about anything, regardless of my name. But I'm right about this. You want to adopt these kids? If you're all in, you know all of us will do whatever we can to help you. But don't up and marry a chick just because you think it'll make you look better in social services' eyes. That's a sure way for the situation to end up FUBAR'd."

"Yeah..." MacGyver said vaguely.

"Wait—you have someone in mind already?" Preacher asked.

"Maybe."

"*Seriously*? Do I know her?"

"No."

"What's her name?"

"Addison."

Preacher waited for MacGyver to say more. When he didn't, he asked, "That's it? That's all I get?"

"That's all you get," MacGyver confirmed. "We've kind of got other things to worry about right now. We need to figure out how to get away from these Russian soldiers, find Maggie and the kids, meet up with the team, and get out of this bombed-out shell of a city, then convince the US authorities to let Artem, Borysko, and Yana into the country. If we manage all that, *then* I can start worrying about how to arrange for them to stay with me."

"Right. But I'm not going to drop this. I want to know more about this Addison woman. Where you met her, and why you think she might be up for this asinine scheme."

"You're annoying," MacGyver bitched.

"And you love me," Preacher said, simply to be *more* annoying.

The makeshift door to the room they were being kept

in was shoved to the side, and three Russians came into the room. One aimed a rifle at Preacher and MacGyver and the other two came over to where they were lying on the ground. They yelled something at them and hauled them to their feet.

Then they were forced out of the room and marched down the street.

Preacher kept his head on a swivel and tried to memorize where they were going. It was difficult, considering the debris and collapsed buildings around them looked the same from one street to the next. But if he and MacGyver had any chance of getting out of this alive, they needed to be ready to make their escape.

It wouldn't be easy. Preacher hurt like hell and his teammate wasn't in any better condition. The soldiers at their side, holding onto them, were already helping to keep them upright as they were force-marched to another location. But Maggie was out there somewhere, and she needed him to figure this out. If he was killed, his team would get her out, of that he had no doubt, but he was motivated to get out with her. He wanted to spend the rest of his *life* with her. And he couldn't do that if Robertson won.

Preacher hated to lose—and this was one battle he was determined to come out on top.

* * *

Maggie lay on a slab of concrete, staring down into the street below. Artem was lying next to her. He'd led her up here after Yana and Borysko fell asleep in another little nook they'd found and made into a home away from home.

She felt exposed and out of her element, but she did what she could to follow Artem's lead. He seemed much older than his eight years. He'd had to grow up fast. Too fast. It made Maggie sad, but she had to admit that at the moment, she was glad he was here. If she'd been on her own, it would've been a disaster. He'd found them water, had scrounged for food in the rubble of what had to have been an apartment building at one time, and was now helping her look for Shawn and MacGyver.

"Where are all the people?" she whispered as they scanned their surroundings.

"They go to safe. West. Away from here."

"Why didn't you go too?"

Artem looked at her with his big brown eyes. His face was filthy, his hair matted and dirty. "This is home. Mother and Father are here." He pointed out into the city, toward the west. "Nowhere else to go."

Maggie's heart broke all over again. "But you would be safe if you left."

"Take Yana away. No family. Not safe. Together safe."

She wanted to argue that they weren't safe right now. Not living in unsanitary conditions, scrounging for food, and hiding from Russian soldiers. But she had no idea what she could do to help the children. She could barely look after herself. She was so out of her element, it wasn't even funny.

"Find Ricky and Shawn. Help."

She nodded. She was still a little fuzzy about what in the world three kids and a woman could do to help two Navy SEALs being held captive by a bunch of soldiers, but at this point she literally had nothing to lose. Without Shawn and MacGyver, she was as good as dead. Roman would win, and that was the last thing she wanted.

She'd gone from never wanting to return to California, to fantasizing about the look on her ex's face when she strolled up to him and said, "Guess what? I didn't die!"

"There! Look, Mag. Soldiers."

Forcing herself to concentrate, Maggie looked where Artem was pointing. He was right. There were people moving through the rubble a few streets over. It was hard to tell if Shawn and MacGyver were with them, but Artem didn't seem to have that issue.

"Ricky and Shawn there. Take them to church. Good. Good. Can get them out."

Maggie wanted to shake her head. Tell the boy that he was crazy. That there was no way they'd be able to sneak the SEALs out from under the Russians' noses. But Artem was already backing off the slanted ledge of concrete. Maggie quickly followed, being careful to keep her head down. The last thing she wanted was to be spotted and shot at.

Once they were back on the ground, she followed

Artem as he weaved his way back to where he'd left his brother and sister.

The entrance to the space they'd holed up in was so small, Maggie could barely fit through the hole in the mangled rebar and steel. Of course, the kids had no problem. If Shawn or MacGyver were with them, they wouldn't have fit at all.

"We get next day," Artem told her, when she was once more sitting cross-legged, leaning against one of the walls.

"How?" Maggie asked.

The next thirty minutes was spent with Artem telling Maggie his plan in broken English—and Maggie trying to talk him out of it. But in the end, she realized she had no choice but to go along with the boy. He knew this city like the back of his hand. If he said his plan would work, she had to believe him.

Her role was easy. She was the bait.

Swallowing hard, she tried not to puke. Not that she had much in her belly to throw up. But thoughts of everything that could go wrong swam through her brain. If she got lost, or if she wasn't fast enough, the Russians would capture her, and if she'd thought she was in deep shit in an American prison, it would be *nothing* compared to rotting away in a Russian cell.

But Artem seemed to think his plan would work perfectly. While she was distracting the soldiers, he, Borysko, and Yana would sneak in through a tunnel they'd found while foraging and get Shawn and MacGyver out. Then they'd all meet up at the edge of the city, in an area she recognized as being near where her crate had landed, when she was pushed out of the helicopter.

This part of the country had a lot of farmland. The city they were in had to have been the biggest around. Not big like a city back home, but large enough for its citizens to have everything they'd needed. Now, the church in the center of the city was one of the only buildings still standing...and even that could be argued. Half of it was destroyed, but the other half was apparently acting as a kind of meeting point for the soldiers. And it was where they'd taken Shawn and MacGyver.

"Next day, I show you where to walk. Where to lead soldiers," Artem told her. In any other situation, Maggie would've found it adorable how he kept saying "next day" instead of tomorrow, but right now? Terror was swimming in her veins.

"Okay."

Yana and Borysko had woken up while Artem was telling her the plan, and the little girl ended up sitting against Maggie's side. She reached over and patted Maggie's hand while saying something in her native language.

"She say it okay," Borysko translated. "Artem keep us safe."

Maggie smiled down at Yana and said, "Thank you."

"You welcome."

The English words coming from the little girl were both surprising and adorable.

"Can you talk us about America?" Borysko asked.

Maggie struggled to come up with something to tell them. Something that wouldn't make their own situation seem even bleaker than it already was. But when she saw the three eager faces looking up at her, it hit home how young these children really were. Because of the role Artem played in keeping her safe right now, she'd temporarily blocked out the fact that they were just kids.

"I live in Riverton, California. It's right by the ocean. The weather is nice almost all year. Not too hot or too cold."

"Ricky live there?" Artem asked.

"Yes. He and Shawn both, and their friends all live there too."

"And there is food store?" Borysko asked.

The question made Maggie sad again, but she kept the smile on her face as she responded. "Yes, there are a lot of food stores. And places that sell wood and hammers and clothes, and everything anyone would need."

"Cost much money," Artem said with a frown.

"Well, yes. Some of the stores are more expensive than others. But there are some places that are cheaper too. I work in a store that gives clothing to those who need it."

"For no money?" Artem asked with wide eyes.

"For free," Maggie confirmed. "But only to those who really need it. For others, they pay. That's how the store can stay open."

"And school?" Borysko asked.

"Yes, there are schools. For kids your age, as well as bigger kids and adults."

"Anyone go?"

"Yes. Anyone can go."

"I like school," Borysko said sadly.

"Danger on road?" Artem asked.

"I'm sorry, I don't understand what you want to know," Maggie told him.

"Here, danger outside house. There, is danger walk on road?"

"Oh, well...yes, I suppose it could be dangerous to walk around. But that's generally only in certain areas. Most places are safe, especially during the day. There are bad guys there, just as there are anywhere, I suppose."

"Put you in jail?" Borysko asked.

"What?"

"Bad guys put in jail?" the boy repeated.

Maggie's heart skipped a beat. She really didn't want to talk about prison because it hit a little too close to home. And she wasn't sure she should talk about jail, because of all these kids had already been through and were *still* going through. But if the question had been asked, it had to be because Borysko was worried about something.

"America is a nice place to live," she told the trio. She wasn't sure how much Yana understood, but she was staring up at her, listening intently, as if she understood every word Maggie was saying. "But there are bad people everywhere. And yes, if someone breaks the law, they could go to jail."

She couldn't believe she was talking about this, but she

needed the kids to know that while the US was a great country, it wasn't free of dangers.

"*You* jail?" Artem asked with big eyes.

There was no way this boy could know that, yes, she'd been in prison. She hadn't talked about it in front of him. But she also didn't want to lie. These kids had probably been lied to way too often. "Actually, yes. I've been in jail. A man I was dating put drugs in my car. The police stopped me and found them and thought they were mine. No one would listen when I said they weren't."

Artem nodded solemnly. "Like here. Police bad."

"No," Maggie said sharply. That was *not* the lesson she wanted the kids to learn. "The police aren't bad. They're there to help. But the bad guy, the man I was dating, is very important. So everyone believed him. The drugs *were* in my car. They had no reason to believe me over the very important man. All I'm trying to say is, no matter where you live, there are bad people. They might seem like they are good, but sometimes they're not. You have to be smart, to lean on those you trust to stay safe."

She was messing this up. Maggie knew that, but she had no idea how to explain well enough to get through the cultural differences.

"Like Shawn. And Ricky," Borysko said firmly.

"Yes, like them," Maggie agreed.

"We smart," Artem said. "We keep you safe."

Maggie's eyes filled with tears. "I know you are, and that you'll keep me safe. Thank you."

"You welcome," Yana piped up with a smile.

Her eagerness to be included in the conversation made Maggie smile. She hugged the little girl against her side.

"I go to America one day," Artem said firmly. "I help people who police no believe."

For some reason, Maggie believed him. That he'd someday get to the US and help those in need like she'd been.

"Next day we get Ricky free. And Shawn," Artem said firmly. "You sleep so you can run."

Maggie wasn't tired. She was thirsty and hungry and too keyed up about tomorrow to even think about sleeping. But she nodded anyway and stretched out on the hard, dirty floor.

Artem fussed over his siblings for a while, then the room went silent.

"Mag?"

She turned her head to see Artem looking at her. "Yeah?" she whispered.

"Take Yana when go?"

"What?"

"Take Yana when go?" Artem repeated. "No safe for baby. She gooder in America."

Maggie had no idea what to say to that. It was obvious Artem loved his little sister. That he'd do whatever he could to keep her safe. And right now, the only way he could think to do that was to send her as far away from this place as possible.

She wished she could reassure him. Tell him that of course she'd take his sister with her. But she had no idea what the future held. It was certainly not legal to take a child out of the country, especially when she wasn't supposed to be here herself. But she couldn't bear to say any of that to the little boy who was doing all he could to survive.

So she simply nodded.

It was apparently enough for Artem. He gave her a solemn nod in return, then turned onto his side, facing away from her.

Maggie wasn't a crier. But it seemed as if she'd cried more recently than she could ever remember doing for her entire thirty-five years. Even when she'd been behind bars, she hadn't allowed herself to get too emotional, for her own well-being. But now the tears ran down her temples into her hair as she stared up at the broken ceiling.

She cried for herself, over her worry for Shawn and MacGyver, about tomorrow's plan—which was surely going to go wrong in one way or another—and for the children sleeping around her. She wanted to scoop up all three and hold them tightly and tell them everything would be okay. But she didn't know if it would be. With a lot of luck, she'd be leaving soon, going back to her life in California, and they'd be stuck here in this bombed-out city, eking out an existence, scrounging for food and water. It was unfathomable. But what could she do about it?

Nothing. And that sucked.

As she lay there, Maggie made a vow to do whatever she could to help Artem, Borysko, and Yana. Shawn had that computer genius friend. Maybe *he* could do something. Get a hold of someone who could come here and take the kids away. At least somewhere safer. Maybe find a kind of foster home for them. She had no idea if that concept existed here, especially in the middle of a war, but there had to be something she could do.

Feeling better, if not great, Maggie closed her eyes. As soon as she did, thoughts of Shawn snuck in. Was he okay? She'd seen the beating he'd received, and it was bad. Would he and MacGyver even be able to walk tomorrow? She had so many questions and worries, and no way of easing her trepidation.

She also wasn't sure about being bait. She wasn't a great runner, and she had no weapon. If one of the soldiers decided to shoot her, she wouldn't be able to do anything about it. Artem's advice about not running straight down a street, but instead using the maze of crumbled buildings to her advantage, was good. But she still worried about going down a dead-end, like they'd done while running from the Russians.

So many things could go wrong, but she'd do whatever it took to help Shawn get free. She loved him. It was a hell of a time to have that epiphany, but she didn't shy away from it. He'd been nothing but supportive, hadn't seemed to mind that she was a convicted felon, had stood up for her, introduced her to his friends, and made her feel as if she was the most important person in his life.

And now he was a captive of the Russian army because of her. He didn't have to get out of that helicopter. He could've called for backup when he saw she was in that crate. But he hadn't hesitated to rush to her side. It was... overwhelming. And proved what kind of man Shawn was. One that she wanted at her side *forever*.

"Hang on," she whispered. "Help is coming."

If she and the kids pulled this off, it would be a story for the ages. One she had no doubt Shawn would tell proudly to anyone who would listen. About the time he was a POW, and a woman with absolutely no military experience and three little kids rescued him and his Navy SEAL teammate. He wouldn't be embarrassed. No, he'd be proud of her.

Maggie wanted to make that happen. Make him proud. Wanted to prove that she was more than the felon society had labeled her. Determination swelled inside as her tears dried up. She literally had nothing to lose tomorrow. And a lifetime of happiness at Shawn's side to gain.

She snorted silently. She was being a dork. There was no guarantee that Shawn felt the same way as she did. Yes, he seemed to like her now, but she was well aware of how life had a way of pulling the rug out from under a person when they felt as if everything was going great. She was living proof of that.

But regardless, she'd do whatever she had to in order to free Shawn and MacGyver, keep Artem, Borysko, and Yana safe, and to live another day so she could make Roman pay for his evil deeds.

It was a lot of pressure, but she'd survived two years in jail for a crime she didn't commit. She could do this. She *had* to do this. There was no other choice.

CHAPTER SEVENTEEN

"We need to get out of here," Preacher said under his breath.

"Yeah," MacGyver agreed.

The day before, they'd been marched through the destroyed town to the church where they were currently holed up. Half of the building was nothing but rubble, but the other half was miraculously still standing. He and MacGyver were currently in what used to be the nave. Pews were on their sides and strewn about the space, the stained-glass windows were broken to pieces, but the space was otherwise intact. There was one bored-looking soldier in the nave guarding them, and the rest were either outside or in the narthex, the small space just outside the worship area.

There were windows they could climb out of, but without any weapons, they'd surely be shot before they were able to get outside. Preacher tried to come up with a plan, but his body hurt, his eye was still swollen shut, and he hadn't slept much the night before. And he couldn't stop thinking about Maggie. Wondering where she was, if she was all right, and how the hell he'd find her when his team showed up.

Preacher still had no doubt they *would* come. He just wanted to try to avoid any one-on-one combat if he could help it. The last thing they needed was to somehow get the US any more involved in this conflict than they were already. World War III breaking out because of his actions wasn't something he wanted to contemplate.

"Can we take him?" Preacher asked, using his head to indicate their guard, who couldn't have been a day over eighteen, if that. It was well known that many Russians were being conscripted into military service. It was entirely possible this kid hadn't wanted to join the army but had no choice. Then again, it was just as possible he was proud to be serving his country.

"Yeah, but then what? His buddies outside will probably hear what's going on and rush in. And while we might be able to get his weapon, I'm not sure that's enough to take on an entire platoon."

"Can't you MacGyver something to get us out of here?" Preacher asked, half joking.

"What? You want me to build us a time machine? A portal like in *Star Trek* that will beam us somewhere else? Frankly, I'd like to beam myself to a beach in the

Caribbean, but since that's impossible, I'd settle for literally anywhere other than this damn building."

"A portal will work," Preacher said calmly.

"You're so weird," MacGyver grumbled.

Preacher couldn't help but smile. He *was* weird, but since his friends were just as odd, he didn't really care. "Think they're going to feed us today?"

"Considering they didn't feed us yesterday, no. Besides, they're looking pretty lean themselves, they'd be smarter to keep any food they have for themselves."

Preacher didn't disagree. He'd just hoped that maybe if someone got close enough, they could somehow overtake them and steal their rifles. Without any firepower, they were definitely at a disadvantage. Their exceptional hand-to-hand fighting skills wouldn't help if they were shot before they could get close enough to knock someone out.

"Right. So we wait?"

"Lookin' like it," MacGyver agreed.

"I hate waiting," Preacher mumbled. "I can't help but wonder where the hell Maggie is. What she's doing. If she's scared to death and hunkered down in some ruin of a building."

"Same," MacGyver said. "Those kids have been through hell. And seeing us getting beaten probably didn't help."

Both men fell silent. Sounds of the building creaking ominously around them seemed loud in the relative silence of the building. The soldiers talked quietly amongst themselves just out of sight, and the guard in the nave with them sighed, as if irritated that he'd been given such a boring assignment.

"I hope Maggie is smart enough to be as far away from here as she can get," Preacher said after a moment. "Heading west is the best thing she can do. She's bound to run into others who can help her, maybe someone who speaks English who can get her in touch with someone from the US."

"She's smart," MacGyver said. "And I have no doubt she's far away from here...and has taken the kids with her."

* * *

What the hell was she doing? Maggie crouched behind a large pile of bricks as she stared at the church across the street. Artem and his siblings had left her about ten minutes ago. They were going to circle around to the back of the church and make their way in through a maze of concrete, rebar, and glass to the back of the nave. They'd seen both Shawn and MacGyver sleeping in there before the sun came up.

It was up to her to provide the distraction they all needed to sneak the guys out of the church and to safety. She would meet up with them at the edge of town, near one of the many fields that littered the countryside. She had no idea what would happen at that point, but she couldn't worry about that yet. She had enough to worry about right this second.

Mainly, why the hell she'd thought this would work.

How was she going to distract all—she counted the soldiers again, hoping against hope the number wasn't as high as it was a minute ago, the *last* time she'd counted...it wasn't—six of the soldiers standing just inside the broken doors of the church.

She couldn't see Artem or Borysko but knew they were waiting on her to do her part of the plan before they moved. But Maggie couldn't seem to make her legs work. She could sneak away, go back to the hidey-hole they'd stayed in last night. She wasn't brave. Wasn't cut out for this kind of thing.

But the alternative was for Borysko to be the bait...or worse, Yana. And that wasn't going to happen, not as long as Maggie had breath in her body. No, she had to do this.

Taking a deep breath, she looked behind her at the escape route she and Artem had scoped out earlier. Over the pile of bricks she was currently hiding behind, down the street, under the precarious-looking slab of concrete, through a confusing maze of rubble, down another street, then going in and out of as many buildings as she could, hiding in or under one of the many burnt-out cars if needed.

Anything she had to do to hide, to keep from being caught, was what she would do.

Her heart was beating out of her chest, her adrenaline was making her feel sick and shaky. But it was now or never.

Taking a deep breath, Maggie stood up.

* * *

One of the soldiers outside the nave shouted something, making Preacher straighten up where he sat and look in that direction. Their guard was also looking where his comrades were gathered—and not at the men he was supposed to be guarding.

Footsteps pounded on the ground as shouts from the soldiers outside got farther and farther away. They were leaving! Chasing after someone was what it sounded like, and at the moment, it didn't matter if it was a rabid hippopotamus leading the men away from the church. All that mattered was that they were leaving the place unattended.

He and MacGyver had no plan, but they weren't about to let this opportunity pass them by. They moved swiftly and silently toward their guard. Because his attention was on the door, he didn't even notice MacGyver before he wrapped an arm around his neck from behind.

Preacher grabbed his wrist, making sure he didn't have a chance to fire off a round. The last thing they wanted was for any kind of ruckus bringing the other soldiers back to investigate.

It didn't take long for MacGyver to render the young soldier unconscious. Preacher relieved him of the rifle as MacGyver eased him to the ground. The kid would be out long enough for them to get the hell out of there. But how? It was likely the soldiers who ran off would be back soon, and Preacher didn't want to get caught slipping away.

As if they shared a brain, both men turned to head to the back of the nave, toward the ruined altar. There had to be a way out that way.

"Ricky! Here!"

Turning, Preacher saw a dirty little face peeking out from behind a huge piece of steel. It had fallen from the building next to the church, piercing through the wall, leaving a large hole and glass everywhere.

"Artem?" MacGyver asked incredulously.

"Yes. We go! Here."

MacGyver didn't hesitate. He got to his knees and crawled behind the steel beam. "Where's Borysko and Yana?"

"And Maggie," Preacher added as he followed behind his friend.

"They here. Come. We go."

This wasn't a time to ask questions, but the thought of Maggie being with them, and safe, was almost overwhelming for Preacher. The boy led them through a maze of rubble and debris. In some places, Preacher wasn't sure he and MacGyver would fit. But somehow they did. And when they emerged, the church was nowhere to be seen. The boy had led them through a maze of destruction that was at least a block away from the church itself. It was genius—and dangerous as hell. But then again, they were living in the middle of a war zone, so the thought was a little ridiculous.

To his relief, Borysko and Yana appeared out of nowhere. They were safe.

"Run now," Artem said.

"Maggie?" Preacher asked again, worried again, now that he wasn't seeing her anywhere.

"She meet. We run."

Preacher didn't like that answer. Not at all. Where the hell was she?

Then a thought struck him. What made the soldiers at the church run off the way they had...?

No. She wouldn't.

Terror hit him *hard*.

"Artem—where's Maggie?" Preacher asked sternly.

"Easy," MacGyver warned. He'd picked up Yana and was holding her against his chest, his other hand on Borysko's shoulder. The kids were safe, and his teammate was obviously relieved, but Maggie was still out there somewhere. Preacher wasn't going to go *easy*. Not until he knew where she was.

"She run. Soldiers run to her. She not let bad guys get her. No jail."

Preacher's mind spun. Artem was confirming his worst nightmare. She'd used herself as bait to lure the soldiers away from the church.

No. No, no, no!

Then he didn't have a chance to say anything else as Artem took off, leading them through the bombed-out city he'd learned to navigate so well. Preacher wanted to shout out his anger and worry. Wanted to go back and find Maggie. It was all too possible that the Russians had captured her already. Were even now beating her, the same way they'd done to him and MacGyver.

But getting himself caught again wouldn't help her. She'd sacrificed herself to free him, and he couldn't ignore that. It was an incredibly humbling feeling. Preacher expected that kind of sacrifice from his teammates. He'd do the same for them. But Maggie wasn't a soldier. Wasn't a SEAL. She'd already been through hell. And yet, she'd been willing to do whatever it took to save him.

Determination filled him as he ran. The second he had a chance to find out what the plan had been, he was going back. To find her. To chew her out for doing something so reckless—and kiss the hell out of her for doing it all the same.

* * *

Maggie was exhausted. In her previous life, she was anything but an athlete. Now, she'd spent hours evading the soldiers. They'd been way more tenacious than she or Artem had thought they'd be. They seemed absolutely determined to find her.

She'd done her best to hide from them, but every time she managed to find a place to catch her breath, the soldiers weren't too far behind. Maggie figured it was because she was leaving footprints or something for them to follow, but even when she climbed up into a building that felt as if it was about to collapse at any moment, or shimmied across an electrical wire that thankfully wasn't live, into another building, the soldiers still found her trail.

She was dehydrated, terrified, and beginning to think it might be easier to just let herself be caught. But as soon as Maggie had the thought, she dismissed it. The soldiers hunting her were *pissed*. She had no idea what they were saying, but it was obvious they weren't happy that she was managing to elude them.

Wanting to go west toward the field where she was supposed to meet up with the others, Maggie had actually turned east instead. The last thing she wanted was the soldiers accidentally running into Shawn, MacGyver, and the kids. But she was running out of places to hide, and she was shaky with the need for water and food.

"This sucks," she whispered softly, simply to hear something other than the ominous creaking and groaning of the rubble around her...and the angry Russian words being yelled as she was hunted down.

Something hit her arm, and Maggie flinched, petrified. It happened again. Then again. Looking up from where she was crouched behind a burnt-out car...she realized it was raining.

The second she had the thought, the gentle rain turned into a deluge.

Smiling, she tilted her head up and opened her mouth. It wasn't a lot of water, but it was something—and it tasted divine.

To her surprise, the shouts of the men looking for her disappeared.

Peeking out from around the car, she saw three of them running the opposite way. As if they were afraid they'd melt if they got wet. Maggie wanted to laugh. Wanted to collapse in relief. But this was her chance to get farther away from the soldiers. To work her way around the city back west. Toward Shawn.

She had no idea if Artem's plan had worked, but she figured it must have, simply because the soldiers had been concentrating so hard on her. If they'd recaptured Shawn and MacGyver, or found them trying to escape, she thought their attention would be on *them*, to make certain they didn't escape again. Not on chasing her all over the city.

Being bait was way scarier than she'd thought, and things hadn't worked out as easily as she and Artem had hoped, but thanks to the rain, maybe, just *maybe*, things would turn out all right.

She slowly made her way through the city, taking short breaks when she could. Trying to stay on the outskirts, away from the church where the soldiers had made their home base.

She'd just crawled out from under another burnt-out car when she came face-to-face with a Russian soldier.

He was soaking wet, just like her, and he looked just as surprised as Maggie.

She froze. The rifle he held seemed more scary up close and personal. She held her breath as they stood there staring at each other in the pouring rain.

Then, to her shock, he said something fast and low—
and pointed at the building behind her.

Maggie turned, trying to figure out what he was trying
to say, with no luck. She looked back to find the soldier
glancing almost nervously over his shoulder. He said something else and gestured to the building more urgently.

She took a step backward, toward the opening in the
rubble, and the soldier nodded quickly and waved his hand
as if to hurry her along.

Maggie had no idea what was happening, but she moved
fast, ducking under the beam hanging precariously across the
doorway and pressing her back against the wall once inside.

As soon as she was out of sight, another soldier joined
the first. Peeking out through a small hole in the wall,
Maggie realized just how close a call she'd had as the
second soldier bent down to look under the car she'd
crawled out from under sixty seconds earlier. The first
soldier said something to the newcomer...then gestured to
the very building where she was hiding.

Her breath caught in her throat. Was he ratting her out
to his friend? Telling him where she'd gone? But she was
shocked again when the second soldier simply nodded and
they both started walking down the street, back the way
she'd just come, stopping occasionally to look inside other
buildings, and under and inside more cars.

The soldier—he'd hidden her! She could only assume
that he'd told his buddy he'd already searched the building
where she was hiding. Maggie didn't know why he'd done

that, she was just grateful that he had. War was a night-mare for both sides. The Russian soldiers weren't bad people; they were doing what they'd been ordered to do. Okay...some of them *were* probably bad. Just as some US soldiers were bad. She knew that from experience. Roman Robertson was the worst example of what an assumed "honorable and brave" military member could be.

Fatigue ate at Maggie. All she wanted was a warm, dry bed, an extra-large supreme pizza, and a gallon of water. And Shawn.

She couldn't have three of the four, but she could have the one she wanted most. She just had to keep moving.

More cautious now, hoping there weren't more soldiers lurking around, Maggie stepped back out into the pouring rain, toward where she hoped she'd find Artem, Borysko, Yana, and MacGyver, and most importantly Shawn, waiting for her.

CHAPTER EIGHTEEN

"Where is she? Something's wrong," Preacher said for what seemed like the hundredth time. MacGyver had physically restrained him when he'd tried to leave earlier, saying it was stupid for him to go and get lost along *with* Maggie. Every-thing within Preacher had rebelled. Wanting—no, *needing* —to find Maggie and make sure she was safe.

But the more practical part of him knew his friend was right. He had to trust that she was not only okay, but that she would make her way to the meeting point when it was safe for her to do so. The rain was coming down almost sideways now, which sucked, but hopefully it would also make it easier for her to get through the city unseen.

It was eerie that there were no other people lurking around. The city had been mostly abandoned after the missiles destroyed it...and no one had even thought about making sure Artem, Borysko, and Yana were safe. That ate at Preacher, but he could tell it absolutely pissed off MacGyver more. He wanted to warn his friend against getting too attached to the children, but he knew it was too late. Hell, the man was thinking about a marriage of convenience just so he could keep them. It was *definitely* too late.

"She'll be here," MacGyver said, answering Preacher's earlier question about where Maggie could be.

The five of them were huddled under a makeshift shelter made out of a piece of corrugated tin and a bunch of the tall grass that grew in the farmlands around the city. Artem had set up a system to gather the rainwater, and every time the empty tin can he'd found filled up, he made sure his brother and sister had their fill before taking any for himself.

But Preacher couldn't concentrate on anything but Maggie. He vaguely heard MacGyver talking to the children, getting to know them better, entertaining them, but he kept his own focus trained on the city, hoping and praying Maggie would appear.

He knew some strong women. Remi, Josie, Wren...they were all tough as nails. Not to mention Caroline, Fiona, Cheyenne, and all the others. But seeing Maggie's strength firsthand was incredible. Never had he met anyone who was able to keep going when the odds were stacked so high against her. Two years was a hell of a long time to be punished for something that wasn't her fault. Technically, yes, she was transporting drugs, but since she didn't know they were there and had no intention of selling them, she'd been punished unjustly. She'd been set up.

And then there was the harassment she'd put up with since her release. She was terrified of Robertson, and with good reason. She knew firsthand the power he wielded... and Preacher had finally learned for himself how absolute that power seemed to be.

And now she'd been kidnapped and dumped in a foreign country in the midst of a violent conflict, and despite being frightened, exhausted, hungry, and out of her depth, and without any experience whatsoever, she'd acted as *bait* to give the kids an opportunity to save him and MacGyver.

Preacher was overwhelmed. Humbled. All he wanted to do was hold Maggie close and never let go again. Tell her how impressed he was. What a great job she'd done. That he'd do better at keeping her safe from now on. Because the truth was, he'd done a shit job so far.

He hadn't believed that Roman Robertson was her ex— and look where that had gotten them. Yes, he'd gotten to her side as soon as he saw her tumble from that crate he'd pushed out of a fucking chopper. But then he'd gone and gotten himself captured.

It was definitely time to step up. To show her that he would go to whatever lengths were required to keep her safe. But first, he needed to find her.

He was done sitting around waiting for her to show up. Fuck the soldiers. Fuck the rain. Fuck it all. With his renewed vow echoing in his head, Preacher turned to MacGyver. "I'm going to go find her."

In response, MacGyver pointed over his shoulder.

Turning, Preacher squinted into the pouring rain and saw a figure standing not too far from where they were holed up, looking around as if searching for something.

Maggie.

Preacher was up and moving before he'd even thought about what he was doing. The rain soaked through his clothes in an instant but he barely felt it. All his attention was on the woman standing in the rain, looking lost and scared to death.

"Maggie!"

She turned, and the absolute relief and joy on her face nearly brought Preacher to his knees.

"Shawn!" she exclaimed, running toward him.

Preacher met her halfway. She slammed into him, but he didn't fall. He wrapped his arms around her, holding her tight. The bruises he'd received at the hands of the soldiers throbbed and his eye was still mostly swollen shut. But the aches and pains were forgotten now that Maggie was back in his arms.

He buried his nose in her hair and lifted her off her feet. Maggie's legs came up and she hooked her ankles together behind him, clinging to him as a child might.

"Maggie," Preacher whispered against her skin.

They stood like that, plastered together as the rain fell around them, for two solid minutes. Then the vow Preacher made to protect her kicked in, and he turned. He needed to get her under cover, and not only because of the rain. The last thing he wanted was one of the soldiers spotting them. They'd been lucky enough to escape once. Preacher didn't think that would be allowed to happen again.

Maggie lifted her head as he carried her toward where the others were huddled in their makeshift shelter, and she studied him. "Your eye," she whispered.

"It's fine. Once the swelling goes down it won't look so bad," he told her. "The tape—you got it out of your hair," he blurted, noticing that the duct tape that had been wrapped around her head was gone.

"The rain got it really wet, and I was able to work it out," she told him with a shrug.

"Are you all right?" Preacher asked with a frown. "What happened? What took so long for you to get here? Are you hurt? Did they see you?"

To his amazement, Maggie chuckled.

How the hell was she laughing? He had no idea. After everything she'd been through, she was in his arms fucking *laughing*. It was a miracle. *She* was a miracle.

"Could you have asked any more questions right in a row?" she asked.

"Yes. I have a million more, but those are the most pressing at the moment," he told her, stopping in front of the small shelter. "Need you to let go so I can get you inside."

Her legs slid from around him and she stood. He helped her crawl under the piece of tin and out of the rain, then cupped her cheeks. He held her gently, staring at her precious face. Her hair was plastered against her head, she had a nasty-looking scrape on one cheek and dark circles under her eyes, but she was here. In his arms. Alive. He'd never been so thankful for anything in all his life.

"I love you." The words came out more as an exclamation than a tender declaration of love.

Her eyes widened as she gripped his wrists tightly. "What?"

"I love you." This time Preacher had more control over the words. "You amaze me. I'm in awe of you. I love everything about you. Your tenacity, your strength, your compassion, your ability to do what's needed no matter what the situation. I haven't done a very good job of having your back, but that changes now. When we get back to California, he's going *down*. You'll stay with me so I can keep you safe. I'll get whoever I need to involved to make sure he doesn't hurt you ever again."

"Shawn," Maggie said. It was hard to tell if the water on her face was tears or raindrops, but it didn't matter.

"I mean it. I made a mistake in not believing you immediately. I'll never make that mistake again. If you tell me the sky is green and the grass is blue, I'll fight anyone who says differently."

"I understand why you had concerns," she said, letting him off the hook.

But Preacher didn't want to be absolved of his sins. "No," he said with a firm shake of his head. "You had no reason to lie about who your ex was. I was just so surprised,

I wasn't thinking clearly." He ran a hand over her head, squeezing out some of the water from her hair. "I can't believe that asshole had the balls to have me and my SEAL team deliver those crates. If he thinks we're going to just let this go, he's dead wrong. That last mission, and this one, he's misappropriated government property. Sending us on unnecessary missions is not only an asshole move, it's fucking illegal. And let's not forget kidnapping and attempted murder."

"It's not going to be easy to put the blame on him. He wasn't the one who showed up at my door. He didn't put me in that crate. And he didn't physically fly the plane."

"Wrong. The list of people who could've gotten you on that plane, inside a crate being sent to the Ukraine on a *SEAL* mission, is tiny. He's fucked himself. He's done, Maggie."

She sighed and leaned forward, resting her forehead on his shoulder. Tenderness swamped Preacher. He'd seen her as a stoic pillar of strength, but at the moment, he could feel that she was finally at the end of her rope.

"Shawn?"

"Yeah?"

"I love you too," she said with a shy smile.

Everything within Preacher shifted at hearing the words. He hadn't told her about his feelings so she'd feel obligated to reciprocate. But now that she had? His entire life changed in that instant.

* * *

It was weird how just having a roof over her head, the man she loved, and their little group all together once more, made the last few hours seem not quite as scary as they actually had been. When she'd first arrived at the rendezvous point, Artem had held out a tin full of water to her, and rainwater had never tasted better. Amazingly, even though there was no food, the water went a long way toward making her belly feel full.

Shawn held her against him, keeping her warm, and she felt safe. It was ridiculous really, because none of them were really safe. But the gray afternoon skies, the fog in the air, and the sound of the rain hitting the tin roof gave the illusion of hiding out in a cozy nook. It was enough to make Maggie relax for a short while. To forget that she was in a foreign country on the other side of the world from California. To forget the man who'd put her there would surely do whatever was necessary to make her permanently disappear next time.

For now, she was content to give Shawn her weight as they exchanged information about what had happened while they were apart. She listened with bated breath as MacGyver told the story of how they'd escaped the church, and how Artem had led them through the city to this little hideaway in the countryside.

Now it was Maggie's turn to tell *her* story.

Knowing Shawn wasn't going to like what she'd been through, she did her best to downplay the entire thing. "I stood up from behind the rubble I was using as cover, and the soldiers near the church saw me immediately. They shouted and I ran. I think most of the guys who were guarding you two came after me, which was the plan. It took a while, but I lost them. I got turned around though, so I wandered for a bit before finally seeing a building that looked familiar. And...here I am."

"No," Shawn said sternly. "I want to hear it all. The *real* details this time."

Maggie sighed. She'd hoped he'd take her story at face value and leave it at that. But she should've known better. Looking over at Yana, she saw the little girl was fast asleep. Both boys had their gazes locked on her though. She didn't want to scare them, but then again, nothing she said would be much of a surprise after everything they'd seen. They'd been living through this hell for quite a while.

"I couldn't lose them," she said quietly. "No matter where I went or what I did, they were right there. I heard a gunshot once, and it scared the crap out of me. I thought they were going to shoot me in the back. I managed to slip through a crack in a building that was too small for them to fit through. But the building was in bad shape. I thought it was going to collapse on top of me. I quickly went out the other side before the soldiers could go around and trap me in there.

"They tracked me for hours. Just when I thought I couldn't run anymore, it started raining. And for some reason, that sent the soldiers running in the *opposite* direction. As if they were scared to get wet. It was strange, but I was definitely happy.

"By this time, I was well and truly lost, and far away

from the route Artem and I had discussed. But I knew I had to head west to find all of you. I went down this one road, and it dead-ended. It reminded me too much of how you guys got captured in the first place. I managed to climb to the top of the rubble blocking my way, then it collapsed under me.

"I thought that was it. That I was dead. But somehow I was able to ride the concrete down instead of getting buried under it. I was sure the noise would bring the soldiers running, so I stayed hidden nearby for quite a while. Finally, when I thought the coast was clear, I started walking again."

Maggie felt Shawn's arms tighten around her.

"I don't know how you guys have done it," she told Artem and Borysko. To her surprise, the younger boy crawled over and took her hand in his. He didn't say anything, but the nonverbal support meant the world to Maggie. Gave her the strength to keep talking.

"I went into one building that didn't seem too damaged. It looked like it had been some kind of office or something. It smelled horrible, like nothing I've ever smelled before. I thought maybe I could find some food or something, so I started looking around. Toward the back, the corner of the room had collapsed. There were bricks and concrete everywhere. There was a desk in the middle of the rubble, and when I got closer, I saw..."

Maggie took a deep breath before continuing.

"An arm. A woman was under there. Dead. That was what I'd smelled. I don't know why it surprised me so much. I mean, there have to be more bodies around with all the destruction, but I hadn't expected to see it. She wasn't hurting anyone. Was simply doing her job, minding her own business, then boom! The bomb hit and the building collapsed around her. It isn't fair."

"Shhhhh," Shawn murmured, nuzzling his nose against her ear.

Maggie realized she was crying. Why, she wasn't really sure. She was safe, for the moment at least, and Shawn and MacGyver were all right.

"Why does he hate me so much?" Maggie whispered, not sure how or why she'd transitioned from talking about her harrowing flight from the soldiers, to Roman. "I didn't do *anything* to him. I was a good girlfriend!"

"Of course you were," Shawn soothed.

"He laughed at me," she said, admitting something she'd never told anyone else. "He came to see me in prison once. I asked him why he'd done it. Why he'd set me up to take the blame for his actions. He shrugged and said, 'Because I can.' Then he laughed. Said it was a rush to have complete control over someone's life."

She felt Shawn stiffen against her, and saw MacGyver's lips press together.

Taking a deep breath, she did her best to rein in her emotions. "Anyway...I left that building and continued heading in this direction. Took refuge under a car for a short break. When I crawled out, I ran straight into another soldier. He was younger. We surprised each other. But instead of shooting me or yelling, he told me where to hide. Then when one of his fellow soldiers arrived, he steered him away from me. That small act of compassion gives me hope for humanity. That's probably stupid."

"It's not," Shawn reassured her.

Borysko squeezed her hand.

"When they were gone, I continued out of the city. Not too much later...I found you. Or you found me," Maggie said with a small shrug.

"We found each other," Shawn said.

And for some reason, those four words resonated within Maggie. Somehow in the shitshow that was her life, she and Shawn *had* found each other. Their lives were polar opposites, and yet...here they were. It was crazy that her ex had kidnapped her, locked her in a crate, and shipped her across the world. And the fact that he'd planned for Shawn to be the one to push her crate out of that chopper just showed how evil Roman was. It was a miracle that the sturdy crate broke open when it landed. That Shawn noticed there was a person inside, and he was able to get out of the helicopter before it took off and left her there.

They were meant to be together. They were going to make it home, figure out how to stop Roman from ruining anyone else's life, and live happily ever after.

She had to believe that. If she didn't, everything she'd been through would be for nothing. And that was unfathomable.

Borysko let go of her hand, patted it, then scooted back over to MacGyver. Yana was in his lap, and Borysko leaned against MacGyver's side as if he'd done it every day of his life. The SEAL lifted his arm and wrapped it around the boy's shoulders.

Looking at them made Maggie happy and sad at the same time. These orphans were desperate for love, and MacGyver obviously had that in spades. But as soon as they were rescued, the children would be alone all over again. The thought was devastating.

Shawn's lips touched her temple, and she looked up at him.

"You're amazing," he said softly.

But Maggie shook her head. "I just did what I had to."

"That's not true and you know it. MacGyver and I would've figured a way out of that church eventually. Or my team would've arrived and gotten us out. You could've stayed hidden and safe with the children."

"At what cost?" she demanded. "You getting beat up some more? No, thank you. Josie has told me stories about how Blink was tortured when they were in those cells. I wasn't about to sit back and let the same thing happen to you, Shawn. Not if I could do anything about it. Besides, I know what it's like to be held against your will. Both from being in that damn crate and from when I was behind bars. It's not a good feeling. I wanted to do whatever I could to help you escape."

He stared at her for a long time, and Maggie couldn't figure out what he was thinking. "What?" she finally asked.

"I love you," Shawn said. "With every word out of your mouth, I think I love you more. You were meant to be mine, just as I'm meant to be yours. When we get back home, I'm going to do a better job of being your partner."

"I don't know what that means," Maggie whispered, even though his words sent warm and gooey feelings throughout her body.

"It means I'm not going to let you out of my sight until Robertson is neutralized."

Maggie gasped. "You can't kill him!"

To her surprise, Shawn chuckled. "Neutralized doesn't necessarily mean killing him. You've been watching too many science fiction shows."

Maggie wrinkled her nose. He probably had a good point. In the shows she loved to watch, neutralize always meant ending someone's life.

"I'm going to use all my contacts to dig into Robertson's life. Expose every dark nook and cranny. I'm going to have every decision he's made in the Navy scrutinized. Interview those who have worked for him. Men on SEAL teams he's had deployed. Find previous girlfriends. Every part of his life will be looked at under a microscope. He's going to suffer for what he's done to you, Maggie, but he should be more worried about everything *else* we're going to dig up. I have a feeling there'll be plenty that's more damning...not that what he's done to you isn't bad enough, just—"

"I know," she interrupted. "He feels as if he's untouchable. There's no telling how many more lives he's ruined simply because he could."

"Exactly," Shawn said with a nod.

They listened to the soothing sound of the rain on the tin roof. After what had to be an hour or more, long after Artem and Borysko had lain down next to MacGyver and fallen fast asleep, Maggie worked up the nerve to ask a question that had been rolling around in her brain. "Do we know when they'll come to get us?"

By "us" she really meant Shawn and MacGyver. She wasn't even supposed to be here.

"Soon," MacGyver said.

"What do we do when they come? What should *I* do?" she asked nervously.

"You stay by me," Shawn said. "I'll get you home safely."

She had a lot more questions, but for once, Maggie swallowed them down. She trusted Shawn. If he said run, she'd run. If he said hide, she'd hide. This was his area of expertise, not hers. She'd learned that the hard way. Hide and seek would never be a game she enjoyed again. Not after it had been a life-or-death thing for her today.

"Okay," she said belatedly.

"Sleep, Maggie," he said.

"What about you?" she asked, suddenly finding it almost impossible to keep her eyes open.

"I'll be fine."

Maggie wanted to protest, tell Shawn he needed to sleep too, but the sound of his heart beating steadily under her cheek was too hypnotizing. One moment she was awake, and the next, she was deeply asleep in the arms of the man she loved.

CHAPTER NINETEEN

There was no way Preacher was sleeping. He was tired, of course he was, but now that he had Maggie back in his arms, he wouldn't do anything that would put her in any more danger than he'd put her in already. And falling asleep would leave her vulnerable, which wasn't acceptable.

The rain had finally stopped and the silence it had left in its wake was almost deafening. But it also allowed him and MacGyver to hear every little sound in the countryside around them. The city they'd been wandering around in was surrounded by farmland. Land that was now filled with rotting vegetables and overgrown fields.

A positive about their current situation was that they'd be able to see any soldiers approaching from quite a distance, but since they had only the one rifle they'd taken off the soldier in the church, they were at a distinct disadvantage.

They also had no way to forage for food, and if it didn't rain again soon, they'd be out of water. Yes, their current situation wasn't great, but Preacher had faith that when Tex checked out their location, thanks to MacGyver's tracker, he'd realize they were in a perfect position to be picked up.

It wouldn't have been ideal to send a team of SEALs into the city, considering they weren't supposed to be here at all. Now, hopefully they could be extracted with little to no fuss...but Preacher had a feeling that wasn't going to happen.

As soon as he had the thought, the faint sound of a chopper coming in hard and fast hit his ears. It was dark now, but that didn't matter to Night Stalker pilots. They could fly in any terrain, weather, or time of day or night.

"Maggie," Preacher said, shaking the woman lying against him.

She woke immediately, and he had the momentary thought that hopefully one day, she wouldn't wake up instantly on guard.

"Time to go," he told her.

She sat up and nodded.

MacGyver had woken up the children, and Preacher could hear them stirring across from where he and Maggie were sitting. They had no flashlight or anything, so their rescue would be a little more difficult, since they couldn't see where they were putting their feet.

"Helicopter," Borysko said.

"Yes. It's our friends," MacGyver told him.

None of the children said anything else, and Preacher had a feeling they were trying to process the fact that they'd soon be on their own again.

He led the way out of the shelter and into the tall grass around them. He couldn't see the chopper, as it was flying without lights, but he heard it get closer and closer.

And so did the Russian soldiers. Shouts sounded from the city, way closer than Preacher had hoped. It made sense that a rescue would come from the farmlands outside the ruined buildings. They'd probably been waiting, just as their small group had.

"Fuck!" MacGyver said. He immediately followed that by adding, "Sorry. Don't say that word, kids. It's not a nice word."

Preacher wanted to laugh at how serious he was taking his role of caretaker, but the situation they were in was no laughing matter.

"You three need to hide," MacGyver told them. "The soldiers will be all over this area. Go back to the city. To one of your shelters."

To Preacher, his friend didn't sound genuine. As if he was saying what he thought he had to say, not what he actually wanted the kids to do.

"We help," Artem said, sounding stubborn.

"No!" MacGyver told him. "You can't help."

"We help," Borysko said, echoing his brother.

"Help," Yana chimed in.

Maggie's hand clenched his, and Preacher was torn. He didn't want the kids anywhere near the chaos that was about to erupt, but sending them back to the city didn't feel right either.

The breeze from the helicopter picked up, and Preacher ducked, urging Maggie to do the same at his side. The chopper arrived out of nowhere in the dark. It landed about two hundred yards from where they were crouched. The length of two football fields. It wasn't very far for him and MacGyver, but with Maggie and possibly the kids in tow, it felt as if it might as well have been miles.

Lights from the chopper turned on and nearly blinded Preacher. He knew that was routine, shining lights to fuck with the eyesight of any nearby tangos, but being on this side of those lights *sucked*. He was used to being behind them, looking out of the chopper.

But the lights also allowed him to see the immediate area. And what he saw made his blood run cold.

The Russian soldiers were closing in on their location. Fast. Sometime in the night, they'd gotten reinforcements as well. It was no longer one platoon they were up against. There were at least four dozen men, all hurrying toward their position.

"Run!" Preacher said urgently, as he got to his feet and pulled Maggie up along with him. He kept his hand on her arm as they ran.

He heard MacGyver behind him as well. He got a glimpse of him holding Yana in one arm as he did his best to keep the boys in front of him.

Five figures fanned out from the door of the chopper,

and Preacher had never been so relieved to see his SEAL team as he was at that moment.

The second he had the thought, the sound of gunfire broke out behind them.

Flinching as the soldiers opened fire, Preacher urged Maggie to run even faster. The odds of none of them being hit were slim to none, but Preacher wasn't ready to give up.

Neither was his SEAL team. They returned fire, doing their best to pick off the soldiers closest to them.

They were going to make it. Preacher could see the opening to the helicopter. They were within fifty yards now. He recognized Kevlar and Smiley, who had taken the outermost positions, doing their best to keep the Russians back.

"About time you got here!" Smiley yelled without pausing his shots.

"That's my line!" Preacher shouted as he ran past him.

"Fuck!"

At the sound of MacGyver's curse, Preacher turned just in time to see Borysko hit the ground. Hard. He fell flat on his face—and didn't immediately make a move to get up.

Everything seemed to happen in slow motion after that. MacGyver made a move that only a stunt double in an action movie could've managed. He leaned down and scooped up the little boy, holding him in one arm and Yana in the other as he yelled at Artem to keep moving.

It occurred to Preacher in that moment that MacGyver had never planned on leaving the kids. No matter what it took, he was going to take them with him when they were rescued. Preacher was glad, because it would've eaten at his soul to leave them behind in this hell to fend for themselves.

He arrived at the chopper then, and with Safe's help, practically threw Maggie into the cargo area. Turning, he grabbed Artem, and was relieved to see Maggie pulling the boy away from the door after he'd been tossed inside.

As if they'd planned it, Blink and Safe climbed in, grabbed MacGyver's arms and hefted him into the helicopter, still holding both children.

Preacher leapt into the door and turned, reaching for his remaining teammates. Smiley and Flash entered the chopper, then it was only Kevlar left to be picked up.

"We gotta go!" one of the pilots shouted over the roar of the rotor blades.

"Kevlar!" Flash yelled. "Now!"

But their team leader was standing with his legs braced, shooting at the Russian soldiers who'd crept closer and closer.

Without thought, Preacher leapt back out of the chopper, ignoring the sound of Maggie screaming his name, and grabbed the neck of Kevlar's vest. He never stopped shooting as Preacher dragged him closer to the helicopter. Even as Blink and Smiley hauled both his and Kevlar's asses into the chopper, their leader continued to shoot.

The lights from the helicopter blinked out and plunged them all into pitch darkness again.

The pilots took off and immediately banked hard to the left. Then right. Then left again. It felt as if they were actually dodging bullets, which wouldn't surprise Preacher in the least. The Night Stalkers were almost scary with what they could do in a chopper. He'd always been in awe of their skills, and he wouldn't want anyone else shuttling him and his team into and out of the dangerous drop zones they frequently experienced.

The ride evened out, and after another fifteen seconds or so, a light was turned on in the cargo area. Thoughts of the pilots flew from Preacher's mind as he turned toward the commotion behind him. MacGyver had placed Borysko on the floor and was attempting to remove his shirt, while Blink was on his knees, cutting off the little boy's pants.

The blood pooling under him was obscene, and the sight made Preacher's guts churn.

"Get an IV started!" MacGyver ordered Flash. The man was already rummaging through the first-aid bag at his side.

Preacher held his breath as he watched his friends tend to Borysko. It looked as if he'd been shot in both his calf and his right side. Moving around, careful not to jostle anyone, Preacher made his way to where Maggie was huddled against the wall of the chopper with Yana in her lap and Artem huddled against her side. For once, the eight-year-old didn't look calm and in charge. He looked like a terrified little boy.

Preacher sat next to Artem and wrapped his arms around both him and Maggie. The boy didn't take his gaze off his brother. Borysko was unconscious now, not moving as the SEALs frantically attempted to save his life.

No one asked who the kids were or why they were involved in the rescue. They simply did what needed to be done. Any concerns about what would happen to the children would come later.

It seemed to take forever to get to the small military base on the western side of Ukraine, where the SEALs had been based during their mission. It was supposed to have been a quick in and out. The longer they were there, the more likely their presence in the country would be noted and advertised. They needed to get the hell out, especially now that gunfire had been exchanged. Russia wasn't going to let an opportunity pass to announce to the world that the United States had broken their unstated agreement not to get involved in the conflict.

But none of that mattered right now. Not when a little boy was lying bloody and fighting for his life.

By the time they landed, the commotion surrounding Borysko had calmed down. The bleeding was staunched and the wounds tightly wrapped for now. MacGyver still hovered over the boy, but some of the terror in his eyes seemed to have dissipated.

Artem had crawled over to his brother and was sitting at his side, holding his hand. But when they landed, there was no time to relax. A plane was already waiting on the runway nearby.

"Load up. We have to get the hell out of the country," Kevlar said.

Everyone began moving quickly, gathering bags and heading toward the plane. Still no one questioned who the children were, or if they were coming with them. They simply assumed as much.

"You got her?" MacGyver asked Maggie, who was carrying Yana.

"Yes."

"We'll take care of these two," Preacher told his teammate, turning to Artem and holding out his hand. To his surprise and relief, the boy took it. He looked uncertain and scared. Preacher couldn't blame him. Things were happening very quickly, and he had to be feeling out of his element. In the bombed-out city, he knew where to go and what to do. He was in charge and in control of what happened to himself and his siblings.

Here? He had no idea what was going on. And his brother was hurt. He had to be terrified.

Making a split-second decision, Preacher leaned down and picked up Artem. The boy didn't protest, simply held on tightly as he was carried toward the plane.

They were still on Ukrainian soil. They could leave the children in someone's capable hands. The fighting on this side of the country wasn't as intense as it was closer to the border with Russia. Someone would take care of the kids. They'd probably be adopted by a loving family and have a good life.

But the thought of simply dropping them off—especially Borysko, who was still unconscious—was abhorrent. And if Preacher was feeling that, MacGyver had to be feeling it ten times worse. He'd bonded with these kids. In a way that was soul deep.

MacGyver carried Borysko up the stairs to the plane, with Safe and Blink at his heels, the former holding the boy's IV. Maggie went next, carrying Yana, and Preacher was behind her with Artem. Flash and Smiley had his back, and Kevlar brought up the rear. The Night Stalkers had already taken off, disappearing into the night, back to wherever they'd been deployed from.

Kevlar paused to talk with someone at the base of the stairs, and after shaking his hand, ran up the steps, taking them two at a time.

"Settle in, everyone. We're going to be taking off hot," Kevlar told them.

Preacher led Maggie to a seat along one of the walls. The configuration of the inside of the plane wasn't like a commercial aircraft. There were seats along both walls, with a large open space in the middle. It was a military bird used for transport of goods and materials. On the way to the Ukraine, it had been filled with the crates the SEALs had delivered as ordered, as well as boxes of humanitarian aid for the besieged country.

MacGyver placed Borysko across three seats near the back of the plane, and the second Preacher put Artem on his feet, he headed for his brother. Yana began to squirm in Maggie's arms, so she put her down. She ran after her brother, and Artem took her hand in his.

MacGyver got them strapped into seats next to him, and they all held on as the plane began to move.

"Holy crap," Maggie whispered.

Preacher took a deep breath, then pulled her into his side. She buried her face in his chest and clung to him as the plane sped up and eventually lifted into the air at a much steeper angle than any commercial aircraft would ever attempt.

"This is intense," she said after a moment.

"We'll straighten out in a moment," Preacher told her as calmly as he could. His heart was still beating way too fast.

"Not the flight. Well, this too, but...everything."

"Yeah," he agreed.

"Are you all right?" she asked, looking up at him.

Preacher couldn't help but snort and shake his head.

"What?"

"You. You're asking if I'm all right?"

"Well, yeah. You're the one who was beaten. Can you even see out of that eye?"

"A little," Preacher said. "You ever been shot at before?"

"Um...yes. When I was trying to make my way through the city to get to you," she said a little cheekily.

"Before that," Preacher insisted.

"No."

"Right. I have. And you probably don't want to hear this, but I'm gonna say it anyway. That was probably about a five for me on a scale of one to ten on the intensity meter, when it comes to an extraction. You've *never* been through anything that intense before. It should be *me* asking if *you're* all right."

"I'm alive," she said simply. "After everything I've been through, I'm taking that as a win."

"Damn," Preacher said on a sigh. "I love you."

She beamed up at him. "I love you too. And for the record...I don't ever want to do that again. Once was enough. And you're right, I don't want to hear that what we just did was normal for you. I'm going to be a basket case every time you're deployed from now on."

Preacher couldn't help but love that. Not that she'd be worried, but that she was thinking so far into the future.

"Is he going to be okay?" Maggie asked.

"Borysko?"

"Yeah."

"It looks like it."

"What happens now? With the kids?" Maggie asked next.

"No clue. But I know that MacGyver is going to fight like hell for them."

"What can we do to help him? Keep them, I mean."

This was just another reason Preacher loved this woman. Her huge heart. She wasn't asking about what happened with herself next. With Robertson. She was worried about the children. And MacGyver. She should be curled into a ball, paralyzed with anxiety over everything that had happened to her in the last few days. But instead, she was thinking about everyone but herself.

"I don't know. We'll play it by ear. But I'm guessing the authorities will want to hear about what happened and the situation we found them in."

Maggie nodded firmly. "Right. Well, whoever I have to talk to and whatever I have to say, I'll say it. They deserve a second chance."

Preacher agreed one hundred percent.

"Where are we headed now?" she asked.

"Probably Germany. Borysko will be checked out, then we'll head home."

"I don't have any identification," Maggie said, looking up at him with a frown. "How am I going to get back into the US?"

"It'll be fine," Preacher soothed. "Trust me."

To his amazement, she simply nodded and melted against his side once again. How this woman could trust him as deeply as she did when she'd had that trust broken so badly in the past was astounding. But he wasn't going to ever take it for granted. He'd give her no reason to distrust him. Ever. He'd be her rock. The person she looked to when she was happy, sad, scared...whatever she was feeling, he wanted to be the man she came to first.

"Shawn?"

"Yeah?"

"I know I should be freaking out about going back to Riverton, about what's waiting for me there. I'll need to get a hold of my probation officer and tell her what happened, talk to your Navy people, face Roman...but all I can feel right now is relief. That we made it out of there. All of us."

"Me too, baby. Me too. We'll tackle whatever comes next together."

"Okay."

"Okay," he agreed, floored again by her trust in him.

As she dozed, Preacher's mind spun with plans.

The threats against his Maggie needed to be stopped. Immediately. He'd do whatever it took to make that happen. Starting with calling Tex the second they landed in Germany. By the time they arrived in Riverton, he needed the ball to already be rolling. Didn't want to give Robertson any sliver of a chance to combat what was coming. He was going to regret not walking away from Maggie and never looking back. Preacher would make sure of it.

CHAPTER TWENTY

Maggie was petrified. But she did her best to hide any emotion from the man at her side. Shawn had been hovering ever since they'd landed back at the naval base. Just being here made her nervous. This was Roman's territory. Even though Shawn and his friends were badasses, what could they do against such a high-ranking officer?

Thankfully, they'd arrived in the middle of the night and the base felt deserted.

She was distracted by Artem and Yana's wide-eyed wonder at stepping foot on US soil for the first time. Now that they'd realized Borysko would be fine, that the bullets somehow hadn't hit anything vital, they were feeling much more curious about everything happening around them.

And Tex had come through in a huge way for MacGyver. He'd somehow arranged for the children to be temporarily placed in his care. There was a long road ahead for the newfound family, but Maggie had high hopes that things would work out for them.

Shawn was taking her to his apartment, and to her surprise, Smiley was coming with them. He said that he didn't think it was smart for them to be on their own, not as long as Robertson was out there gunning for them both. The woman who owned the house where Shawn rented a room had another tenant who'd just left, so there was an empty room next to Shawn's. It was one more way that things simply seemed to be working out. Maggie didn't want to dwell too long on the hows and whys. She was just trying to be grateful instead.

Shawn explained that it was likely Roman had already learned how badly his plans had gone, and that he was probably even now trying to figure out how to spin what happened to his advantage. That didn't exactly give Maggie warm and fuzzy feelings, but she couldn't think about it... otherwise she would break.

So after the short ride to his home, she let Shawn lead her into the house and up the stairs to his room. The woman who owned the place was obviously asleep. The rental rooms were on the third floor, and Smiley followed behind.

"Don't forget, we're meeting with Kevlar and the rest of the team tomorrow at ten," he reminded them.

"I know," Shawn said.

Maggie bit her lip. Everyone had to be exhausted, and she suddenly felt guilty that she was the reason why.

"Don't answer the phone, your door, or talk to anyone other than Preacher," Smiley lectured her.

She nodded. "I don't have my phone, and I'm going to crash the second my head hits the pillow. Smiley?"

"Yeah?"

"Thank you for staying here tonight. Roman...he's...I'm afraid of him." It was a huge admission, but after everything that happened, she didn't think her terror would be a surprise to either of these men.

"He fucked up," Smiley said with a fierce expression on his face. "He put all his cards on the table and now we all know who he really is."

Maggie swallowed hard. She wanted to believe that, but she also had a feeling he wouldn't go down without one hell of a fight.

"Get some sleep. We'll figure things out tomorrow," Smiley told her. Then he gave Shawn a chin lift and turned toward the open door in the hallway.

Shawn pressed on the small of her back, urging her toward the other door. He unlocked it, then stepped back to let her enter first.

Maggie was surprised by the room. She'd expected a normal bedroom, but this was a suite, and it was huge. A queen-size bed was against the left wall, with a small, old-fashioned table on each side in place of nightstands. There was what looked like a fairly large walk-in closet, with a dresser inside and all of Shawn's clothes hung neatly. Across from the bed was a seating area, complete with a leather couch, an oversized chair, and a large flat-screen television. There were also shelves filled with books and knickknacks.

There was even a small kitchen area with a sink, a two-burner stove top, a microwave, and a refrigerator.

"Wow!" Maggie exclaimed.

"When Jane's husband died, she realized she was lonely in this big house all by herself. So she had this floor remodeled, making the rooms big enough to basically be apartments. In my opinion, she doesn't charge enough to rent them out, but I'm grateful I was able to get one. Come on, you need to get cleaned up."

Maggie let Shawn lead her over to another door, and this time she wasn't surprised at the size of the bathroom. This Jane woman had outdone herself in designing the rental spaces. The bathroom she was standing in was large. There was no bathtub, but the walk-in shower was oversized and had not only a rain showerhead on the ceiling, but also another showerhead coming out of the wall.

"I don't have any clothes that you can put on other than mine, but I'll call Kevlar in the morning and see if he can go by your apartment and grab some things for you, and bring them over before we need to leave to meet with the team. Is that all right?"

Maggie nodded. She hadn't thought much about personal hygiene in the last few days, having more important things to worry about—namely, not dying. But now that she was standing in front of this amazing shower, she suddenly couldn't wait to get clean.

She vaguely heard Shawn chuckle as he brushed past

her and opened the shower door. He reached in and turned one of the knobs, then water poured from the ceiling. "There's a clean towel right outside the door. Take your time."

He turned as if to leave—and panic hit Maggie like a tidal wave. She reached out and grabbed his arm in an iron grip. Her mouth was dry, her stomach churned, and she realized she was breathing with short, fast gasps.

"Maggie? What's wrong? Shit! You're okay. You're safe. Slow your breathing." Shawn turned back to her and pulled her against him. The feel of his tall, hard body against hers made the panic recede as if it had never happened.

"Shower with me?" she mumbled. It was ridiculous that at just the thought of being alone in a bathroom, she'd panicked so badly. But if she was by herself for even a second, she felt as if Roman would somehow find her again. Get a hold of her. Finish what he'd started. There was no telling where he'd send her next. Siberia? North Korea? Somewhere no one would ever find her this time.

Or he'd simply blow her brains out and bury her body six feet deep in the mountains around the city.

Shawn didn't answer verbally, simply took a step back and began to strip.

Following his lead, Maggie quickly took off her clothes. It felt as if it had been years since they'd made love. She should've been embarrassed to be naked in front of this man, but she wasn't. Not in the least. After they were both nude, he opened the shower door and stepped inside, testing the water to make sure it was perfect before holding out his hand to her.

Maggie took it and stepped into the glass enclosure. Steam from the shower fogged up the walls, and it felt as if she and Shawn were in their own little world. Showering with someone else could be awkward, but he made it feel as if they'd done this a thousand times already. He stepped into her personal space and held onto her hips, urging her under the spray. As she tilted her head back to get her hair wet, Maggie felt his gaze running down her body.

When she opened her eyes, she saw that he was frowning as he studied her torso. Looking down, she realized why he looked so unsettled. She was covered in bruises. Even had some scrapes here and there.

"I'm okay," she told him.

"You aren't, but I'm going to make sure you get that way," Shawn said, then he leaned over and grabbed a bottle of shampoo. "Turn," he ordered.

She wanted to assure him that she really was all right. That a few bruises and scrapes were a small price to pay for being alive, for surviving what she should never have survived. But instead, she did as Shawn asked and turned her back to him.

The next ten minutes were surreal for Maggie. Shawn was gentle as he thoroughly shampooed, rinsed, and conditioned her hair. Then he soaped up a washcloth and washed her from head to toe. Kneeling at her feet, he gently ran the cloth up and down her legs. He didn't shy away from cleaning between her thighs either. And while it made Maggie blush, she didn't protest. Then she returned the favor, although it was difficult to reach his hair.

Cleaning each other wasn't about sex, it was about taking care of the person they loved. But when Maggie wrapped a soapy hand around his cock and gently cleaned his balls, the warm shower turned red hot.

His cock hardened, and Shawn moaned as she stroked him. Desire hit Maggie hard and fast. She'd forgotten that he'd been a virgin not too long ago. She wondered if he'd ever had a woman get him off in a shower like this. She moved her hand faster, squeezing his cock as she stroked him.

"Maggie," he said, his voice low and raspy. "You don't have to..."

"I know," she said. "I want to. Stop thinking and enjoy."

As the water cascaded over his shoulders, Maggie concentrated on making him feel as amazing as she did right that moment. She hadn't seen Shawn lose his cool even once in the last couple of days. He'd been her rock. Even when he was getting beaten by the Russian soldiers, he'd kept his head.

But now? He was putty in her hands, and it gave Maggie back some of the confidence she'd lost. Knowing she was bringing Shawn pleasure enough to make him shake where he stood was heady.

"I'm not going to last long," he warned.

"Good. I want to see it. Feel your come all over my hand. Feel it on my skin," Maggie said, feeling sexy as hell. She was standing close, and the thought of his come spurting out and hitting her skin was as erotic as anything she'd ever done.

He wasn't wrong. It didn't take long for his pleasure to overwhelm him.

One of his hands shot out and grabbed the nape of her neck in a strong grip. The other went to her waist, where his fingers dug into her skin. She felt surrounded by him, completely in tune with him.

His hips pushed forward as his orgasm hit. Come burst out of the tip of his cock and splashed against her belly. It was hot and creamy, and Maggie couldn't hold back her smile. She'd done that. Made him lose that iron control that turned her on so much.

She milked his cock, making sure to get every drop of come out of him. To her surprise, he was still half hard when he suddenly grabbed her wrist, stopping her now gentle caresses.

He turned her hand, placing it on her own belly. Then the two of them rubbed his come into her skin. His gaze was glued to their hands and her body.

"So fucking sexy," he murmured before stepping to the side and letting the water hit her torso. His come was quickly washed away, and he turned and shut the water off. He opened the door to the shower and grabbed the towel he'd placed there earlier, then briskly and efficiently began to dry Maggie.

"I can do that," she told him.

"I know, but I want to."

He was acting a little weird, and Maggie wasn't sure

why. So she stood still and let him dry her off. Then he quickly ran the towel over his own body before throwing it to the floor and stepping out of the shower. He had Maggie's hand in his, and he practically dragged her out of the bathroom, toward his bed.

He flung the comforter back and said in a guttural tone, "Get in."

Swallowing hard, having a hard time reading his mood, Maggie did as ordered. She was no sooner on her back than Shawn was hovering over her. His cock brushed against the hair between her legs, and she squirmed under him.

"That was...I don't know what that was," Shawn said as he gazed into her eyes. "Perfection. A dream come true. A miracle."

Every muscle in Maggie's body relaxed. For a moment, she thought he was upset about what happened. But it seemed that wasn't the case.

"I'm not the most experienced guy, but I want to make this good for you. What do you need? My mouth? My fingers? I know you're exhausted, so you probably just want to sleep. Tell me, Maggie. What do you need from me? Name it, it's yours."

"You, Shawn. I just need you."

"You have me."

Maggie smiled at that. "*Inside*, Shawn. I need you inside me."

"How? Soft and easy? Or hard and fast?"

Maggie could feel the aches and pains from the last few days deep in her bones. She wasn't used to as much physical exertion as she'd had recently. "Soft and easy," she told him.

"Your wish is my command," he told her.

Then he proceeded to do just that. He made love to her gently and reverently. Maggie had never felt so cherished.

He'd coaxed two orgasms out of her before she urged him to take his own pleasure. Even in the midst of his orgasm, he didn't pound into her. He simply planted himself deep inside her body and came long and hard.

Then he rolled over and held her tight, covering them both with the comforter.

Maggie sighed against him. His arms around her felt amazing. She'd gone so long without human touch that this felt like a miracle. *Her* miracle.

Tomorrow, the shit might hit the fan, but for now, she was content to soak in Shawn's love. She felt his lips on her forehead and she sighed with contentment.

"Sleep, Maggie."

"Do we need to set an alarm?" she asked sleepily.

"I already did."

"Did you call Kevlar?"

"I'll take care of it. Don't worry."

Don't worry. When was the last time she'd been carefree enough not to worry? Before she'd met Roman, for sure. Dating him had been...stressful. Maggie always felt as if she had to live up to what he'd thought was his greatness. That she was somehow falling short whenever she was around him. With what she wore, how she acted, what she said. But with Shawn, she could just be herself.

Maggie was still trying to figure out who she was, as being incarcerated had changed her. She was more wary, less trusting, less willing to take people at face value. But somehow with this man, his friends, she was coming into her own.

"I need to call Julie," she mumbled.

"We'll do it tomorrow. Go to sleep, Maggie. You're exhausted, and frankly, so am I. Tomorrow is soon enough to worry about the real world."

"Okay," she slurred.

"Love you," Shawn said.

"Love you back," Maggie said with a small smile. Then she fell into a deep sleep, trusting the man whose arms were around her to keep her safe.

CHAPTER TWENTY-ONE

Preacher took a deep breath and tried to relax. It was fifteen minutes after ten and the team was gathered at Safe's house to discuss the situation with Robertson. Josie was at MacGyver's house with the kids. Maggie was sitting nervously at the table just off the kitchen. Kevlar had picked up a few things for her before the meeting, then called Dude and Benny to go with Wren and Remi to Maggie's apartment to pack up more of her stuff. She'd agreed that morning to temporarily move in with Preacher until things with Robertson were resolved.

He should be ecstatic that she'd be in his space for the foreseeable future, but he was also concerned that she felt as if she had no choice. It wasn't lost on Preacher that Maggie had no real home. She'd been staying with Adina after being paroled because she had nowhere else to go. And now she was being shuffled to his place because of circumstances beyond her control once again. The last thing he wanted was her agreeing to move in with him because she felt cornered. He wanted her there because *she* wanted to be. She'd told him that morning that she was happy to stay with him, but he still worried.

Then there was Robertson. The man was a threat. A big one. Not only to Maggie, but to his SEAL team, other women, and even other Navy personnel. There was no telling what he'd do in order to evade justice. He'd already proven he had no problem setting up others to take the blame for his actions.

"I've been talking to Tex this morning, and what he's been able to dig up so far...it's not good," Kevlar said.

"This morning?" MacGyver asked. "Thought he was joining us via phone for this meeting?" His teammate had dark circles under his eyes, and Preacher wondered if he'd gotten any sleep at all. He was obviously stressed about Artem, Borysko, and Yana, but he was here, which meant the world to him.

"Yeah, he is. But I was up early, and I didn't want to wait to update him. The thought of Robertson messing with not only our careers, but other SEAL teams, is so fucking wrong it's not even funny."

Preacher nodded, as did all the other men. Nothing about the rear admiral using his power inappropriately sat well with any of them.

"He's not going to do anything himself," Flash said. "He's a coward. If he's going to come after Maggie again, he'll send one of his flunkies."

"I agree. Which is why Tex has been trying to figure out who Robertson has doing his dirty work. So far he's found a few enlisted sailors, as well as a convicted drug dealer or two."

"Really?" Maggie asked.

"And he thinks that's just the tip of the iceberg," Kevlar said with a nod. "Tex has a couple of his hacker friends working on this too. A woman out of Texas, another in New Mexico. And also Rex, who we all know...the leader of the Mountain Mercenaries. It's their top priority at the moment. They're looking especially hard at the cold case of his missing wife. Including combing through reports of unidentified remains that have been found in the area where he lived, to see if any of them can be traced back to the wife, and thus to Robertson."

Maggie looked down at her lap, and Preacher realized she was trying not to cry. He went to her side and pulled out the chair next to her. He took her hand in his and put it on his thigh.

"So...what now?" he asked. "What do we do while we wait for Tex and his friends to do their thing? It's not exactly safe for us to go back to work."

"I talked to the commander as well," Kevlar said. "He's pissed. He agreed that Robertson had to have a hand in Maggie ending up in a crate on that plane. He's put us on a no-deploy list for now. Of course, Robertson has the power to rescind that order, but if he does, it'll be even more obvious that he's guilty of everything we're accusing him of."

"And Maggie? How do we keep her safe?" Preacher asked.

No one spoke for what seemed like minutes, but was probably only a few seconds. Preacher felt Maggie's hand tighten in his grip.

At that moment, Kevlar's phone rang. He answered it and put it on speaker. "Tex," he said briefly, acknowledging the former SEAL on the other end.

The conversation continued as if it hadn't been interrupted.

"She's not to be alone. One of us needs to be with her at all times," Safe said.

"Working is probably a bad idea too," Smiley agreed.

"He's going to do everything in his power to make sure she can't testify against him when he eventually goes to trial. And he *will* have to own up to what he's done. Tex will make sure of that," Kevlar added.

"No."

It would've been comical the way everyone's head swiveled around to stare at Maggie. But nothing about this was funny. Preacher did his best to stay calm. "No what, Maggie?"

"He put me in prison once. I won't let him do it again. I don't want to hide away like a coward. I don't mind having someone with me, because I'm not an idiot, and I don't want to risk being snatched again and being sent to some other war zone just so he can get rid of me. And I don't want to quit my job. I *like* it. But I know being near me puts other people in danger. That's the last thing I want.

It's bad enough that *your* association with me has put all of you in his sights. This needs to stop. *Now*."

Preacher's gut rolled. "What are you saying?" he asked.

"He won't be able to resist talking to me if he has the chance. He'll want to exert his power over me. Threaten me. Probably brag about all the things he's already done. Gloat about what he's *going* to do. If we can get that on tape, that'll help prosecute him. Oh! And I completely forgot. I still have the recording from that last phone call he made to me."

"That's right," Tex said from the phone. "Can you send it to me? Like...ASAP?"

"Sure. It's on my laptop at my apartment though."

"I can go get it and send it to you, Tex," Kevlar said.

"Good."

"I still think it would be a good idea to get him to admit what he did to me. The Ukraine thing," Maggie said. "The phone recording is pretty bad, incriminatory, but what if a lawyer says it's not him? There's no other proof he's the one threatening me. If we can get both audio *and* video recordings of him bragging about what he did—"

"No," Preacher said firmly, interrupting her before she could finish her thought.

"Probably not the best idea," Blink agreed.

"I'm with them," MacGyver said.

"She might have a point," Smiley said.

Preacher gave his friend a death glare.

"I'm not saying let her waltz into his office and have a showdown...although, now that I think about it, that's not the worst idea either. He won't be able to do anything if she's on his territory. He seems to work best outside the boundaries of his job. So if she shows up on base, where there are people around, he won't be able to snatch her again or do anything that would hurt her."

"Are you fucking kidding me? You can't be that stupid," Preacher told Smiley.

"I'm guessing he wouldn't risk saying anything someone could overhear in his office," Safe interjected.

"Okay, good point. But what if they 'accidentally' run into each other in a parking lot on base? With no one in hearing distance, he might feel empowered enough to tell her what he has planned for her next. And obviously, we'd all be there watching, recording, out of sight. Just in case."

Preacher took a deep breath. He wanted to beat the shit out of Smiley for even suggesting that Maggie confront Robertson face-to-face. But he also had to admit that the idea had some merit. On one hand, there was a good chance if the man knew he was being investigated, he'd be paranoid and even *more* careful about what he said, and to whom. On the other, he was a cocky bastard. Someone who thought he was smarter than everyone around him. He might make a mistake. And as long as they controlled how and when he and Maggie met up, the rear admiral couldn't do anything to hurt her.

"Yes. Let's do it," Maggie said.

Kevlar frowned. "I'm not so sure about this. I don't trust the man as far as I can throw him."

"Me either," Maggie told him. "But I also don't want to

spend my life looking over my shoulder, wondering when he'll strike. He could put drugs in any of *your* cars next. 'Forget' to order bullets to be packed on your next mission. Or worse, leak your location to the bad guys. I admit that being bait was pretty horrible back in Ukraine, but the end justified the means. I'm here, MacGyver's here, and so is Shawn. I've felt helpless against him for so long. Please let me help take him down."

"Fuck," Blink muttered. "How can we argue against that?"

"If we do this," Preacher said forcefully, "we need the agreement and assistance of NCIS. There's no way we're going to do anything that might end up not being admissible in court."

"Agreed," Kevlar said. "I'll talk to the commander. He was going to contact NCIS anyway, so he can arrange for them to be part of the operation."

"Thank you," Maggie said softly to the group. "I can't stand the thought of anyone else being caught up in his lies and accused of something they didn't do."

Preacher didn't like this. Not at all. But he couldn't think of anything else they could do to keep her safe, other than fleeing the country, which in the end would get her in *more* trouble, not less. But honestly, this was no longer just about her. Robertson was abusing his power and there was no telling what he'd do to other Navy personnel in the future. He needed to be stopped for the good of the institution, the country, and every man and woman who could be affected by his orders.

Never had Preacher heard of someone abusing their power as badly as Robertson was doing now. He knew exactly what he was doing when he'd sent their SEAL team to deliver those crates. They'd questioned the mission even before they'd discovered Maggie in one of the boxes. The man was unhinged, and clearly feeling utterly invincible if he thought he could get away with smuggling a person out of the country and leaving her to die in a war zone.

The group broke up not too long after the decision to let Maggie meet with Roman face-to-face. Preacher wanted to take her home, to hide her away, but she insisted on stopping at My Sister's Closet to talk to Julie. That, in turn, led to Aces Bar and Grill for a late lunch. Jessyka, Caroline, and Alabama happened to be there, and somehow they ended up commandeering Maggie and telling Preacher to shoo, that they had women stuff to talk about.

Since Maggie seemed happy to talk to the women, he backed off. He kept her in his line of sight at all times, but slowly as the afternoon went on, he relaxed a little. No one would touch one hair on her head as long as he was there. She was...

Preacher couldn't think of the best word to describe the woman he'd fallen head over heels for. She was everything he'd ever wanted in a partner. And he'd be damned if he'd lose her to some asshole who got off on wielding power over others.

It was around three-thirty when Maggie's phone rang. Preacher had been staring at her, attempting to gauge where she was at mentally, when he saw her pull out her phone, the one Kevlar had brought over that morning with a change of clothes for her.

And he saw the instant all the blood drained from her face as she listened to whoever was on the other end of the line.

Adrenaline spiked within Preacher and he stood up so fast, his chair teetered on its back legs. He rushed over to the table, and he noticed that the other women were looking just as concerned. But all his attention was on Maggie.

"Yes, sir. I understand. I can explain everything. Uh-huh. Okay. Now? All right." She looked at her watch. "I can be there in twenty minutes? Yes, sir. Bye."

"What? Who was that? Where can you be in twenty minutes?" Preacher asked.

Maggie's hands shook as she put her phone back into her purse. "That was someone from my PO's office. They heard I took a trip out of the country, which is against the terms of my probation. He said I needed to come in immediately so she could assess what happened...and whether I would be going back to prison."

"That's bullshit!"

"No, that's not fair! You didn't *want* to leave the country!"

"I'm calling Tex. He'll straighten this out."

Preacher blocked out the other women. It wasn't as if he didn't share their outrage. He did. But he was more concerned about the freaked-out expression on Maggie's face. He pulled a chair over from a nearby table and sat, then took Maggie's face in his hands. "Look at me," he ordered.

Her gaze immediately found his.

"We're going to straighten this out."

"I can't go back there," she whispered in anguish. "I just can't!"

"You won't."

"Damn straight she won't," Caroline said as she scrolled on her phone. "Tex will make sure of it." She hit a button, brought the phone to her ear, then pushed her chair back and stood, stalking over to a quieter corner of the bar.

Tears fell from Maggie's eyes, and each one tore at Preacher's heart. "What do you want to do?" he asked.

"Do?" she questioned with a frown.

"Do we head to Mexico? Wait and meet with your PO tomorrow, after we make arrangements to bring the commander and a lawyer with us? Or the pilot of the chopper who was there when that damn crate you were in burst open after landing on the ground? Whatever you want to do, I'll make happen."

She stared at him for a long moment. "You'd go to Mexico with me?" she asked softly.

"In a heartbeat."

"But that would ruin your career. You'd probably be charged with aiding a fugitive."

Preacher shrugged. "Don't care. All I care about right now is making that horrified look on your face disappear."

Maggie closed her eyes and sighed. "I can't run. A lifetime of being hunted sounds like the worst kind of hell.

Besides, I suck at foreign languages. I almost didn't grad-uate college because of French." She opened her eyes and stared at Preacher. "I need to go in now. If I don't, they'll issue an arrest warrant. That's what the guy on the phone said. I'll go in and talk to them, explain what happened. Maybe you can give me your commander's number on the base for my PO? Maybe he can vouch for me?"

"Done. And Caroline is right, Tex will come through. We just need to stay calm. Okay?"

Maggie licked her lips. "Okay."

But Preacher could tell she was anything but calm. He could literally see her heartbeat in her neck. Could feel the slight shaking of her body under his hands.

He hated this. Loathed it. He'd never been the kind of SEAL who enjoyed taking another person's life. But if Rear Admiral Robertson was standing in front of him right now, he'd break his neck without feeling an ounce of remorse.

"Come on, let's go. Cheyenne, will you call Kevlar and let him know what's happening?" Preacher asked.

"Of course."

"And I'll call Abe. He'll rally the rest of the troops. Don't worry, Maggie. Our guys'll figure this out," Alabama told her.

Maggie nodded and attempted to smile, but everyone could tell it was forced.

Preacher took her hand and led her through the bar to the door. His mind spun. He needed to figure out what to say to Maggie's probation officer to make her believe that she hadn't gone on a pleasure trip to Ukraine. It was a ridiculous thought, but the bottom line was that leaving the country *was* against the terms of Maggie's probation. The state had every right to put her back behind bars until this mess was sorted out. But he hoped that wouldn't happen before it could be proved that Maggie had no choice. That she'd been fucking *kidnapped* and locked in a crate.

Hell, he'd bring in Artem, Borysko, and Yana if he had to. Anything to make this nightmare end for Maggie.

Her fingers clasped his with a grip so tight, it almost hurt. But Preacher didn't say a thing. He'd go to the ends of the Earth for the woman at his side, and it killed him that he didn't have the magic words right this moment to make everything better. To fix this. Not being able to help the woman he loved through one of the most stressful times of her life was as painful as anything Preacher had ever experienced.

His heart hurt as he drove them toward the government building in Riverton, but Preacher vowed that no matter what happened, he'd be Maggie's rock. Her protector. The one person in the world she could rely on.

CHAPTER TWENTY-TWO

Maggie was freezing. It wasn't cold outside, but she felt frozen from the inside out. This was literally her worst nightmare come true. She'd done everything in her power to stay on the straight and narrow. To not do anything wrong so there would be no reason to put her back behind bars. Okay, using Adina's ride-share account wasn't exactly legal, but she hadn't been hurting anyone. Especially because she'd had her friend's permission to do what she'd done.

She'd never in a million years thought she might be thrown back behind bars for being freaking *kidnapped*. She didn't have any say in what happened to her. God, she'd been *unconscious*. But no one believed her when she'd said she had no idea those drugs were in her car. Why would anyone believe her now?

The only reason she wasn't screaming at the unfairness of it all was because of the man holding her hand. Shawn was literally holding her together. The truth was, she was terrified. More scared than she'd been to stand up and let those Russian soldiers see her. Back in Ukraine, she had control over what she was doing and what would happen next. She'd been able to hide, to run, to use her brain to get away.

Now? She couldn't do a damn thing. There was no running, no hiding, and what happened next was literally up to someone else. Her probation officer was generally pretty laid-back. The woman had been kind anytime she'd met with her in the past. Maggie just had to hope she still felt a little compassion toward her when they met in a few minutes.

Just walking up to the building made her feel sick. As the door closed behind them after they entered, Maggie felt the weight of it down to her soul. She prayed she'd be able to walk out the same door in the not-so-distant future.

"Tex is on this," Shawn said softly as they stepped into the elevator that would take them to the third floor. "Caroline texted and said he's pissed way the hell off. There's no way the state can lock you up for leaving the country against your will."

Maggie nodded, still numb inside. It felt really good that she had such staunch supporters, but she wasn't convinced it would make a difference in the short run. Rules were rules, and she was petrified that she might be spending the night, or the next several, behind bars.

She suddenly wanted to pull away from Shawn. Insist that she wasn't good for him...but she wasn't that strong. She needed him. He was the only thing keeping her from sinking to the floor in a puddle of despair.

The elevator dinged as it reached the third floor, and Shawn led her toward the person sitting behind the reception desk.

"Maggie Lionetti here for an appointment," he said confidently, as if he'd done it a million times.

Looking down at the computer screen, the woman nodded. "Go through the double doors here and have a seat inside. Someone will come for her in a moment."

The sound of every door she went through closing behind her was like a death knell. Maggie could still remember the sound of her cell door clanging shut every night, and while the glass doors didn't sound even close, the imagery was the same.

They sat, and Maggie did her best not to hyperventilate.

"It's okay. You're okay," Shawn said, squeezing her hand.

She wasn't. She wasn't okay in the least. But Shawn thought she was strong, had told her so more than once. And she didn't want to do anything that would make him think otherwise.

The truth was, she was terrified of Roman. The man had proven time and time again what he was capable of. How he'd use anyone and everyone to exert his dominance.

They needed more than the recording of his threats over the phone to take him down. Proof that he'd killed his wife would be a good start, but if Roman was going to be held accountable for the things he'd done, she needed to be brave and face him.

Being bait for the Russian soldiers had been scary, but necessary. She'd told Shawn that she never wanted to do anything like that again, but frankly, if she had to make the same decision twice, she'd do everything just the same to protect those she cared about.

And now that she thought about it, Roman was probably the one who'd called her probation officer and informed her that she'd left the country. It was an easy thing to do, calling in an anonymous tip. If she was going to confront Roman face-to-face and get the proof needed to make sure the man didn't exploit and hurt anyone else, she needed to get through this meeting with her PO. Explain what was going on, give her the contact info for Shawn's commander so she could verify everything Maggie told her. Luckily, the woman was reasonable and not prone to report her probationers for every little infraction. She believed in second chances, which right now would hopefully be Maggie's salvation.

Her little internal pep talk made her feel a little more confident. This place scared the hell out of her. The building itself felt as if it was a portal straight back to prison. But she'd done everything she was supposed to do in regard to her probation. Every drug test had come back clean, she reported to her PO right on schedule, was never late to her meetings. This meeting would work out as well...it *had* to.

"Maggie Lionetti?" a man called from another doorway.

Shawn put his hand on her cheek and turned her head so she had no choice but to look at him.

"I'll be right here. We'll call Tex when we get home and see what he thinks about the recording you made. This is gonna be over soon, Maggie. I swear."

Swallowing hard, she nodded.

Shawn leaned forward and kissed her. "You've got this," he reassured her.

She took a deep breath, then stood and headed toward the man who'd called her name. He nodded at her but didn't smile. The door behind them clicked as it closed. Shivering at the sound of the lock engaging, Maggie tried to block it out.

She was thinking about the most succinct way to explain to her PO what had been going on in her life when the man she was following suddenly turned. He took hold of her upper arm—and she felt something prick against her side.

"Don't say a word," he hissed quietly. "If you do, I'll gut you right here and now."

Looking down, Maggie saw a wicked-looking serrated knife at her side. Instinctively, she attempted to pull away from him. He jerked her close and the knife he was holding penetrated her shirt. She gasped at the instant pain that bloomed when it broke her skin.

"I'll do it. I have nothing to lose. This isn't personal. Robertson is holding all the goddamn cards—my career, my marriage, my literal fucking life. So come along nicely and you'll be just fine."

She wouldn't be. Maggie knew that better than most. But it was obvious this man would hurt her too, if she didn't do what he wanted. She was screwed either way.

He dragged her down the hall and through a door that led to a stairwell. She almost tripped several times as he practically ran down the three flights to the ground floor. Every other step made the knife prick her skin, and Maggie could feel blood soaking her black shirt and making it stick to her skin.

Leaving a trail of blood drops would be good, but she didn't think her wound was that bad...or at least she wasn't bleeding that badly *yet*.

Then something else occurred to her. Cameras. Looking up, she saw one in the corner of the stairwell aimed at the door that led outside.

"They aren't working," the man holding her said almost nonchalantly. "The cameras. I see you looking. You think he wouldn't have thought of that?"

Shit. There would be no trail of where she'd gone. Shawn would eventually get concerned when her meeting ran too long, and when he realized she wasn't in the building, he'd do everything in his power to find her. But how could he?

Maggie was beginning to think she'd end up just like Roman's wife had so many years ago. Gone without a trace. The police would be baffled, her new friends would be worried and pissed off. But it wouldn't do any good. If Roman had his way, she'd never be found.

Despair filled her. She supposed she should be scared or trying to figure out how to escape this latest predicament, but at the moment, all she could think about was how she'd miss out on spending the rest of her life with Shawn. She'd never get to know Remi, Wren, and Josie better. Would never be a mother. Wouldn't grow old with Shawn at her side. All the dreams she had for her life were disappearing in a puff of smoke.

The man holding her was surely leaving bruises on her upper arm. He was gripping her so tightly, it felt as if he was cutting off the circulation to her entire limb. He exited the building and walked toward a black four-door vehicle that was sitting at the curb. The windows were tinted, and Maggie couldn't see who was behind the wheel.

The man wrenched open the back door and practically threw her inside. He didn't say a word, simply slammed the door behind her and turned back toward the building. As the car pulled away from the curb, he disappeared through the stairway door, probably to go back up to the third floor and pretend he didn't see anything after leading her to a room to wait for her probation officer to arrive.

"Hello, Maggie."

She spun around, gaping at the man behind the wheel in disbelief. She'd been so fixated on the asshole who'd forced her out of the building that she hadn't thought to look at the driver.

"Roman," she breathed.

"You're a hard woman to make disappear," he said almost lazily.

Maggie couldn't believe he was here. That he had the guts to participate in her kidnapping firsthand. She wanted to claw his eyes out. Leap into the front seat and attack him, make him crash so she could get out of the car and away from his evilness. But there was a metal barrier between the front and back seats. She couldn't do a damn thing to him as he drove.

"I told you to keep your mouth shut," he said. "You didn't. I warned you that if I heard even a peep that your SEAL boyfriend or his friends were asking about me, it wouldn't end well for you. But they aren't going to take me down. No one can. I'm untouchable."

"You're wrong," Maggie managed to say.

He laughed. The sound made the hair on the back of Maggie's neck stand up.

"What are you going to do about it? Looks as if I have the upper hand right now. The back doors can't be opened from the inside, and you can't do anything to make me wreck this car. You aren't going anywhere until we get to where we're going."

"And where's that?" Maggie couldn't help but ask.

"There's a nice little beach that I know of. Deserted, out of the way. Not too far from your apartment, actually. It'll be a shame when people find the suicide note you left behind before you drown yourself in the ocean."

"No one is going to believe I killed myself," Maggie

said, her voice wobbling a bit instead of sounding as firm as she wanted it to.

"Doesn't matter. Not when your body will never be found to verify anything. Besides, even if they did find it, an autopsy will confirm water in your lungs. Classic drowning."

Roman really was insane. He was talking about murdering her as calmly as he would discuss the weather.

"You aren't going to get away with this," she said almost desperately.

"Of course I am. You have no idea how many contacts I have. In the police department, the Navy, local government, drug dealers...everyone I come into contact with owes me, or I have something I can hold over their heads. Everyone does *what* I want, *when* I want it done. Haven't you learned that yet?"

Maggie swallowed hard. It was sinking in for real now that she was going to die. "Leave Shawn and his friends alone," she said in a low voice. She wasn't above begging. Anything to make sure the man she loved was safe.

"Not happening," Roman said almost gleefully. "I have plans for them. They think they're such hot shit. News flash—they aren't. They might have a no-deploy tag on them right now, but eventually that'll be removed...and I know just where they're going next." He laughed again. A sound so evil, Maggie shivered in terror.

"Sit back and relax, love. We'll be there soon."

Maggie was having trouble breathing. There seemed to

be no stopping this man. He was evil incarnate, and she was stuck in his vile web.

Turning slightly to look out the window, Maggie flinched. Her side ached. One of her hands touched the wound there, and she saw blood smeared on her fingers. Instinctively, she wiped them on the leather seat. She watched a lot of crime TV, and it occurred to her if she could leave DNA behind, maybe someday, someone who wasn't under Roman's thumb would find it.

Trying to be as sneaky as possible, Maggie put her fingers under her shirt, gathered up more of her blood, then wiped it under the lip of the seat, behind the handle of the door, even on the seat belt she hadn't bothered to put on. Trying to leave some sort of trace for some crime tech to find that she'd been in this backseat, even if it was a decade from now.

As the streets of Riverton went by, Maggie's hope that someone would come to her rescue quickly faded. Yes, Shawn would realize she was gone, but it would be too late. And there was no way to track her. His computer friend, Tex, would try, but there was no way he'd find her quickly enough. They were halfway to the apartment she'd shared with Adina. If the beach Roman was taking her to really was near where she'd lived, she didn't have much longer.

Her emotions were all over the place, seesawing between anger and sorrow. But the longer she sat there, staring at the back of Roman's neat military haircut, the angrier she got.

How dare he play God like he was! This wasn't fair! She might not live through this, but she'd do whatever she needed to in order to leave her mark on him. NCIS wouldn't be able to overlook scratches on his face, bruises on his body. She'd fight. It might not do any good in regard to the outcome of her life, but maybe, just maybe, she could do enough damage to prove that he'd had something to do with her supposed suicide.

"Not long now," Roman taunted.

Lips pressed together, Maggie went over in her head her next moves. As soon as he opened the back door, he'd find out that she wasn't the docile, cowed woman he'd manipulated and had sent to prison two years ago. She'd changed. And this asshole wasn't going to take her new life from her without one hell of a fight.

Preacher looked at his watch. Ten minutes had passed since Maggie had gone behind the door to speak to her probation officer. Barely any time at all...but the longer he sat there, the more uneasy he felt. And he'd spent too many years as a SEAL to ignore his gut.

He'd heard the click of the door lock engaging when Maggie had gone through, so he waited until a man near him was called and got up to follow the officer through the door—then Preacher made his move.

He caught the door before it shut and entered the secure area.

"Hey! You can't be back here," the officer told him sternly.

But Preacher ignored him. "Maggie!" he yelled, using his "SEAL" voice, as he and his friends dubbed it. Dominant, harsh, loud.

Heads began to pop out from behind office doors.

"Maggie!" Preacher repeated.

"You need to leave, sir," the officer tried again. The man who'd been called back for his appointment was leaning against the wall, his arms crossed. He didn't seem alarmed in the least by Preacher's actions. In fact, he seemed amused.

"I came here with my girlfriend. Her name is Maggie Lionetti. Where is she?" Preacher demanded.

The officer wasn't the same one who'd retrieved Maggie. He shrugged. "No clue."

"Find her."

"You're going to be in big trouble for coming back here," the officer said, instead of doing what Preacher asked.

"Maggie!" Preacher shouted yet again.

A middle-aged woman came out of an office and headed toward him. "What's going on here?" she asked.

"I'm looking for Maggie Lionetti. She came back here ten minutes ago for an appointment with her PO. I'm trying to find her."

The woman frowned. "I'm her probation officer, and Maggie's not on my schedule for today."

Every muscle in Preacher's body tensed. He had no idea

what was going on, but he had a feeling it had everything to do with Robertson. It wouldn't have been hard for him to call Maggie, or have someone else call, and tell her she had to come in for a meeting, intercept her, and take her right out from under his nose.

"Are there stairs in here?" he barked.

The woman still looked confused, but she turned and pointed toward a door at the end of the hallway.

Preacher ran toward it, ignoring the male officer telling him to stop.

The felon who'd watched with amusement joined in the confusion by saying loudly, "You go, man!"

Bursting through the door, Preacher cursed. It would've been easy to get Maggie out of the building without anyone seeing her leave. He pulled out his phone as he ran down the stairs. He wanted to call his team, their assistance would be invaluable right about now. But there was only one person on his radar. Tex.

"I just got the recording," Tex said in lieu of a greeting. "I haven't had time to analyze it yet."

"He's got her!" Preacher practically yelled as he raced down the stairs.

"Fuck!" Tex didn't ask who; he knew.

"I slipped one of my trackers into her purse," Preacher said. "I didn't want to freak her out, so I didn't tell her. I need you to find her."

"On it," Tex said.

Preacher heard the man's fingers clacking on a keyboard as he burst out of the government building. He looked up both sides of the street as he stood on the sidewalk but saw no sign of Maggie, Robertson, or anyone who looked out of place. He took off at a dead run toward the parking lot where he'd left his Malibu not too long ago. Thank God the lot wasn't too far away.

By the time he'd unlocked the door and thrown himself behind the wheel, Tex spoke.

"Got her."

The relief that hit Preacher was instant. Her purse must not have been left behind in the abduction. There was still a chance it wasn't with her now, but Preacher couldn't even think about that possibility.

"She's headed southeast. About to pass her apartment." His voice was steady. This was the most important mission of Preacher's life, and he was glad for Tex's calm professionalism.

He tore out of the parking lot, ignoring the honks from the cars he'd cut off. He flew down the street, driving recklessly but with purpose. He could only hope a cop got behind him. He'd need all the firepower and witnesses he could get when he caught up to whoever Roman had tasked with taking Maggie.

"Where is she now?" Preacher asked. He was panting, breathing way too fast. He couldn't control his emotions or his body's reaction to the stress and fear he was feeling. Roman wasn't going to give Maggie another chance to get away from him. This was it. If he didn't catch up with her, and fast, he had no doubt she wouldn't survive.

"Going the same way," Tex told him. "She just passed the apartment complex."

"Any ideas where he's taking her?"

"Not yet. He could go south toward Mexico, but it's unlikely he'd try to take her across the border. I just put out an alert for her, so if he does think that's the best route, she'll be found. He could also hit the interstate, then go north toward LA, try to get lost there. Maybe give her to one of the drug dealers he was attempting to sell to when she was pulled over years ago. That seems like something he'd feel was appropriate."

"Asshole," Preacher muttered.

"I'm watching her, but I'm going to call Kevlar. Give me a minute."

Preacher nodded, relieved that backup would be on the way but hating to lose the connection to Tex, and thus to Maggie, at the same time.

Preacher took the time while Tex was radio silent to say every curse word he could think of, trying to relieve some of the tension he felt. It didn't help. By the time Tex came back on the line, Preacher was even more wound up than he'd been when he realized Maggie was gone.

"She's slowing down. Oh shit."

"What? Tex? Where is she?"

"On the road map, it looks as if she just pulled over on the side of the road, but when I look at the satellite, there's a small strip of sand. There's thick vegetation blocking the beach from the street."

Preacher pressed his foot down harder on the gas. "Where?" he barked.

"Two miles past the parking lot of her apartment, take a left," Tex said.

Preacher's heart was in his throat as he followed Tex's directions. Time was running out. He could feel it. Every second it took for him to get to Maggie was one second too long.

"I'm comin'," he said under his breath as he drove like a maniac to get to the woman he loved. "Hang on, Maggie. I'm comin'."

CHAPTER TWENTY-THREE

Maggie's heart was in her throat when Roman slowed the vehicle. He pulled off the side of the road, thick bushes and small trees scraping against the side of the car as he did. She prayed they'd leave a mark; it would be one more piece of evidence against Roman.

He shut off the car and turned to look at her. The smile on his face made her blood run cold. "Ready for some fun?" he asked. "Well, fun for me maybe, not so much for you." Then he laughed as he opened his door and got out.

Maggie braced herself.

The second he opened the back door, she was moving.

She leapt forward as best she could from her seated position and raked her nails down his face.

He stumbled backward but grabbed her as he fell. They both landed on the asphalt, and Maggie immediately tried to get up and run.

Roman caught her ankle and she went down, hitting her chin on the street so hard, her teeth rattled in her head. Roman was on her then, holding her face down, wrenching her arms behind her until her shoulders felt as if they were being pulled out of their sockets.

It was just her luck that there was no traffic at that moment. Any other time, there would probably be tons of people driving by, but it felt as if she and Roman were the only two people on the planet right then.

Roman yanked her to her feet, still holding her hands behind her, and shoved her toward the bushes.

Maggie opened her mouth and screamed as loud as she could, hoping against hope that someone, somewhere, would hear her and call the police. But almost as soon as sound left her throat, Roman's hand clamped over her mouth and nose. Cutting off her air.

He was taller than she was by almost a foot. Stronger too. Maggie couldn't win in a physical fight against him, and right now, all she could think about was getting air into her lungs.

She didn't notice the scrapes of the bushes against her body as Roman pushed them through to the small strip of sand on the other side. The early-evening sun glinted off the water, and she vaguely noticed how pretty the sunset was with the clouds.

She thought of a different beach, a different time. When she and Shawn had lain on the sand and looked up at the stars. She'd loved that beach, and didn't want the feel of sand on her back to forever remind her of this moment...if she survived.

Just when Maggie thought she was going to pass out, Roman removed his hand from her face.

She gulped in air, trying not to hyperventilate. In her desperate attempt to get oxygen to her lungs, she didn't notice how close they'd gotten to the water until she felt the wetness on her feet.

She tripped over the rocks at the shore, making it easy for Roman to push her to her knees. The water lapped at her thighs as she renewed her struggle to get away from her would-be murderer.

But he simply laughed at her attempts to escape. "You're more trouble than you're worth," he said as he bent her farther, so her face was almost touching the water.

"You were an easy mark," he said quietly. "Pathetic. Desperate for attention. You were the worst I ever had in bed too. Cold as a fucking fish. I've had limp whores who were better than you. I hadn't counted on you getting pulled over, but it was fun to watch you go down for those drugs. I got off just thinking about you being miserable, crying behind bars. *I* did that. *Me*.

"And I'm looking forward to reliving *this* moment so many more nights in the future. The way you're going to squirm and thrash as I hold you down. The moment your lungs fill with water and your heart stops beating. I can't fucking wait. The quickest way to die will be to just inhale as soon as I shove your face under the water. I want you to fight, because it's more exciting that way. But if you're smart, which I know you aren't, you'll just give in to the inevitable."

Maggie was crying now, her tears falling into the ocean inches beneath her face. She tried once more to loosen Roman's grip around her wrists held at the small of her back, but it was no use.

"Fuck you, Maggie. You're *nobody*. A loser. And I regret ever meeting you and wasting one goddamn second of my time on you. But I'm sure going to enjoy the aftermath of your death. Of fucking with your SEAL and sending him to *his* death. I'll make sure to leak all the plans of the next mission I send him on to the enemy. They'll be waiting. Loverboy and his team will soon be dead. Blown to pieces. Never to be found—just like you."

Then without warning, he shoved her forward.

Maggie's head went under the water, and all plans she'd had to try to get her DNA on Roman, or to mark him further, went out the window. She couldn't breathe, the sandy bottom scraped against her cheeks as she did exactly what he wanted, thrashed and flailed, doing everything she could to get her head above water, to no avail.

Blackness crept into the edges of her vision, and just when she'd held her breath as long as she could and was about to inhale in a desperate attempt to live a few more precious seconds—the weight on her back disappeared.

Maggie whipped her head out of the water and sucked in lifesaving oxygen.

She wasn't aware of anything but the feel of being able

to breathe again, her pulse beating loudly in her ears... when something finally caught her attention to her right.

Turning her head, she saw Roman and another man fighting in the shallow surf.

Fight or flight finally kicked in, and she frantically crab walked backward, away from the water, away from the man who'd just tried to kill her. Who would've succeeded if it wasn't for whoever had obviously ripped him off her.

It didn't take more than a few additional seconds for Maggie to recognize the other man.

Shawn.

What...? *How?*

It felt impossible that he was there. That he'd arrived exactly when she needed him most. But Maggie didn't know why she was so surprised. Shawn was her knight in shining armor, the man who, in the short time she'd known him, had *always* been there for her, and who she had a feeling always *would* be in the future.

She had no idea what to do. How she could help him. Looking around, panting heavily, she scrambled on her hands and knees and picked up one of the heavy rocks near the shore. To do what with, she wasn't sure. Bash Roman's head in? Throw it at him?

But honestly, it didn't look as though Shawn *needed* help. The two men were about the same height, but Shawn obviously had more experience in hand-to-hand combat—and he was clearly more motivated.

The men didn't speak, they were only grunting as they fought.

It was brutal, but Maggie didn't take her eyes off them for a moment. Her chest heaved with her need to continue to replenish the oxygen in her body, and she impatiently scraped her wet hair out of her face so she could see what was happening more clearly.

The sound of screeching tires up on the road was a huge relief. Others had arrived. They'd help Shawn. Make sure Roman wouldn't escape and somehow come after her again. Follow through with his threats of treason against his country just to make Shawn and his SEAL team disappear.

Even as she heard several people moving through the thick bushes toward them, Roman picked up a rock to use as a weapon, aiming right for Shawn's head.

She drew back her own arm, about to throw her rock at Roman, but Maggie had time to do little more than gasp when Shawn ducked, then used his right leg to kick her ex—hard.

His boot connected with Roman's throat.

Maggie heard a gurgling noise come from her ex—then he fell backward into the water, landing with a huge splash.

To Maggie's surprise, he didn't immediately leap up and go after her or Shawn. He lay in the water, unmoving. Face up, eyes unblinking.

Then Shawn was in front of her, blocking her view of the man who had literally made her life a living hell. His hands gripped her head tightly. "Maggie? Are you all right? Can you breathe? Put down the rock, I've got you. *Fuck*, I need to get you to the hospital."

She reached up and gripped his wrists. "I'm okay." At least, that was what she'd meant to say, but as soon as the first word was out, she started violently coughing.

"Preacher!"

Both her and Shawn's heads swiveled to see Kevlar bursting through the vegetation. Followed closely by the rest of the SEAL team.

"Is she okay?" Safe asked, dropping to his knees beside them in the wet sand.

MacGyver joined his teammates on her other side, and Maggie felt Blink's hand on her shoulder as he stood behind her. She was completely surrounded by the men. They'd closed ranks, and she had no doubt that she was protected...and loved. These men had become her family, and she couldn't help but tear up again.

"He's dead," Kevlar said, dragging Roman's body out of the water and onto the sand.

"Shit," Flash swore. Then he looked at Maggie. "Not that I'm upset he's dead, just that this is going to be hard to explain."

Her mind spun. She was a convicted felon. Being anywhere near a dead body wasn't going to look good for her. She knew how the world worked. The first thing the cops did was check everyone's records. And the fact that she'd blamed Roman for planting the drugs during her criminal investigation gave her a very good reason to want him dead.

Before anyone could say anything else, Kevlar's phone

rang. It was a strange sound in the middle of the chaotic scene.

"Kevlar here. Uh-huh. Yes. Right...No shit? Damn, Tex, you're amazing! Oh, it wasn't? Well, I'm going to want to meet this chick and thank her personally." He chuckled a bit. "New Mexico. Right. We can do that. Yeah, I'll let them know. We'll talk soon."

The second Kevlar clicked off the connection, he turned to the group. "That was Tex. He said that a computer chick in New Mexico hacked into the government's spy satellites and recorded everything that happened here. Video's grainy, but it clearly shows Maggie and Robertson fighting along the road, before he brought her to the water and held her under until you showed up, Preacher."

Maggie frowned in confusion. A videotape from space? It sounded too crazy to be true.

"Seriously? Good. No, *great!*" MacGyver said.

"I'm calling NCIS," Smiley said. He'd pulled Roman's body farther away from the water, and Maggie hadn't missed how he'd "accidentally" kicked the man in the side while doing so.

NCIS...She tensed. The authorities had to be contacted, Maggie knew that, but the ramifications could be bad for her.

"I'm sure Tex is transferring the video to them right now," Shawn told her gently. "It'll be okay. I'm more worried about you. Your chin is bleeding, and he had your head underwater. How much water did you inhale? I need to get you to the hospital."

But Maggie shook her head. Her chin was throbbing where she'd hit it on the asphalt, and her side ached from that asshole's knife...but amazingly, she felt good, all things considered. "You got here in time. I didn't swallow any water."

"Thank fuck," Shawn breathed.

"How did you find me so fast?" she couldn't help but ask.

"I put a tracker in your purse," Shawn told her sheepishly. "Are you mad?"

"Mad?" Maggie asked. "No. Why would I be? You saved my life." And with that, she burst into tears once more. All the emotions she'd felt in the last ten minutes had her feeling shaky and definitely unstable. She'd almost *died*. Her tormentor was dead, and Shawn was safe from whatever nefarious schemes Roman had planned for his future.

Even though she was physically okay for the most part, Maggie couldn't stop crying. After the police, NCIS, and the paramedics showed up, she was borderline hysterical. Eventually, the medics gave her a shot to calm her down, and Shawn insisted she be transported to the hospital to get checked out.

It wasn't until hours later, after getting two stitches in her chin, the knicks on her side cleaned by the doctor—they weren't deep enough for stitches—talking with the NCIS detectives, speaking with her probation officer—

who'd been frantic after finding out that she'd been lured to her office, and apparently kidnapped as a result—and after reassuring Wren, Josie, Remi, Caroline, and all the other women who'd shown up at the hospital when they'd heard what happened, that Maggie was finally able to fully relax.

Shawn had brought her back to his place, and she'd met Jane Hillman, his landlady, who'd insisted on bringing two huge bowls of Shepard's pie she'd made earlier that evening to their room. Finding she was starving, the comfort food really hit the spot. Then she and Shawn had taken a shower to wash off the salt from the seawater that had dried on their skin, and climbed under his covers.

Shawn held her tightly against him, almost desperately.

Neither spoke, but at that moment, it wasn't needed. They both knew how close they'd come to losing one another. Maggie had literally been seconds from dying. Roman had almost succeeded in his evil plan to get rid of her once and for all. If it hadn't been for Shawn's quick thinking at her PO's office, and putting his tracker in her purse, he never would've made it to her in time.

To her surprise, she heard Shawn's breath hitch. Looking up, she saw tears soaking into the hair at his temple.

Without a word, knowing exactly how he felt, Maggie lay her head on his chest and tightened her arm around him. Tomorrow would be soon enough to talk about everything that happened, to work through it all.

For now, all she wanted to do was hold the man she loved, and be held in return.

EPILOGUE

Maggie stood in Aces Bar and Grill a week later and marveled at all the people who were there. She had a huge circle of friends now, and it still felt almost surreal.

The investigation into Roman was ongoing, and would be for years, considering how many special forces missions the rear admiral was involved in, and every afternoon when Shawn came home, he had another instance to share of how her ex had fucked with someone. SEAL teams, other Navy personnel, former girlfriends...his reign of terror wasn't limited to just her. Which made Maggie a little sad.

Tex's computer genius friend—whose name was Ryleigh, and she lived at what sounded like a kickass resort in New Mexico called The Refuge, for people who suffered from PTSD—had finally found Roman's wife. She'd combed through NamUs, the National Missing and Unidentified Persons System, and used her skills to narrow down the possibilities to five bodies. She was identified as being found in West Virginia. A hunter had come across her body years ago, but her hands had been cut off, and with no tattoos or other distinguishing features, she hadn't been able to be identified...until now.

She'd been murdered. Strangled. While Maggie wasn't happy in the least that the poor woman had ended up dead, she was relieved she'd finally been identified and could be returned to her family.

With all the horrible things Roman had done coming to light, Maggie and everyone else had been relieved to discover the rear admiral hadn't been the one to send Blink's team on that ill-fated mission. So while he had a lot of things to answer for, the deaths and injuries of Blink's teammates wasn't among them.

How one man had been able to pull the wool over so many people's eyes was confusing. How had he gotten so much power in the Navy? He seemed to have no soul, took delight in tormenting others, and his favorite thing to do was blackmailing those he considered beneath him.

Tex's friend Ryleigh had also found Maggie a new lawyer, who was doing her best to get the felony conviction overturned. The phone call Maggie had recorded—where Roman had threatened to put "another" stash in her car—was clear proof that her ex had set her up, as far as her lawyer was concerned.

It wasn't an easy or quick process to get the charges dismissed. But while her case was churning through the courts, and because of the extenuating circumstances, her probation had been knocked down from one year to six months. So she only had a couple more months left to meet with her PO, then she was done.

Even if the felony conviction *was* overturned, Maggie didn't think she'd go back to being a pharmacist, but strangely, she was all right with that. She felt like a completely different person than who she'd been a few years ago. She didn't want to go back to her before life. Maggie wanted to move on. Put her past behind her.

"You look like you're thinking really hard over here," Shawn said as he came up beside her. He handed her a glass of water and wrapped an arm around her waist. "You good?"

Maggie nodded and took a sip of the water. In the last week, Shawn had hovered. Constantly asking if she was all right, offering to take her to a psychologist if she felt she needed it, driving her to work and picking her up...generally being a perfect partner. Of course, she'd reciprocated. After all, *she* hadn't been the one to kill Roman. Even though Shawn said it didn't bother him in the least, she still worried about the long-term ramifications on his psyche.

She'd pretty much moved into his apartment at Jane Hillman's house, but since most of her things were still in storage, she didn't have a lot to move in. Adina would be coming back from her deployment in a couple months, and Maggie was happy her friend would have her apartment all to herself when she returned.

Things were going surprisingly well in Maggie's life...

but she needed to talk to Shawn about something. And she couldn't do that in the busy bar, where they were surrounded by their friends and would likely be interrupted every few minutes.

As if her thoughts conjured her, Caroline walked toward them.

"You look happy," the older woman said as she approached.

Shawn took a step back, reaching out and plucking the glass of water out of her hand but not walking away entirely. He was giving her space, but still hovering nearby in case she needed anything. Maggie loved him all the more for it.

She hugged Caroline and said, "I am."

"Good. You also look like you wouldn't mind leaving."

"Oh, but—"

Caroline chuckled and held up a hand. "I remember the days after Matthew and I first got together. All I wanted was to be alone with him, and yet we were constantly hanging out with his team here at Aces. Don't get me wrong, I love this bar and I love the guys, but after everything I went through, being alone with my man fed my soul in a way nothing else could. Go on...sneak out the back. I'll cover for you."

"I shouldn't leave without saying something," Maggie argued, wanting more than anything to take Caroline up on her offer. She *did* want to be alone with Shawn, and not simply because she loved him. They needed to have a serious discussion. "I don't want anyone to think I disappeared again."

"They won't. They know Preacher is stuck to your side. Go. I'll talk to Remi, Josie, and Wren, and will make sure no one else freaks and heads out on a rescue mission."

Maggie chuckled. "Caroline?"

"Yeah, hon?"

"Thank you." There was more Maggie wanted to say, but she wasn't sure where to start. Everyone had been so great in the aftermath of her near-death experience...well, her *second* near-death experience. But Caroline had picked her up at My Sister's Closet a couple days ago and driven her to a busy beach, not too far from the naval base. Not the one she and Shawn had visited, and *not* the one Roman had tried to kill her on. Just a busy, apparently popular stretch of sand full of people enjoying the warm weather and calm water. She'd encouraged Maggie to take a walk on the shore. Somehow, she'd known how uncomfortable she'd become with beaches.

They'd walked together, not saying a word. And by the time they'd gotten back to her huge SUV, Maggie felt ten times better.

"The water and sand aren't your enemy," Caroline had said once they were back in her car. "I've been where you are. I almost died in the ocean, and I had a hard time getting anywhere near it for the longest time. But after a while, I realized that it's not the beach that tried to kill me. It was a man. That's who I should project my negative energy toward, not the beautiful water. Not that it's good to have negative energy at all, but...shoot, you know what I mean."

Caroline had been wise and funny at the same time, and Maggie was grateful for her insight and help.

They hugged again, then Caroline turned Maggie around and gently pushed her toward Shawn, who was standing patiently not too far away. "Get," Caroline ordered. "That's an order."

Maggie rolled her eyes but didn't hesitate to walk into Shawn's arms.

"Ready to go?" she asked.

"If you are," he told her. He placed the glass of water on a nearby table, then steered Maggie toward the front door.

"Caroline said we should go out the back," Maggie said.

"No way in hell. The last thing I want is a SEAL contingent breaking into the house because they think you disappeared again," Shawn said with a chuckle.

"We're never going to get out of here anytime soon," Maggie moaned, as people began to notice them heading for the exit.

"Sure we are," he said. Then he brought two fingers to his mouth and let out a shrill whistle. Everyone stopped talking and turned toward the two of them.

Maggie could feel her cheeks heating up with a blush at the attention now focused on her and Shawn.

"We're heading out!" he yelled. "Talk to you all later!" He gave the room in general a chin lift, then turned and walked with Maggie toward the door.

"I can't believe that worked!" she exclaimed as they headed to his car in the parking lot.

Shawn chuckled. "You were right, we would've been there forever saying bye to everyone, I figured that was a lot more expedient."

Maggie loved this man. So damn much. She felt like a new person around him. She wasn't the shell of a woman she'd been when released from prison. She wasn't the carefree, almost naïve one she'd been before meeting Roman. With Shawn, she felt free to be whoever she wanted to be. And sitting with him in the evenings and sharing about their days, cooking together, watching TV, and laying in his arms at night was exactly what she'd been looking for all her life.

It had only been a week since she'd almost been drowned, but it felt as if it had been years. The freedom she felt thanks to Roman's death made her feel a little bad...but she was moving on.

The conversation she needed to have with Shawn would decide if the happiness she was feeling right now would continue. Nerves hit as they drove toward his house, but she couldn't and wouldn't put this off anymore. Shawn deserved to know what was going on with her.

He parked, and they walked into the house hand-in-hand. Instead of going in the front door, Shawn took her around the back to the stairs Jane had installed so her renters could come and go without feeling as if they were bothering her in the main house.

He led her into his room and shut the door behind them.

Maggie spun and blurted, "Can we talk?"

"Of course," Shawn said, not looking or sounding worried about what was on her mind. He went to the small kitchen and grabbed a bottle of water from the fridge and handed it to her, before putting his hand on the small of her back and leading her into the sitting area. He sat with her on the couch and pulled her feet into his lap, then took off her shoes and started rubbing her arches.

Maggie moaned a little. She loved having her feet massaged. Ever since he'd learned that little fact about her, Shawn took every opportunity to do so.

"Was tonight too much?" he asked.

Maggie shook her head. She didn't want to get into a guessing game with him. She just needed to come straight out with what was on her mind. "How attached are you to this place?" she asked.

Shawn's hands froze on her feet. "*This place* meaning...?" he asked.

"This room."

He resumed his massage. "Not at all. I mean, I like Jane, and this place is close to the base and convenient. But I can honestly live anywhere." Shawn leaned toward her. "Why? Do you not like it? I don't care where I live as long as you're there."

Maggie swallowed. This was harder than she'd thought it would be. "I love this place. It's cozy and fits you really well. I just...when I was first released, the only thought I had was to get the hell out of California. I hated everything about this state."

"I can't leave," Shawn said quietly. "I go where the Navy sends me. And right now we're in a long-term contract here in Riverton."

"I know!" she said quickly. "I'm not saying this very well. But...I don't want to leave anymore. That's what I was getting at."

"Thank fuck," Shawn breathed.

Maggie smiled. He was adorable, but the hard part of this conversation wasn't over yet. "I was asking because, well...this apartment isn't the ideal setup for a baby."

There. She'd said it.

Shawn stared at her for a moment with no expression on his face. "You want to have kids with me?" he finally asked with a small smile. "I'm all right with that. I want them too. We've got plenty of time to find the perfect place. Maybe a small house. It'll be farther from the base, but that won't be an issue. Maybe we can ask Caroline for advice and help. She's been here a while and—"

Maggie reached out and put her hand on Shawn's. He immediately stopped talking.

"I love you," she whispered.

"I love you too," he returned immediately.

"But we don't have plenty of time to find the perfect place," she told him. Then she took a deep breath and said what she'd been beating around the bush about. "Because... I'm pregnant."

Shawn stared at her again.

"I mean, it's early. Probably too early to really get excited, but I was feeling weird and for some reason, the thought that I might be pregnant hit me, I don't know why, and so I peed on one of those sticks and it came back positive. I haven't seen a doctor or anything, and I *swear* I thought it wasn't the right time of the month when we had sex but...I guess I was wrong. And if you don't want this right now, a baby, I understand. The last thing I want is for you to feel trapped into anything. I'm not doing that—trapping you, I mean. I just...*I* want this baby. So much. It feels as if it's a new start for me, and I'm terrified, because what do I know about being a mother? But I already love it so much."

Shawn surprised her by suddenly lifting her feet off his lap, and for a second, Maggie froze in panic. Was he pissed? Going to tell her to get the hell out? She had no idea. He walked over to the table where he'd put his phone when they'd arrived home and picked it up. He clicked on the screen then brought it up to his ear. His gaze bore into hers as he spoke.

"Hey, Caroline, it's Preacher. Yeah, she's fine. I need your help though. Maggie and I need a house. Preferably one with three bedrooms. Two baths would be nice. If possible, if we could be near you guys, I'd love that... Because Maggie's pregnant, and we're going to need more space than I have here."

Maggie's lips twitched when she heard Caroline's excited screech all the way across the room.

"I just figured you've been here for years, you might

have some connections...okay. Thanks. Gotta go. Talk to you soon."

Shawn clicked off the phone, threw it on the table, then walked back to where Maggie was sitting on the couch. He got down on his knees in front of her, shuffled forward between her legs, then wrapped his arms around her waist and buried his face in her lap.

Maggie's hands came up and cradled his head.

After a long moment, Shawn lifted his head. "A baby," he whispered.

Maggie nodded.

"You're a gift. A miracle. I was happy—no, *thrilled* having you by my side. But this? You giving me a child? I can't...I have no words."

"But...you aren't upset?" Maggie asked tentatively.

"I'm the opposite of upset," Shawn said, his smile growing. "I'm ecstatic! So fucking happy...er...*freaking* happy." Then he frowned. "Wait—is it okay? You were without oxygen for a while last week! Shit, we need to go to the doctor!"

"It's eight-thirty at night. We can call tomorrow. I don't even know who to call though," Maggie said.

"We'll call Jessyka. Or one of the other girls. They'll give us the name of a good obstetrician. I love you, Maggie. So damn much."

Relief swept through her. She'd been so worried about telling Shawn about the baby. As she'd said, it was still very early. But she didn't want to hide anything from him. And... a part of her thought if he didn't want a child, it would be easier to make the break from him now rather than months down the line.

"A baby," he breathed, then leaned down and kissed her flat belly. "We'll get married as soon as I can arrange it. What kind of wedding do you want?"

Maggie's breath caught in her throat. "What?"

"Wedding. Do you want something big and fancy? Or maybe something more low-key, like at Aces? Or we could just go to the courthouse...maybe that would be best. The sooner I officially get you added as my dependent, the better—"

"Shawn," Maggie said, stopping his babbling. "Married?"

His gaze flew to hers, and he went up on his knees and scooted forward a little more. "Yeah. Married. To me. Do you not want that?" he asked with a frown.

"I do. More than you'll ever know. But things have moved crazy fast for us. Are you sure you don't want to wait?"

"I was sure after knowing you a week. No, I think I was sure that first night, when the guys and I crashed your ride share."

Maggie could only stare at him.

"Marry me, Maggie. Make an honest man out of me."

She could only nod.

"Yes?"

"Yes," she confirmed.

Shawn smiled huge, then stood. He reached down and

picked her up off the couch, and Maggie let out a girly screech.

It wasn't a long walk to the bed, considering it was right behind the couch. Shawn dropped her on the mattress and immediately began to undress her.

"What's the rush?" Maggie asked with a laugh as she did her best to help him with her clothes.

It wasn't until they were both naked and he was braced over her that Shawn said, "I can't wait to get inside you. I want at least three."

"Three?"

"Kids. Maybe more. I can't wait to see you round with our child. To get up in the middle of the night with them. To watch you breastfeed. To experience Santa Claus and the Easter Bunny. To trip over toys and step on Legos. I wish we could have this baby tomorrow, that's how excited I am."

He was being adorable, and that wasn't a word Maggie usually associated with her SEAL. "Well, he or she will need to marinate for quite a bit longer before coming out," she told him.

Shawn's hand eased down her body, stopping between her legs. He began to play with her clit as he spoke. "So... what kind of ceremony do you want? Big and lavish?"

Maggie's hips pushed upward into Shawn's hand. It was ridiculous how easily he could arouse her. How fast she got wet when he stroked her clit, just as he was doing right now. "Courthouse. Then a party at Aces."

"Done," Shawn said with satisfaction. "I love you, Maggie. You have no idea how much."

"I do, because I love you the same way."

Then he moved, pressing his cock into her. She wasn't quite as wet as she usually was, but he managed to bury himself inside her to the hilt.

"A baby," he breathed. "At least we don't have to worry about birth control anymore."

Maggie chuckled. "True."

"Thank you," he whispered. "For being strong enough to withstand that asshole's attempts to silence you. For not giving up when shit got real. For loving me. For giving me a baby."

"I think you were the one who gave *me* the kid," Maggie joked. It was getting harder to concentrate on what he was saying as he made love to her.

"We did it together. The way we'll do everything from here on out."

"Uh-huh. Shawn?"

"Yeah, love?"

"Less talking and more moving," she ordered.

Shawn barked out a laugh but nodded. "Yes, ma'am."

Their lovemaking was deeper in that moment. Maybe it was the commitment they'd just made to each other, maybe it was the knowledge that within her body, a new life was forming. Whatever it was, Maggie knew she'd never forget this night. Being arrested and sent to prison had felt like the end of her life. But in actuality, it was the start of something beautiful.

* * *

Bree Haynes crouched behind a dumpster and peered out into the dark parking lot. He'd found her again. She'd thought this time she'd finally been able to evade her ex. The asshole who'd fucking *sold* her. If asked just a few months ago, she would've scoffed at the very notion of someone selling a person in this day and age. And yet, here she was.

She had to get out of Vegas. But she had a feeling that wouldn't stop her ex. He'd been given a lot of money for her, and since whatever asshole he'd sold her to hadn't actually received their purchase, they were threatening Carl. Saying he either gave back the money they'd paid him, or find their property.

She knew all this because Carl had told her the *last* time he'd found her. She'd managed to get away, but Bree knew she'd just gotten lucky. She wouldn't be able to get away the next time. Carl would hog-tie, gag, blindfold her, and cart her ass to the sex trafficker before she could even think about escaping again.

His car drove slowly around the casino parking lot as he searched the dark nooks and crannies for her. Easing back behind the dumpster and ignoring the stench coming from it, Bree pressed her lips together and tried to think about her next steps. She had money, but that wouldn't protect her from Carl.

Even leaving Vegas wouldn't necessarily guarantee her safety. Carl wouldn't give up—ever. He felt as if he owned her. He'd track her down. And she couldn't go to her sister's place in Washington. That would be the first place he'd look.

She needed a protector. Someone who wasn't afraid of standing up to Carl and his criminal friends.

A face flashed in her brain.

Jude Stark. She didn't remember a lot about the night Carl had sold her, or the scary ape who'd beaten and tied her up and shoved her into his car. He'd told her as he drove away from Carl's apartment that he had one more pickup to make, then he was going to deliver both women to an underground brothel.

Then Jude Stark had shown up. Gotten her out of the man's car and taken her to safety. But she hadn't stayed where he'd put her. She was too scared. Too freaked out. Just wanted to get away.

And yet, Jude's face was burned in her memory. As was everything he'd told her. He was a Navy SEAL stationed in Riverton, California.

That's where she needed to go. Jude would help her. Maybe. He had once, maybe he'd do it again.

Bree had no idea how she'd find the man. The possibility that he'd been moved to another naval base, or was deployed, or hell, was even married to someone who'd be less than thrilled to find a random woman on their doorstep...all those thoughts flitted through her brain. But she ignored them.

Jude Stark was associated with safety in her mind, and that's who she needed to find.

Peeking out from behind the dumpster, Bree saw that Carl was nowhere in sight. But she knew he wasn't gone. No, the asshole was always lurking. Him or one of his cronies. She couldn't use her identification to stay in a hotel, but she could use her money to at least get to River-ton. She'd play things by ear once she arrived.

Scared, dirty, and freaked out, Bree stood cautiously. She might be making another mistake—Lord knew she'd made plenty recently—but she didn't think so. Jude Stark would either be her salvation or another colossal fuck-up. Either way, she'd be better off in Riverton than here in Vegas, where Carl's minions were everywhere.

"Just once, I need a break," Bree whispered, before blending into the shadows and disappearing into the night.

* * *

Addison Wentz looked down at her hands, currently being held by Ricardo "MacGyver" Douglas, and wondered what the hell she was doing.

"By the power vested in me, I now pronounce you husband and wife. You may kiss your bride."

Looking up, she caught a glimpse of hazel eyes and a very serious expression on Ricky's face before his lips were suddenly on hers.

She hadn't regretted making the decision to marry the man until this exact moment.

Electricity shot down her arms and legs, making her feel almost light-headed.

She'd always liked Ricky, thought he was funny and kind, but also gruff and grouchy at the same time. She'd met him at the car repair shop. Her VW Bug was acting up, and he was getting new tires on his Ford Explorer.

Surprisingly, they'd kept running into each other. At a gas station, coffee shop, diner, and one time, they even ended up next to each other at a stoplight. Ricky eventually insisted they exchange numbers, and they'd actually gotten together quite often since then. She'd watched over his house when he was deployed with the Navy, and he'd even pretended to be her boyfriend once when her parents were giving her a hard time for being thirty-six and still single.

Ricky was one of the few people she'd met in her lifetime who didn't make jokes about her height. She was six feet tall and had absolutely no athletic ability whatsoever. So she'd spent her life laughing off questions about whether she was a basketball player, or how the weather was "up there." Ricky was the same height as her, and he'd never, not once, made her feel as if she wasn't pretty simply because she was tall. And yes, plenty of other men had done just that. They'd obviously felt their masculinity was threatened because she was taller than them, and while intellectually, she knew it was *their* problem, not hers, she'd been teased her entire life because of her height, so it always hurt.

Then there was Ellory. She was twelve going on twenty-six. Her daughter was Addison's life. Wise beyond her years, introverted and shy. Somehow, Ricky had broken through her thick shields and made her smile the first time they'd met. Addison didn't talk about Ellory much. About her chronic illness and how many nights they'd spent in various hospitals. But Ricky knew. Ellory herself had opened up to him, told him all about how much she hated being sick.

What her daughter didn't know was that Addison was struggling with money. And if Ellory got sick again, and had to go back into the hospital, it would start a cascade of financial issues that would most likely result in them losing their apartment. Addison had no idea what to do, she'd never *not* give Ellory the medicine she needed, never *not* take her to the doctor.

When Ricky had called and said he needed to ask her something, Addison had immediately driven out to his house to meet him. He was one of her best friends, and anything he wanted or needed, she'd be happy to help him with. The house he lived in, he'd bought on a whim, and he was currently working on fixing it up. He was amazing with his hands, and Addison had always been impressed with how he could turn something old and rundown into something new and beautiful. It was usually a mess, however, filled with gadgets and wires and other things he used to "tinker."

He was a genius, and Addison thought he was adorable.

She hadn't been prepared for his question though. Never in a million years did she expect to walk into his house and see three children. One boy was sitting on his couch with a blanket over him, a younger girl was sitting next to him, playing with a Barbie doll as if it was the most fascinating thing she'd ever seen. And a second, older boy was watching TV as if it held all the answers in the world... not that she herself didn't love *Mythbusters*, but the boy was so entranced, he didn't even look up when she entered.

Ricky had brought her into his kitchen, and without fanfare or even much emotion, had asked her to marry him.

And here she was.

Saying yes had been out of necessity. For both of them. Ricky needed her so he could keep the kids, and she needed him for his health insurance. Addison had initially thought it wouldn't be a big deal. That she was doing her friend a favor, and in a year or so, they'd quietly get a divorce and go their separate ways.

But the second his lips touched hers in that room in the courthouse, it hit home just how much of an idiot she was.

Addison loved Ricky. Had since the moment they'd locked eyes in that waiting room at the repair shop.

He'd married her because he needed a nanny for the kids he hoped to adopt one day, and she'd married *him*... well, there were many reasons. But first and foremost—she was head over heels for the man.

And he saw her as a friend. Someone who'd done him a massive favor.

He pulled back and stared at her with a look Addison couldn't interpret. Then he licked his lips and turned to Artem, Borysko, and Yana, the three children he'd rescued in Ukraine, and asked, "Anyone want to stop and get some ice cream on the way home?"

As the kids enthusiastically said yes, Addison tried to pull her hand out of Ricky's, but he didn't let go. In fact, his fingers tightened around hers. He looked at her with that funny expression again, then turned to answer a question Borysko had asked him.

Licking her own lips, Addison could taste Ricky on her skin. Lust shot through her, and she almost moaned.

She couldn't do this. Wouldn't survive living with this man and acting like his wife for a whole year.

But it was too late. She'd said yes, and from now until an undetermined date in the future, she was Mrs. Addison Douglas.

If she survived with her heart intact, it would be a miracle.

* * *

A marriage of convenience? Two strangers, four children, and a whole lot of shenanigans. Find out how it all plays out in the next book in the SEAL of Protection: Alliance series...*Protecting Addison*!

Scan the QR code below for signed books, swag, T-shirts and more!

Securing Zoey
Securing Avery
Securing Kalee
Securing Jane

Delta Force Heroes Series

Rescuing Rayne
Rescuing Aimee (novella)
Rescuing Emily
Rescuing Harley
Marrying Emily (novella)
Rescuing Kassie
Rescuing Bryn
Rescuing Casey
Rescuing Sadie (novella)
Rescuing Wendy
Rescuing Mary
Rescuing Macie (novella)
Rescuing Annie

SEAL of Protection Series

Protecting Caroline
Protecting Alabama
Protecting Fiona
Marrying Caroline (novella)
Protecting Summer
Protecting Cheyenne
Protecting Jessyka
Protecting Julie (novella)

ALSO BY SUSAN STOKER

Shelter for Quinn
Shelter for Koren
Shelter for Penelope

Ace Security Series
Claiming Grace
Claiming Alexis
Claiming Bailey
Claiming Felicity
Claiming Sarah

Mountain Mercenaries Series
Defending Allye
Defending Chloe
Defending Morgan
Defending Harlow
Defending Everly
Defending Zara
Defending Raven

Silverstone Series
Trusting Skylar
Trusting Taylor
Trusting Molly
Trusting Cassidy

Stand Alone
Falling for the Delta
The Guardian Mist

ALSO BY SUSAN STOKER

Nature's Rift
A Princess for Cale
A Moment in Time- A Collection of Short Stories
Another Moment in Time- A Collection of Short Stories
A Third Moment in Time- A Collection of Short Stories
Lambert's Lady

Special Operations Fan Fiction
http://www.AcesPress.com

Beyond Reality Series
Outback Hearts
Flaming Hearts
Frozen Hearts

Writing as Annie George:
Stepbrother Virgin (erotic novella)

ABOUT THE AUTHOR

New York Times, *USA Today*, #1 Amazon Bestseller, and #1 *Wall Street Journal* Bestselling Author, Susan Stoker has spent the last twenty-three years living in Missouri, California, Colorado, Indiana, Texas, and Tennessee and is currently living in the wilds of Maine. She's married to a retired Army man (and current firefighter/EMT) who now gets to follow *her* around the country.

She debuted her first series in 2014 and quickly followed that up with the SEAL of Protection Series, which solidified her love of writing and creating stories readers can get lost in.

If you enjoyed this book, or any book, please consider leaving a review. It's appreciated by authors more than you'll know.

www.stokeraces.com
www.AcesPress.com
susan@stokeraces.com